KILL
TEAM

THE FIRST BOOK IN THE
BLACK OPS VIETNAM SERIES

ERIC MEYER

FOREWORD

June 1966, Hanoi

Tran Quang was a rising star inside the Communist Party of Vietnam. Early on in the conflict with the French and the resolution about to split the country apart, he'd sensed his future would lie in Hanoi, rather than in his native Saigon. He traveled North immediately after the Geneva Conference in 1954. The Party welcomed him with open arms, recognizing a true believer, and allocated him a comfortable house close to the Hall of the People, and the Politburo. They'd promoted him to the rank of commissar and lately had offered him a further promotion to Senior Regional Commissar. The snag was he'd need to return to the South to take up his new post to continue the struggle the Communists swore had ended after Geneva.

He declined. He had a pleasant life in the capital of the fledgling People's Republic, and he'd married Trieu, the daughter of a Party Cadre. After many barren years, his wife was, at last, expecting their first child. Each day when he arrived home after work he admired her growing belly.

He always greeted her with the same question. "Will it be a boy or a girl?"

Each day, she'd suppressed a feeling of anxiety at the thought it could be a boy. She didn't want a boy. Boys often traveled South, to throw away their lives in the never-ending war. "My husband, it is too soon to know. You must wait until the baby is born."

"But…"

"You must wait. Perhaps it will be a girl. You will not be disappointed?"

Quang was no fool, and he understood her nervousness. "Do not worry, my darling. If it is a boy, I will make sure he never becomes a soldier. To travel South means death for most of our young men. When he becomes an adult, our son will take up a post here in Hanoi, working for the Party, like most sons of senior Party cadres. No son of mine will end his life in the South."

This day was like no other, and she'd relaxed when he gave her the same assurance he always gave. They ate their evening meal and spent the evening listening to the radio. This time, it was a recorded speech of Ho Chi Minh, and Quang listened enraptured by the words of the man whose name meant Bringer of Light. When he joined his wife in their bed, he reflected on how lucky he was; his future in the Party assured, and his family safe in Hanoi, the capital of North Vietnam. His son would grow up in the Communist Paradise they were creating, and nothing could stop it. Provided he resisted the attempts to send him South, and he was already making contacts with those able to shepherd his son through the labyrinth of bureaucracy necessary to ensure the young man was steered into a safe career; an arrangement most senior Party leaders made for their own sons.

He was almost asleep when he heard a strange droning overhead that became louder as each second passed.

Could it be a storm? No, storms are frequent here, and the sound is different.

The droning grew even louder, and he thought about pulling on his clothes and going outside to see what was causing the noise when the first bombs fell.

He dressed hurriedly in pants, shirt, and sandals after hearing more explosions. Before he left he ordered his wife to go down to the basement, which he'd prepared the year before for just such an eventuality. She told him to be careful before she dressed and climbed down the narrow staircase into the underground shelter.

She glanced at him as she disappeared into the depths. "Be careful, my husband. I don't want anything bad to happen to you. Our baby needs a father."

"I will be careful. For you, and him."

She smiled. Despite everything he was convinced he would soon be the father of a son. She dutifully descended to their basement shelter. Quang rushed outside into the street, in time to hear the whistling of more bombs falling. When he looked up at the clear sky, he was just able to make out the groups of eight contrails. There could be no doubt, American bombers, which was no surprise. They were aware of the potential threat of the B-52s. Part of his work for the Party involved theoretical calculations about blast areas, potential damage, and how to protect the civilian population, especially the senior members of the Party. The theory had become practice, and bombs began to explode close by.

A nearby building collapsed, and men and women were running to help the trapped and injured. He went with them, knowing it was his duty as a member of the political administration to show a willingness to work shoulder-to-shoulder with the people. The cries and screams of the injured were appalling. He dragged out broken bodies, pulled them to safety, and returned to pass chunks of masonry in a human chain to clear the way to those who were trapped beneath.

In the meantime, the bombs continue to fall, and he noted the terror of the populace. He didn't show fear. It was his duty to show defiance in the face of the enemy attack. He continued working for a further three hours, until tired, covered in soot and dust, he staggered home to take a shower and change his clothes. There was no question of going back to bed. He would hurry to the Hall of the People in anticipation of them calling an immediate meeting to discuss the implications of the bombing.

When he returned to his house, he stopped fifty meters away. It was no longer intact. Instead, half the house had been reduced to smoking rubble, and his wife would be buried beneath it. With a cry of anguish, he rushed at the rubble, pulling aside what remained of his house, clawing his way to the staircase. He found his way into the basement and switched on a flashlight. In the beam, he could see his wife's face, unmarked, as if she was sleeping. She wasn't sleeping. When he felt for a pulse, it wasn't there. She was dead, killed by the enormous pressure of the blast that had demolished their house.

There was no question of the baby surviving. Two months before the birth was due, he knew his son lay dead inside her womb. An immense sadness swept over him, and he was unable to stop the tears flooding down his face. After an hour, he pulled himself together, for he had work to do. He pulled her body toward the staircase, intending to get her out of the wrecked house. Before he reached the first step a rumbling announced more of the house collapsing, and masonry and dust showered down the staircase, half filling the basement room. In the chaos and confusion, he dropped the flashlight, and the bulb shattered as it hit the ground.

In total darkness, he cowered in a corner. Entombed, alone, except for the bodies of his wife and unborn son. They would come for him soon. He knew they would come. All he had to do was wait. Yet for hour after hour, nobody came. He had no watch, and he could only estimate the time that had elapsed. He remained trapped in the basement for three days, and the body of his wife was starting to decompose when he heard the first sounds of rescuers trying to reach him.

An hour later they helped him out from the remains of his house, and a handcart carried away his wife's body. Most of his neighbors' houses had survived intact, and he fervently wished it had been one of them the bombs hit, instead of his. And another woman had died, not his wife. That another unborn baby had perished.

A comrade invited him to occupy a room in his house, and after he'd showered, eaten a meal, and borrowed a change of clothes, he went straight to Party Headquarters to report for duty.

The place was in chaos, but he found his way to his boss, the Deputy Minister who greeted him. "Comrade Quang, I'm sorry to hear of your wife. What can I do for you?"

"Are you still looking for a Senior Commissar for Northeast Saigon?"

"That is correct. You will cover the area the Americans call the Iron Triangle." He smiled, "Above and below ground. You're aware of the Cu Chi tunnels, and of their importance to our struggle? They will be part of your remit."

Quang fought down a shudder. After spending three days trapped in the ruins of his basement with his wife's corpse, there was no way he could face the prospect of spending time in one of those dank, dark, stinking, disease-ridden places.

"If you still want me, I will go."

But not in the tunnels. Not that, anything but that. I would sooner die.

"The job is yours."

* * *

Any man who'd fought there could never forget the stench of Vietnam, the ever-present stink of unwashed humanity. Of human manure, of strange spices, of the peculiar scent of Vietnam no man who'd ever fought in that distant Asian war would forget. Above all, there was the humidity. There was the rainfall, and it was always wet. Wet, so the water seems to soak into a man's ODs through to his skin. The scent of mildew and mold became so familiar men learned to ignore it, like the poisonous insects, snakes, and spiders. And the Vietcong.

Men used different mechanisms to cope with the constant dread. Bravado was common, a scorn for the enemy. VC, Vietcong, Victor Charlie, or just Charlie. Sometimes Mr. Charles. Gooks, and they were there to be killed. They did kill them, in their hundreds, and their thousands. Yet still they came, in a human tidal wave. And still they killed them. Many soldiers used drugs to cope with the ever-present stress. To wipe out the nightmare of imminent death lurking with every step they took. Others made a determined effort to become better soldiers, tougher, more skilled, so they'd see out their tour and go home inside the cabin of the chartered airliner instead of the cargo hold.

PFC Paul Farrell was one such soldier. He was a relaxed kind of guy, with an unruly mop of hair, long, like a California surfer. At least it was until an Army barber shaved it to a buzz cut. Before he enlisted he was a devoted outdoorsman and liked nothing more than hunting for game in the mountains of his home state of Virginia. He was lean and rangy, with muscles like whipcord, his skin tanned and leathery after so much time spent in the outdoors. His wary eyes were piercing, a deep, dark blue, in contrast to his dark hair.

He'd enlisted to follow his brother Mark, who'd achieved a commission and was engaged in heavy fighting inside South Vietnam. Paul Farrell wasn't interested in a commission, all he wanted was to serve his country. He worked hard, trained hard, and fought hard. Six months after his arrival in country they promoted him to sergeant following a series of successful patrols. Patrols where his unit came back with an impressive body count, a genuine body count, unlike so many.

He called his older brother every month. The two men were close, which was no surprise. Orphaned after their parents died in an auto accident, they had no other close relatives. Mark Farrell, a captain in the First Air Cavalry, told Paul he intended to stay in the military and make it a career. He advised him to consider doing the same.

"If you can survive Vietnam, you can survive anything, and it's a good life. Provided you steer clear of drugs. You get into that stuff, and you won't even know when you're walking into an ambush. If you're stoned out of your brains, Charlie will make mincemeat of you."

He'd taken his advice and steered clear of drugs, mainly marijuana that circulated freely. Often, a cloud of richly scented smoke hung over Bien Hoa Air Base so pungent it almost blotted out the perpetual stench of burned aviation fuel. But he'd listened to his brother, avoided the temptation, and became a better soldier.

Saying no to drugs didn't save his older brother. Mark was his only relative and after he died he realized how much he'd been his rock, how much he'd depended on him. For advice, guidance, and friendship. He was family, his only family. And he was dead. Not killed in action, but murdered when he responded to a call from a nearby strategic hamlet to assist with the evacuation of a Vietnamese woman about to give birth. She was experiencing serious difficulties with her labor, and they said she needed urgent medical treatment. Captain Farrell's squad was ordered to cover the medevac helicopter detailed to convey her to the hospital.

At the time, MACV was making a determined effort to turn the strategic hamlet program around, and make people believe the system worked. The mission would demonstrate to the Vietnamese the humanitarian credentials of MACV. When Captain Farrell entered the hut to check it out, and ensure it was safe before the medics went in, the pregnant woman detonated a grenade as he stood close. The grenade killed her, killed her unborn child, and killed Mark Farrell. It wasn't war. It was butchery.

Sergeant Paul Farrell learned of the tragedy a week later, and in his grief, he looked for comfort. Booze didn't cut it, and when they offered him marijuana, he accepted with alacrity. It wasn't long before he was swallowing amphetamines to offset the soporific effects of the Mary Jane, and when he needed more of a kick, he turned to cocaine. He'd spent ten months acquiring promotion, acquiring the toughness and skills of a professional soldier. Within ten days he'd lost it all. Vietnam had stolen his soul.

FLAMES OF THE PHOENIX

Chapter One

The order was issued by the commissar sent from Hanoi to harden the campaign of terror and intimidation inside the area known to the Americans as the Iron Triangle. Tran Quang was the right man for the job. From the first day, he demonstrated how much he could terrorize and intimidate, starting with his own men. The message was clear. Obey orders or die. Enslave the peasants, force them to assist the regime, and kill as many noncombatants as you wish to make clear the penalty for disobedience.

"Le Duan, the General Secretary of the Communist Party of Vietnam, has issued an order to set the South alight. You will spare nobody, man, woman, or child until Vietnam is one country. The people will swear their allegiance, or they will die."

The Vietcong were following the orders of Tran Quang when they entered an anonymous village, a collection of crude huts not marked on any map. The inhabitants were peasant farmers, men and women who'd cultivated the surrounding fields for generations to grow crops to feed their families. The twenty men who arrived that day were a platoon of black pajama Vietcong. Like they always did, they went to the house of the village headman, Nguyen Tien Minh, a fanatical supporter of the red tide that flooded south from Hanoi.

The village huts were wretched constructions of bamboo and thatch, patched with anything the villagers could find. The dwelling of Nguyen Tien Minh was different. The headman received a bounty from the United States government in return for administrating the strategic hamlet. He also received regular favors from the Vietcong, in return for providing them with food and shelter when required. Like now, when they were on the run from a company of United States Marines who they'd encountered unexpectedly, almost one hundred heavily armed soldiers, and they needed somewhere to hide.

After he'd greeted them, his wife brought food and drink for the visitors, who stayed out of sight inside his house. While they enjoyed his hospitality, Minh took two villagers with him and visited each hut in turn. Collecting items of clothing from the inhabitants, and scared people handed over what few rags they possessed. Kalashnikov assault rifles were a powerful incentive to cooperate, for most, but not for all.

An older villager, Phan Nam, had a son Phan Tan serving in the ARVN, the Army of the Republic of Vietnam. Nam was fiercely patriotic and despised the ravages of the Communists as they rampaged across South Vietnam, looting, raping, and killing. He told Minh in no uncertain terms there was no way he was about to part with any possessions, his clothes, his food, or anything else. They should go and leave the village, and preferably South Vietnam, in peace.

Two VCs held him while Minh attacked him with a machete, and when he'd finished Phan Nam was dead. He was a grisly sight, his arms and legs almost dismembered, and his face unrecognizable. Minh ordered the VCs to drag the victim into the open and tie him to the tree next to the well that gave shelter from the sun while the villagers drew water. He remained there for three days, his body becoming black and stinking, invaded by hordes of insects. When the ARVN arrived on a routine patrol, they vomited on finding what was left of him.

Their report of the incident found its way to Lieutenant Phan Tan, who happened to be the local liaison with MACV. He kicked up a fuss and insisted they find out what had gone wrong in the strategic hamlet where they'd assured him his father would be safe. MACV sent a patrol after Nguyen Tien Minh, making him a priority target. When they arrived at the strategic hamlet, Minh had disappeared.

* * *

They ordered him to locate and eliminate a man responsible for a series of bloody killings of innocent civilians. It led to him losing everything. After the court martial, he'd become a nobody. Busted down to private soldier, and they'd given him a prison number instead of his name. His world was a tiny cell inside the stockade at Leavenworth. Ten feet, or three meters square, with a concrete floor, concrete walls, and a concrete roof. His bunk was steel-framed, the mattress as hard as the floor, so it made little difference where he slept.

They'd handed down a severe sentence to make an

example of him. To prove to the government of South Vietnam they took his crime seriously, so he was to serve his sentence in solitary confinement.

Ten years! Ten years for killing a man who needed and deserved to be killed.

He'd shot him dead in a fit of rage and passion, his mind in a drug-fueled haze. It shouldn't have made a difference. It did. The death of one man, a traitor, was insignificant compared to the total of what went on in Vietnam. Who would care? Unless the man he killed happened to be the son of the National Police Chief in Saigon. Then it made a difference.

His brother was dead, and the men he'd fought with who had yet to complete their tours were somewhere in Vietnam. Fighting that endless war, but at least they had each other. He had nobody. No family, no friends, he was just a number. Although that wasn't entirely true. He had made one friend since he'd been banged up in Leavenworth. One friend, and one enemy. The torture that wracked his body day and night. The urge to snort cocaine to satisfy the tremors racking his body, an urge he couldn't satisfy.

He was sitting on the floor with his back resting against the wall, and he looked up and grinned when his one friend appeared. "Hi Colin. How're things?"

As usual, Colin didn't reply. Colin was a cockroach, and although roaches weren't everybody's favorite critter, when a man is banged up inside a secure stockade, he had to take what he could get. Maybe Colin was an insect, but he was also a living, moving creature, and Farrell had struck up a kind of rapport with him. Talking to Colin filled some of the long, cold, lonely hours, and at least he didn't talk back. It helped. Especially when the urge raged through his body, and he could share his despair.

The nights were worse. He'd think of his dead brother, Mark Farrell, and of the times they'd spent together growing up in Virginia. Hunting in the mountains, the hot summer sun blazing down on them as they chase and shot game. Returning in triumph with a deer or a wild pig, and their father would take out his sharpened steel knives and clean and butcher enough meat to feed the family for the coming weeks. He recalled his father's pride when he learned Mark had been accepted for West Point.

That was before they died in the auto accident. A delivery truck pulled out of a street without looking and rammed the side of their vehicle. The collision didn't kill them, but it burst into flames, and they died in the resulting conflagration. Ever since he'd been unable to witness a napalm strike in Vietnam without visualizing those final terrible moments when his parents died.

He'd even lost his girlfriend. Kate Seldon had promised to wait for him when he flew out to Vietnam. When he got back they would get married, and they had plans to buy a small house, and he'd set up a business doing the thing he loved most. Hunting; taking parties of city dwellers up into the mountains, teaching them the skills of survival, of tracking, and killing game.

After his conviction, she wouldn't even speak to him, never bothered to write or return his calls. All he had left were memories. His arrival at Tan Son Nhut and his brother had come to meet him. They'd gone into Saigon for drinks, and he recalled them drinking cold beer while they watched the pretty girls flutter past in their ao dais. That was the last time they'd been together. They were never again in the same area at the same time, and all they had was the monthly call when they discussed their plans for the future.

That was then, and this was now. Mark's remains lay in Arlington Cemetery, and his cell in Leavenworth may as well have been a grave. The lock rattled, the cell door opened, and he assumed it was time for lunch. As usual, the guard ordered him to stand at the back of the cell while he placed the tin plate and tin mug on the floor just inside the door.

"Chow time, Farrell." He was one of the friendly ones who called him by his name rather than his number. Some just called him 'shitface,' which he guessed they called all the inmates so they didn't need to remember names or numbers.

"What is it this time?"

A shrug. "The usual. Stew. No idea what's in it, but there's nothing else so what difference does it make?"

"What's in the mug? Fresh coffee?"

He chuckled. "It's coffee, that's all I'll say."

"Tastes like shit?"

"Worse. I'll be back in an hour for the plate."

He swallowed the food, and the coffee was every bit as bad as the guard had said. When he'd finished, his mind went back to Vietnam, and he sat on the floor chatting to Colin.

"Whatever you do, don't go there," he murmured, "The natives are not friendly."

His mind wandered, he was back in South Vietnam. And the memory was nothing good.

* * *

It was the conclusion of a Search and Destroy mission that saw him leading his platoon into enemy territory. The mission was to investigate a reported sighting of a bunch of VCs entering villages and attempting to disrupt the Strategic Hamlets Program. The Lieutenant had called in sick, which was SOP for the sonofabitch who avoided combat like the plague. They'd entered a village, and in the center, he came across a dead body. But this was no ordinary dead body. The guy had been hacked to pieces, aping the historic 'death by a thousand cuts.' The man's wife was sitting next to him, weeping, and her children were looking on, their innocent faces filled with fear and uncertainty.

He questioned the villagers, and they said the man responsible, whose name was Van Dam, had run into the jungle when he heard the platoon arrive. Dam was a known supporter of the Vietcong, a committed Communist, and the villagers were glad to see him go after this latest atrocity. He'd killed the man because he supported the South Vietnamese regime. Van Dam had made an example of him to ensure the loyalty of the rest of the village.

As far as Farrell was concerned, he did what any red-blooded American would do. He went after him and found him cowering in a bamboo thicket about one klick from the village. He gave him a chance, put down his rifle, and produced his combat knife. The guy was armed with a machete, so it was a fair fight. More than fair, most people would regard a combat knife against a machete as a win-win for the machete.

The long blade was still covered in the blood of the man he'd hacked to pieces, and Farrell lost his head and went in hard. He should've arrested him and taken him back for trial, but his brain wasn't functioning the way it should. He'd snorted cocaine the night before and couldn't sleep. Knowing he'd be on patrol at dawn, he snorted more cocaine than was good for him. Enough to keep an elephant awake for a week, and he stormed out of Bien Hoa with enough pent-up aggression to single-handedly charge down a battalion of North Vietnamese regulars.

His brain was still buzzing when he confronted Van Dam holding the machete. He attacked like a crazy man, brushed aside the machete, and stabbed with his combat knife. Not once, not twice, but repeatedly, slashing the guy to ribbons. They found him crouched over the body, sobbing. Not for the death of the man he'd killed, who more than deserved it. He'd been thinking of his brother Mark. Picturing him on that last, humanitarian mission, murdered by a pregnant Vietcong suicide bomber. Fighting a crazy war to save a beleaguered people in a country floating on the sea of blood.

* * *

He couldn't finish the evening meal and left the remains for Colin while he paced backward and forward. All through the long night, his tormented mind unable to think straight. What was he? A drug addict, and often a prison number, nobody. His only company the cries and screams of other inmates elsewhere in the prison. Desperate men caged like animals. Tearing apart their very souls, driving themselves insane. Like wild birds trapped in tiny cages, unable even to flap their wings.

Shortly after dawn, his eyes red-rimmed from lack of sleep, he was seated on the cold floor when the key rattled in the lock. He looked up, expecting to see his breakfast arriving. Colin scuttled out, looking forward to mealtime, but he retreated. This was a new man, a stranger. Unlike the guards, he wore civilian clothes, and Farrell's brain screamed a warning. He was too neat, too preppy. Hair stylishly cut, his features smooth, his eyes calm and relaxed. Chinos, polished brown brogues, button-down Ralph Lauren shirt, and he looked like the Hollywood image of a college professor. The kind of image a man would adopt if he wanted to disarm those he came into contact with.

He assumed a polite expression like they were meeting in a restaurant over lunch. "Do you mind if I sit down?"

"Knock yourself out."

The man smiled and seated himself. "I guess you're wondering who I am."

"Nope."

A shrug. "Fair enough. Mr. Farrell…"

That's new, calling me Mister. Not just Farrell, or private, or sergeant, or my prison number, or even shithead. Mr. Farrell. Progress.

"How're you finding things in here?"

"I've known worse."

A grimace this time; "Nam? I guess you had it bad over there." He didn't reply, "Bad over there, bad in here."

"Uh-huh."

"Right. The thing is, I have a proposition for you. Something that could appeal to you, Mr. Farrell, especially considering your current predicament." He glanced around the tiny cell as if to emphasize the point.

"Not interested."

"Excuse me? I'm offering you a way to get out of this place. Dammit, anything would be better than this."

"You ever fought in Vietnam?"

He gave an evasive answer. Which meant he hadn't fought in Vietnam. "I've been there."

"If you'd fought, you'd know there are things worse than this."

"Of course, of course." He smiled and modulated his voice, so it was as smooth as his appearance, "All I'm asking is that you listen to my proposition, hear what I have to say. Make up your mind and…"

"Fuck off."

His face fell. "You're being a tad hasty, Mr. Farrell, and in your position, you don't have anything to lose. You're not exactly busy, so why not listen to what I have to say, it could…"

"Me and Colin are waiting for breakfast. You're interrupting our schedule, so get out of here."

"Colin?" The expression became sympathetic, like a wealthy man tossing a few cents to a homeless man so he could buy some food, "Is he some kind of imaginary friend?"

"I told you to fuck off."

He gave out a long sigh. "I'll be back tomorrow, see if you're in a better mood."

"Don't hold your breath."

The guy left his cell, and presently the guard arrived with his breakfast. The solitude suited him, rather than eat with the other prisoners. A kind of self-imposed exile from real life. Besides, he wasn't alone. He had Colin, who'd scuttled out and was waiting patiently to be invited to eat.

That night his mind was back in Vietnam, a crazy country when nothing was as it seemed. Where up was down and down was up. Where the ARVN, supposedly defenders of South Vietnamese democracy, frequently refused to carry out routine missions. Where his government was prepared to throw him to the wolves to appease the locals. Or in his case, the National

Police chief.

* * *

He'd been building up to doing something crazy for several weeks. The constant, grinding pressure of patrols into enemy-held territory, speculating whether every time you placed your foot on the ground you'd tread on a pressure mine, a booby-trap, or a pit filled with poisoned punji stakes. On those occasions when the platoon lieutenant accompanied the men, it was worse. His name was Jameson, Second Lieutenant Oliver Jameson, and he wasn't suited to the life of a soldier.

He came from a long line of soldiers, one of whom had served under George Washington. There were ancestors who'd fought in the Civil War, through the Spanish-American War, the First World War, the Second World War, the Korean War. None had reached the rank of general, and they'd put their hopes on Oliver Jameson, expecting great things. The pressure was on, and it was too much. Lieutenant Jameson would have been more suited to a career teaching high school, or maybe junior high, perhaps elementary.

He suffered frequent bouts of illness, which his men suspected were mainly in his head. He couldn't help it. Whenever he heard the sound of a shot, he developed a heightened tic at the corner of his eye, and his right arm started twitching. In the early days, he'd report for duty with the stink of alcohol on his breath. That was before he stopped reporting for duty, and responsibility for leading the platoon fell on Farrell's shoulders.

It was soon after he'd learned of the death of his older

brother. He'd been leading the platoon, chasing down a bunch of Vietcong who'd set an ambush across the main route from Saigon to Binh Long. A cart pulled by water buffalo had overturned and was blocking the carriageway. A jeep slowed before it reached the ambush, and the Viets fired too soon from a concealed machine gun nest hidden inside the edge of the jungle. One soldier died, and one was wounded. Fortunately, the driver was unhurt, and he flung the jeep into a tight turn and raced back to Saigon.

They dispatched Farrell's platoon by helicopter to head them off, and they landed close to the intersection where the highway forked for Dalat. They were easy to track. They'd fled toward an area known to be controlled by the Vietcong, and Farrell had simply returned the favor and set an ambush, which they promptly fell into.

He remembered it all in vivid detail. The line of ten pajama-clad men walking along the narrow path, laughing and joking with each other. Smoking and spitting, some drinking rice wine from improvised flasks, and he gave a signal to the men on the opposite side of the track. They'd brought along an M-60, mounted on a tripod, and the gun roared out its message of death. They had nowhere to run to, for the foliage grew thick and tangled on either side, like a wall. Men went down like ninepins, and inside of a minute, most were dead or dying on the path.

But not all. He counted eight bodies, which meant two had got away. Not enough, he'd wanted a clean sweep, and he took off on his own, charging along the path, leaping over the bodies of the dead and dying. In his drug-fueled fury, he ran like the wind, his muscles developed during years of hunting through the mountains of Virginia carrying him along so fast he felt he'd sprouted wings. He caught up with them after the first ten minutes. They were unaware he was so close, and they'd stopped, bent over, trying to recover their breath.

It didn't occur to him to take the shot, not then. He wanted to get close, to tear them limb from limb. These men fought for the same regime responsible for the murder of his brother. As he closed with them, they brought up their rifles to shoot him dead. One rifle jammed, the other fired a short burst before he unslung his M-16, stood in the open, and fired several three-round bursts that knocked down the shooter. He didn't care whether he lived or died, for everything he cared for had gone when Captain Mark Farrell fell victim to the pregnant suicide bomber.

As if sensing he was faced with some powerful, elemental force, something unearthly, almost inhuman, the VC froze. His rifle had jammed, but he could've picked up the rifle dropped by his dead comrade. He didn't, and when Farrell closed with him, he grabbed him by the front of his shirt and pulled his face close.

"You want a fight, you backstabbing motherfucker? You're good at getting sick women to kill American officers with grenades. How about you fight it out with a real, live American soldier who ain't afraid to take you on face-to-face? Mano a mano, come on, use that knife, and let's do this right."

The rest was a blur. Until he heard a voice saying, "Sarge, the guy's had enough." PFC Jed Fisher was standing over him. Jed, short for Jedediah, from a family that held deep-set Christian beliefs, beliefs that included strong hatred of Communism, which had prompted Jed to enlist. He was a good soldier, and he was also a man with a conscience, "You should clean yourself up, and I'm not talking about the blood on your ODs. Stop taking that stuff. It's screwing with your brain."

He looked down, and he was covered in blood, the blood of the VC. He'd stabbed him so many times it was impossible to count them, not that it mattered too much. He was dead. Several times afterward Jed tried to persuade him to quit the habit that was playing havoc with him, and he didn't listen. Not until it was too late.

* * *

The civilian returned the next morning. Neat and prim, with the warm, confident smile fixed on his face, like a surgeon who'd just performed a successful operation to remove a tumor and was about to impart the happy news it had been successful.

"Hello again, Mr. Farrell. I trust you had a comfortable night." Before he could toss a surly reply, he held out his hand, "By the way, I have the advantage of knowing your name, but I haven't told you mine. Charles Curtis, and I represent…"

"CIA."

His eyes widened in surprise. "How did you know?"

"Pal, it's the uniform. You guys all look the same."

He forced a grin. "Maybe I should pass that on to our people at Langley. Okay, you worked it out, but why don't you hear what I have to say? I may as well tell you, Mr. Farrell, there's an offer on the table. It's an offer you shouldn't refuse. Not if you want to get out of here any time soon."

"I'm not interested."

Farrell observed him, and the strange thing about Curtis

was his eyes. Despite his prim, straightforward appearance, they looked everywhere, except right at you. Maybe he could've looked more dishonest if he'd worked at it, but somehow Farrell doubted it.

He gave another long sigh and smiled again. "I hear you, but being as you're a captive audience. You're gonna hear it anyway. Especially as it's something that should appeal to a man like you. I read your file and discovered the reason you carved up that Viet. Frankly, I don't blame you. He was one bad dude. It's just a pity he happened to have a father who headed up the National Police." He shrugged, "Shit happens, but that's history. What I'm offering you, Mr. Farrell is a chance to get out of here and do the same thing as you did to that Viet. Seek out the men who are prolonging the war in Vietnam, betraying their own people, and frequently butchering them. You should know that CIA has put into effect a program to seek them out."

Despite his misgivings, he was interested to know more. He was also amused. "Seek them out and what?"

Curtis didn't pull any punches. "Kill them. They're a disease, a blight on the land, like a plague of locusts. Kill them, and the Communists lose their support in the towns and villages." He spread his hands, palms upward, like a bazaar merchant who'd just made his final offer, even if it would bankrupt him and cause his family to starve, "There's a place for you in this program. We call it Phoenix, the Phoenix Program. Early signs are promising. We're recruiting men prepared to enter enemy-held territory in small groups, sometimes alone. Often they go in at night. Take out senior Vietcong commanders masquerading as friendlies, and leave with no trace of them ever having called. Except for the corpse, of course."

He didn't reply. He was too astonished at what he was hearing. This jerk was suggesting he'd jump at the chance to go back to Vietnam, back to the green hell, back to the blood and the slaughter. Back to a war fought by a generation of brave Americans, on behalf of a generation of South Vietnamese, many of whom refused to lend their support.

"The answer is no."

Curtis ignored the refusal. "If I were you I'd give it some thought."

"I have, and the answer is no."

He paused, eyeing Farrell with a steady gaze. "Don't you care about your brother?"

It was like he'd slapped him across the face. "Excuse me?"

"Your brother. I'd have thought you'd jump at the chance to find out who was responsible for his murder."

He felt like putting his hands around Curtis' throat and strangling him. "The woman who murdered him, along with her unborn child, was torn apart when the grenade exploded. She's dead."

He nodded. "That's all in the report, but there's a lot it doesn't say; like who persuaded that woman to kill herself and her baby to kill an American officer. We believe we can track him down, and he'd be a perfect target for the Phoenix Program."

"Do you have a name?"

"What difference would it make to you, Mr. Farrell? Even if we had a name, there wouldn't be a damn thing you could do about it." He glanced around the bare, concrete walls, "Unless you're planning on breaking out of here, and I doubt Houdini could manage it."

"You didn't answer me. Do you have a name?"

He paused, apparently thinking hard. "Not yet. It's something we're working on. If you agree to help us, we could get you out of here. Arrange to commute your sentence, strike you from the Army records, and you'd become a civilian employee of the CIA. Free and clear to return to Vietnam with the Phoenix Program. Who knows, maybe you could find that guy and take him out?"

He wasn't fooled, not for a moment. The guy didn't have a name. If he did, he'd have used it as leverage.

"What's your answer, Mr. Farrell?"

"If you're asking me to become an assassin, the answer is no."

He shook his head. "You're making a big mistake. During your service in Vietnam, you demonstrated considerable talent for asymmetric warfare."

"You mean killing."

"If you like. You're an ideal candidate for the Program, and frankly, I believe you could make a difference to the progress of the war. Why don't you think about it?"

"I have. Unless you can come up with a name, the answer is no."

He sucked in a breath, fighting back his frustration. "I'll tell you what I'm gonna do. I'll give you one last chance to make up your mind. Think about it overnight, and I'll be back in the morning for your answer. I can't waste any more time. I have other men to contact. It's up to you, Farrell. Last chance."

He was amused that he'd managed to piss the guy off. It was no longer Mr. Farrell, just Farrell. He grinned to himself. If he told him no in the morning, he'd probably call him by his prison number, or maybe 'shithead.' He didn't care. But he had a lot to think about, and the day seemed to last forever. The food looked and smelled even more disgusting, and even Colin didn't show for the evening meal. He tossed and turned all night, thinking about his brother. Looking around the darkened cell and wondering if by refusing Curtis he was making a mistake. It hadn't worked out so well the last time he was in Vietnam.

Would it be any different next time? Sure, anything's possible. I'd be a civilian. That's true. Which would give me more freedom of action than when I belonged to the Army. The involvement of CIA would likely be a two-edged sword, but maybe, just maybe, the Phoenix Program would work out. And maybe, just maybe, I'd find the man who ordered that woman to slaughter Mark.

In the early hours, Colin put in an appearance. The plate was gone, and he was disappointed to find there was no food. He grinned. "You should've come earlier, pal. You'll have to wait for breakfast." As usual, he didn't reply.

Curtis was late the following morning, and a new guard put his tin plate and mug on the floor before backing out of the cell without saying a word. Although he was hungry, he couldn't eat the food. For some reason it made him feel more nauseous than usual, even more nauseous than the stink of South Vietnam, and that was saying something.

An hour later, the CIA man returned. "I need an answer. What's it gonna be?"

He still hadn't made up his mind. His mind swirled at lightning speed with a million thoughts.

Mark, what should I do? Would you want me to go back to that hellhole and attempt to track down your killer? Or stay here and rot in this cell?

He didn't have to wait for an answer, although he knew what Mark's answer would've been. If the CIA wanted him to become an assassin inside Vietnam as the price of his freedom to track down his killer, go for it. Forget the lawyers, forget justice, forget the courts, forget the whole mechanism of the judicial process. All that did was put him in this shithole. Mark would want him to take revenge in the most fundamental way.

He looked at Curtis. "How does this work?"

The man relaxed and smiled, and he saw a hint of triumph in his expression. "I'll arrange to get you out of here by the end of the week. When you've been sworn in and filled out the paperwork, we'll put you on a plane for Vietnam, where you'll meet up with the other members of your unit. There're normally four men, but one was wounded, so they're shorthanded. The guy in charge is Clarence Dorsey, a former Marine, and he's good people. His body count is one of the best, and with more men like him we'd have won the war years ago."

He put out a hand. "Welcome to the squad, Mr. Farrell."

Mr. Farrell again, I wonder what it would've been if I'd refused.

He shook hands, feeling as if he'd just made a pact with the devil. When Curtis left the cell, he recalled an old Chinese proverb.

'He who seeks revenge should first dig two graves.'

Deep inside the prison, he heard a door clang shut, and it sounded like a coffin lid closing.

Chapter Two

Two days later Curtis returned with a sheaf of paperwork, several forms for him to sign. He didn't bother reading them and just scrawled a signature.

What difference does it make? I'm a condemned man, condemned to rot in a cell in Leavenworth or condemned to return to Vietnam, and probably end up rotting in a shallow grave in the jungle.

Things moved fast, so fast he was in a daze. Except this time there were no drugs inside him, coursing through his veins. Not that he didn't crave them, crave the release into oblivion, release from the torment his life had become. One day confined in a tiny concrete box inside Leavenworth, and the next they gave him back his clothes and booted him out. He left wearing his battered brown leather flight jacket and flew first-class with Curtis to Washington. A limo transferred them to Langley, and he was inside the vast and impressive CIA headquarters. They swore him in, and he felt like a package being processed on an assembly line. Passed from person to person, department to department, photos, fingerprints, and so many questions he lost track. He guessed frozen chickens felt the same way.

He eventually had to fight down his irritation when they repeated the same questions again and again, until it was done, and he spent the night alone in a budget hotel in Washington. A cab picked him up to convey him to Washington National, where he would fly Braniff International onboard a Boeing 707 bound for Vietnam. He should've slept during the flight, except he couldn't sleep. Wondering what he'd let himself in for.

Who are these Phoenix Program operators? What kind of men are they, former elite soldiers, or cynical mercenaries, paid killers? Decent men on a mission, or ex-cons, like me?

The difference in time zones and lack of sleep left him feeling spaced out, struggling to come to grips with the reality of his situation. Not that he'd slept much since his court martial and conviction. There didn't see much point. The 707 bumped onto the tarmac at Tan Son Nhut and he was back, the air reeking of oil, jet fuel, and sewage. Gripped by the incredible humidity, which often reached one hundred percent, like an invisible glue. The arrangement was the leader of his assigned Phoenix team, the man named Clarence Dorsey would meet him, and as he climbed down the aircraft steps, he looked at the mix of vehicles approaching to convey passengers to the terminal.

One was a Willys jeep like the mainstay of World War II, but this was the more modern M151 Military Utility Tactical Truck, or MUTT for short. Unlike most military jeeps, a man drove this one in civilian clothes. He eyed Farrell with a fierce expression like he was sizing him up in the ring to decide where to place the first punch.

"You Farrell?"

He nodded. "Dorsey?"

"Get in."

He climbed into the passenger seat, and before he was seated Dorsey stamped on the gas pedal, let go the clutch, and the jeep leaped forward across the airfield. He drove straight past the terminal buildings, heading toward the hangars.

"Back at Langley, they told me I needed to check-in on arrival."

He grunted a reply. "No need."

"If you're sure."

"Waste of time. Most of the guys on duty are gooks. I wouldn't give them the time of day."

"Uh, okay. So what's the deal, where do I start?"

"I introduce you to the other guys, kit you out with weapons, and we go out and do some killing." His mouth twisted into a sneering smile, "Or did you think you were here to admire the scenery?"

"Nope."

"Good. Let's get one thing straight from the word go. You're here to kill gooks. Nothing else."

He didn't reply. He could've reminded Dorsey that many of the gooks were South Vietnamese allies of the United States. That despite the dismal performance the Army of the Republic of Vietnam, the ARVN, there were still plenty of good Vietnamese. On balance, he let it go. Dorsey didn't look like the kind of man who would take kindly to having someone mention his prejudices.

When they reached their destination, he braked so hard

Farrell was flung forward. He had to grip the windshield to prevent him from slamming into the hard steel frame. Dorsey climbed out and strolled through the narrow wicket door of a hangar. He had time to get a good look at him. Clarence Dorsey was one of those guys you set eyes on and disliked on sight. Of medium height, hair thinning, and skin as oily as his expression. He moved in a loose kind of disjointed way, like a cowboy who'd spent most of his life on a horse, so when he got off it looked like he was swaggering, or maybe staggering. When he smiled, he looked like a rattlesnake moments before it struck. He looked mean. Mean and nasty, with enough prejudices to fill the cargo hold of the 707 he'd arrived in.

It occurred to Farrell that Clarence was in Vietnam for one reason only, to benefit Clarence Dorsey. He had a brisk, cold manner, spitting out orders like he was a senior officer about to send his men into battle. He wasn't a senior officer. He wasn't even military. And they weren't going into battle. Clarence was an assassin, bought and paid for like the rest of them, with one difference. He made it clear right from the start how much he enjoyed it. Farrell afterward found out he didn't give a damn who he killed. Man or woman, friend or foe. They were counted the same. Meet for the grinder. He followed him, and there were two men inside, who he assumed were the other two members of the team.

He waved a hand toward them. "You'll be working with these men. Pablo Batista and David Ashe."

He nodded a greeting and looked them over. Pablo Batista, as his name suggested was Hispanic, and he later discovered he'd crossed from Cuba to Florida on a flimsy raft. He was swarthy and short, with a bushy beard that made him look somewhere between a young Fidel Castro and Che Guevara. He looked tough enough, with long, apelike arms, and he stared back at Farrell with a hard, expressionless gaze. The eyes were soulless, cold, the eyes of a stone killer. He suspected CIA had chosen wisely when they recruited Batista. He afterward discovered Batista had a huge chip on his shoulder after the Bay of Pigs disaster, much of which he blamed on the CIA, who he claimed had sold his country down the river. He never explained why he worked for CIA, and nobody asked.

David Ashe was somewhat different. Tall and lanky, in a kind of Clint Eastwood way. A craggy, lined face, etched with what looked like suffering. The eyes were more human than those of Batista, yet they gave little away. Instead, they stared past Farrell into the distance, the Vietnam, 'thousand-yard stare.' A man who'd been in country for too long and had seen plenty of action, as well as too much pain, too much horror, and too much death. Yet for some reason he'd elected to stay on. Maybe the reason was the same as his, to escape a long prison term, although it turned out to be something altogether different. Money. Ashe had gambled away every cent of his severance pay, and his gambling addiction had made him near destitute, until he took the only route left open to him. To sell the skills and experience he'd acquired in Vietnam to the highest bidder. CIA.

He shook hands with both men. Batista glared at him without saying a word. Ashe was friendly enough. "Call me Dave."

"Paul."

"Welcome to the team." He grinned, "Did they tell you about the health plan?"

He recalled some of the paperwork they'd shown him at

Langley. "They did mention something about it."

"Just kidding. If you're not healthy, you won't make it back. No health plan is gonna save you."

Dorsey bullied his way between them. "Okay, that's enough of the pleasantries. Ashe, get him kitted up. We're due out at dawn. Get yourselves moving."

Farrell stood his ground. "What's the deal? What're we getting into?"

"We hitch a ride on a Huey heading out to Binh Long, and we hike into our destination, a strategic hamlet about ten klicks from the base. The target is a guy by the name of Duy Tan. He used to claim he hated the Communists. Until he showed his true colors and hacked a man to death for refusing to assist the Vietcong. They sent in a patrol to get him, but by the time they'd arrived he'd disappeared. Our orders are to find him and bury him." He gave a savage grin, "When I say bury him, I'm talking dead or alive. Preferably alive."

Batista chuckled, looking forward to the prospect of inflicting such brutal cruelty. Ashe wore a neutral expression, and he guessed he was used to it. Killing was like that. After a while, it was like eating dinner. Routine. Except it didn't taste so good.

"What's so special about this particular killing? I mean, we're in the middle of the Vietnam War. We're killing hundreds of men every day, so why this guy?"

"All you need to know is they gave the job to us, and we'll get it done. Get your gear together, weapons, ammunition, helmet, field pack, the usual stuff. We won't be out for long, so there's no need to draw rations. Make sure you're on the stand at 06.00. No later, Charlie works the night shift, and we should catch our target, Duy Tan, on his way home. If we're late, we'll miss him."

"I still want to know what this guy did to piss off MACV."

"He runs the local brothel."

"Since when has that been a reason to kill a man?"

"Since he rounded up the local girls to give aid and comfort to the enemy. This is no ordinary brothel. When their testosterone is overflowing, Charlie pays a visit to Tan's brothel during the night. They get what they want, and the VC pays him a stipend to keep the business running. Everybody's happy." He grinned, "Except for the girls, of course. They're all prisoners, and they get raped several times a night, especially the better-looking ones. Their families complained to Saigon, Saigon handed it to MACV, who passed it on to the CIA, who gave it to us. Is that reason enough for you, Mr. Farrell?"

He started to walk away, and Farrell called after him. "Say, where do I sleep?"

He shrugged. "Who gives a shit? It's up to you to find somewhere." He chuckled, "Ask Ashe, maybe he'll share."

He stalked away, and Batista followed him out of the hangar. Ashe went to a steel cage, opened it, and began pulling out equipment. "Combat pants, T-shirt, armored vest, helmet, and canvas pack."

"What about a jacket?"

He raised his eyebrows. "What for? That jacket looks okay. Clarence likes to sell unused equipment to the locals. It's a kind of sideline."

"I get it. I thought I'd ask."

"Sure. You'll need weapons, and we use AR-15s. More reliable than the M-16, and they fire on full auto. There're times when you need to spray plenty of bullets." He pulled an assault rifle from a rack fixed to the wall and handed it over, "I'll issue some spare mags when we're done. Handguns are Colt M1911s, and you have a choice of a belt or a shoulder rig."

"I'll take the shoulder rig."

He nodded. "No sweat. They keep your gun clean when we're wading through mud and shit."

"I know."

Farrell regarded the familiar weapon with interest. He'd used the same gun when he was in Vietnam before, and the pistol had proved itself solid and reliable. It was also heavy, heavy enough to batter a man over the head if you ran low on ammunition.

"Dave, I don't want to push too hard, but I need to catch up with some Zs. Do you have any ideas where I can bunk down for the night?"

"There's a spare couch in my place. You're welcome to use it until you get fixed up. There is room on the base allocated to the squad. Clarence refused to allow anyone to use the room that's going spare. He said to keep it empty for when the guy who sleeps there comes back."

"You're saying this gig is temporary?"

"Kind of. It depends on Melvin, that's Clarence's brother. He stopped a bullet in the belly, and he'll be in the hospital until he makes a full recovery. Clarence tends to be protective of his brother, and he wants to keep his job open."

"Is he that good?"

"Depends on what you call good. He's a psycho, worse than Clarence. Shoots everything that moves. Come to that, he shoots everything that doesn't move. I wouldn't get too attached to this job. There're plenty of other jobs going inside the Program. Men don't tend to last long in Clarence's outfit."

"They burn out?"

"They die."

He loaded the spare magazines into the pack and followed Ashe across the air base, carrying the equipment he'd issued. He lived in a bungalow several hundred meters outside the main gates, and the couch he offered was a comfortable double bed, albeit in a dilapidated condition. When he put his weight on the mattress the frame creaked alarmingly, and the mattress sagged so low it almost hit the floor. But it was somewhere to lay down his head, and he was so tired he wanted to fall asleep right there and then.

He stowed his gear ready for the morning and went back out to find Ashe, who was in the tiny kitchen. "Dave, I'm beat, I'm gonna hit the sack."

"I was about to heat a couple of burgers with fried onions. There's fresh bread rolls, and you're welcome to share."

He shook his head. "I'm bushed. Where do you eat breakfast?"

"Right here." He grinned, "Last night's burgers with fried onions, bread rolls, but not so fresh."

"That sounds good enough to me. And thanks."

He went back to his room, removed his boots, and before he'd taken off his clothes he was asleep on the bed. His dreams were nightmarish and a kaleidoscope of vivid images. Napalm strikes, flames and smoke shooting up after fighter-bombers dropped several tons of ordnance on Charlie, or where they believed Charlie to be. Which wasn't always the same thing, a night patrol, and tracer rounds hacking toward them, forcing them to take cover, and finally, a grenade exploding close to his brother Mark. He watched his body get ripped apart by hot metal fragments, and when the smoke and dust settled, it was hard to work out who was the American officer and who was the pregnant woman.

Like before when he was in Vietnam, he slept with his Colt underneath the pillow, and when he felt a hand on his shoulder, he was awake in a split second, snatching for the gun. And looking at Ashe's amused face.

"It's 05.00, and I've fixed fresh coffee and burgers. As soon as we've eaten, we need to get over to the stand and join Dorsey and Batista."

They ate breakfast in silence. He had a hundred questions he wanted to ask, but he'd just arrived, and this wasn't the time. When they'd finished, Ashe tossed the dirty dishes into the sink. "I have a maid who comes in every day. She'll take care of them. Let's go."

He strapped on his Colt, pulled on his leather jacket, shrugged into his pack, and picked up the rest of his gear. Rifle and armored vest. He was about to walk outside when Ashe stopped him. "About that vest, I wouldn't bother. In this job, you need to move fast and keep silent. If they see or hear you, no vest on earth is gonna do you any good. Those things are too damned heavy, and they slow you down when you're in a hurry. Which is most of the time, especially when the bullets start to fly."

He dumped the vest and followed Ashe outside. They had a half-hour before they were due to meet Dorsey and Batista, and they strolled through the gates onto the air base. Dave gave the sentry, who seemed to know him, a friendly wave, and he passed them through. It was all familiar, a kind of déjà vu. The odors, the soldiers running everywhere like ants, all of them looking the same, clad in ODs. Green-painted jeeps buzzing around aimlessly, and the roar of several jet engines startled the birds as four McDonnell Douglas F-4s, their hardpoints loaded with ordnance, prepared to embark on yet another mission. He wondered where they were headed; guessing the area around Cu Chi was a strong candidate.

They reached the stand where several Hueys were clustered on the pad. As they approached, a squad of infantry appeared and boarded four of the helicopters. The engines started with a roar of turbines, and they took off, flying northwest. A cargo aircraft touched down on the tarmac, followed by a Cessna Bird-Dog O-1 returning from a reconnaissance mission, or maybe spotting for artillery. Ashe led the way to a Huey some distance away, and unlike the others this one carried no military markings.

"This is our ride, but they're not here, so we'll have to wait."

He looked around for any sign of Dorsey and Batista, checked his watch, and it was almost 06.00. There was no sign of them.

"I thought Dorsey said it was important we got away on time?"

"Yeah, that's what he said. If he had a skinful last night, he'll likely be late. Batista, too, they generally spend their evenings together. Booze, drugs, girls, you name it. Working for CIA the pay is good, and they like to spend it."

"What happens if they don't turn up?"

"Nothing happens. Dorsey will make up some lame

excuse about an important mission up country." He grinned, "I guess it's not like the Army."

He thought about that for a few moments. "Dave, it's just like the Army."

They waited and waited some more. Hueys took off, several landed, and there was still no sign of them. Until 07:20, and they swaggered in without a greeting.

"We need to get into the air. We're running late." He looked at Farrell and belched loudly, "We had important stuff to take care of."

"Yeah, sure."

They climbed into the Huey, and the first thing he noticed was the bright patches of aluminum riveted over the bullet holes. If somebody had told him this Huey had been in the war for the past five years, he wouldn't have been surprised. In places, there were more patches than original panels, but when they were aboard, and the pilot started the Lycoming turboshaft engine, it came to life, roaring just the way he remembered. The pilot turned his head a fraction, stared at them through mirror shades, looked back through the windshield, and gave the collective a savage jerk.

The UH-1 leaped into the air, and minutes later they were flying north over the endless, green jungle canopy. The destination was the sprawling air base at Binh Long, and more than anything this told him he was back. Not far from where his brother had died so cruelly.

The last time I was in action, I had the satisfaction of staring down at the bloody body lying dead on the jungle floor. After that, everything went wrong, and I wound up in Leavenworth in a tiny concrete cell, but hey, shit happens. Now I'm back!

He had serious misgivings about the other members of the team. At least, about Clarence Dorsey, who seemed to regard everything as some kind of joke. Forgetting the guy they were going after gave aid and comfort to the enemy by capturing local young women and forcing them to prostitute themselves for the Vietcong. Never mind the suffering these women endured, and he guessed a few would've killed themselves. Being raped inside a country where many girls valued their virginity above life itself would for some be a dishonor impossible to bear.

He glanced at Dorsey, at Batista, and at Ashe. Finally, he caught his reflection in the Perspex canopy of the Huey, and he didn't like what he saw. They were death, all of them, including him; men who wore no uniform and carried no means of identification. They could commit whatever atrocities they pleased, and who could complain?

'Mr. Diem, you said a bunch of men murdered your wife and children and burned your hut? The Army takes this kind of thing very seriously. Just give me their names and unit, and I'll find them and make sure they're punished. What was that? You didn't see any names? What about unit identification, anything to help me find out who they were? Nothing? I'm sorry, Mr. Diem, there's nothing I can do.'

The pilot glanced back at them, his eyes hidden behind the mirrored glasses, and he spoke in a toneless voice, empty of any expression, like a recording. "We land in ten." He glanced back through the Perspex.

Farrell looked around again, and he was beginning to wonder if he'd made the right choice. He'd swapped his cell inside Leavenworth and the company of a cockroach named Colin for this, the company of a bunch of hired thugs and cutthroats, even though Ashe didn't seem as bad. Time would tell, and he had a feeling the taint would be bad.

He recalled a line from some German philosopher.

'When you stare death in the eye for long enough, death stares back at you, and you become death.'

That's what I've become. Death.

Before they landed at Binh Long, the pilot detoured to overfly the village they were headed for, and he looked down with interest at the dismal collection of hooches. Just like ten thousand others in Vietnam, the peasants living in abject poverty, ill educated, and deprived of any healthcare. It was a depressing sight, and he wondered what would make these people want to fight for either side. They reached Binh Long Air Base, and the skids touched down on the concrete hardstand. The pilot didn't even look around as they disembarked. Didn't wish them good luck, didn't grin, and thank them for flying Army Aviation. Just ignored them. Dorsey led the way through the base, stalking out the gate without a word or a glance at the sentries on duty as they left and headed along the highway. They followed in a single line. Farrell was in the rear, and he noticed Clarence took occasional swigs from a small flask. He wasn't surprised. He'd smelled the booze when they arrived at the helicopter, and all he could wonder was how much it affected his judgment when the shit started to hit the fan.

Despite the booze, he seemed to know where he was going. After walking north for two klicks, they came to a path that led into deep jungle. He turned onto it, walking as if he didn't have a care in the world. This was bandit country, and Farrell had plenty of cares. Like staying alive. He dropped back so there was plenty of space between him and the next man. If Charlie started shooting and they were too bunched up, they could take them down in a single shattering burst.

After an hour, Dorsey held up a hand for them to stop and took out a map. He gestured for them to gather around, and they squatted on the ground.

"The village is about two klicks further along this path." He belched, and the stink of booze was overpowering, "With any luck, we'll be in time to catch Tan on his way home from running his underground brothel. By day, he's the local tax collector, so he'll be heading back to grab a few Zs before he starts his day job. By the way, the word is he's built up a big pile of cash that he keeps hidden inside his home. It's a bamboo hut, but bigger than most of the others. They say it's comfortable and well furnished from his ill-gotten gains. When we get there, the hut is mine."

He gave them a terse smile, "Anything I find I'll split between the four of us. You men make sure you grab Tan, and you know what to do with him." He drew a hand across his neck. They knew.

The more time Farrell spent with these men, the more uncomfortable he felt. He also had a bad feeling about this mission, and when Dorsey talked about a stash of money, that feeling got worse. He wondered about the main reason for targeting Tan. Was it because he whored the local women for the Vietcong? Or was it an excuse to shoot him dead and steal his loot? He'd no way of finding out, and he suspected if he asked too many questions, Dorsey and Batista would find a way to shoot him dead. The 'accidental' victim of friendly fire. He'd talk to Ashe later, but in the meantime, he had to go along with it. This was the wrong place to get into any arguments. They had enough to handle with Charlie.

They started walking again, and a half-hour later they came upon signs of civilization. Or what passed for civilization inside Vietnam. The palm-thatched roofs of the hooches, and soon they'd see the huts. With any luck, they'd find Tan. And kill him.

* * *

Duy Tan had heard the beat of rotor blades and the roar of a turbine engine. The unmistakable sound of a Huey heading toward the village, and Hueys were bringers of bad news, especially for a man such as him. He'd recently returned from an education and indoctrination course outside Hanoi, and before he returned, they'd informed him of his promotion. He was now Commissar Duy Tan, with overall command of his home village and the area around it. Which included the local Vietcong.

The Americans called villages like his strategic hamlets. He smiled to himself, for they believed the strategy of these supposedly safe places was successful. It was successful, but not for the Americans. Although they'd offered some protection from the Communists in the early days, it had mostly been an illusion. The North began inserting their people into the villages and forcing the inhabitants to swear allegiance to Hanoi. Forcing the population to feed and house the gallant fighters of the Vietcong, for fear of the brutal alternative.

Of course, there was the other thing, his brothel, which had caused problems. Families loathed their daughters being whored to Vietcong fighters, but he'd explained they were there to help bring about the glorious reunification of Vietnam. When the Americans were gone, everybody would enjoy tremendous benefits, prosperity, health care, good housing, and sanitation. It meant making certain sacrifices, like their younger daughters, but it would be worth it in the end. They were skeptical at first, but after he'd arranged for a few dissenters to be shot, the objections faded.

He considered sounding a warning about the Huey, but the local commander, Nguyen Ninh, had emerged from his hut with his son Trung, who'd indicated they'd heard it and were taking precautions. The younger man was a complete contrast to his father. Bespectacled, with a serious expression, he looked more like a student than a Vietcong fighter. "Commissar, my father has alerted his men, do you believe they will come here?"

He nodded. "I do." He looked at the father. "Commander Ninh, we can anticipate an American patrol arriving sometime soon. One helicopter means there'll be no more than a dozen men, perhaps less, and I doubt they'll be expecting too much trouble. This could be a good chance to kill some of the enemy. Disperse your men to their spider holes and get ready to ambush them when they arrive."

He looked troubled. "If they find out what we've done, they'll send in more troops, and you know what happened in Binh Can last month. They torched the village, killed every man they suspected of being Vietcong, and moved the women and children to a camp outside Saigon."

"They won't find out, Commander. Tell your men to prepare."

He stood his ground. "There was also My Lai. They killed them all."

A shrug. "My Lai was of no importance. We execute entire villages all the time if they refuse to swear allegiance to Hanoi.

Those villagers they killed at My Lai weren't Communists, so who cares?"

He stood firm. "Four hundred people died. They were Vietnamese, women and children, as well as men, shot by American soldiers. Even their General Westmorland approved. He said the men responsible had carried out an 'Outstanding Action.' Commissar, my wife and my children live in the village. I do not want them hurt. Or killed."

Tan jabbed a finger into Ninh's chest. "Commander, I have full authority over this village and this region. Hanoi has given me the authority to punish any man who fails to follow my orders to the letter, and I just gave you an order! Disperse the men to their spider holes, and when the Americans appear, kill them. All of them." He softened his tone, knowing he needed the cooperation of this man, "Don't worry, we will hide the evidence and bury the bodies deep in the jungle where they will never be found. They will never know, and the village will be safe. Your family will be safe."

He stood for a few seconds longer, and Tan wondered if he'd have to pull out the Tokarev automatic they'd given him in Hanoi and shoot the man dead for disobedience. But, eventually, he walked away with his son Trung in tow and began shouting orders. Men appeared from the huts and dispersed to their pre-prepared positions. Spider holes, typically shoulder-deep, round holes, often covered by a camouflaged lid, from which a soldier could suddenly stand and fire a weapon. Men rushed to obey the command they'd practiced many times, and within minutes they'd disappeared. Tan smiled to himself.

When the Americans arrive, AK-47s will rake the area with a hurricane of bullets, impossible to withstand. They're as good as dead.

Hanoi will be pleased.

* * *

He began to feel uneasy, that familiar feeling of déjà vu. He'd been in too many villages like this one, and each time he swore he could smell trouble before they got close enough to inhale the rank stench of poverty, decay, and lack of sanitation. Clarence's order to the pilot to overfly the village to check it out was stupid. If Duy Tan was in there, he'd have seen the Huey, and it would have given him ample warning of trouble. The chances were he could call on local VCs to back him up, which meant they'd be walking into an ambush.

He caught up with Clarence. "Don't you think we should check it out, see how things are before we go in?"

He halted and stared at Farrell, his lips twisted into a sneer. "What's on your mind? You scared?"

He didn't rise to the bait. "They're bound to have heard the helicopter, and they'll have had time to prepare a hot welcome."

He sighed. "Farrell, we're here for one man, the local tax collector by day, and whoremaster by night. We don't need to be scared of one man."

"Clarence, there's being scared, and there's being careful. I suggest we split up. How about I cut through the jungle with Ashe and come in from the north? You circle around with Batista from the south, and if Charlie got there before us, we'll know about it."

He shrugged. "Play it your way if you want to be a Boy Scout. Me and Pablo are gonna kick in the front door, and if any

51

gooks get in our way, we'll waste them. That's what I call being careful."

He gave him a final, contemptuous glance and continued along the path.

Farrell dropped back with Ashe. "I don't know what you want to do, but I'm cutting around to the north and make sure we're not walking into an ambush."

He shrugged. "Why not?"

They left the path and started walking through the trees, cursing the tangles of vines and undergrowth that held them back. They changed direction several times to find a way through the foliage, and as they got closer, Farrell found the silence ominous. He'd encountered something similar before, and it usually, not always, but usually meant one thing. The shit was about to hit the fan. Big time.

"Do you hear it?"

"I don't hear anything."

"That's the thing. Me, either, everything is too quiet. I'm asking myself why."

The other man glanced around as if he was about to see a fierce, slant-eyed face peering out from behind a tree, with an AK-47 pointed right at him. "You think it's an ambush?"

"I think it's possible. There's something funny going on here, and if it isn't an ambush, it's near enough. You locked and loaded?"

"Affirmative."

"Okay, let's go find Charlie."

The first sign of trouble was a reflection, the result of a shaft of sunlight glinting through a gap in the foliage on something shiny. It could be glass. Like a lens, the kind they used in binoculars, spectacles, and telescopic sights. He put up a hand, and Ashe paused. "Twenty meters ahead, there could be someone there."

"VC?" he whispered.

"It ain't the Hanoi Young Socialists Choir, that's for sure. Cover me. I'll get closer, and if it's what I think it is, try to nail the bastard before he starts shooting."

He dropped to the jungle floor and snaked forward, pushing his way through bushes beneath tangles of vines, and across a tiny stream with a trickle of water in the bed. The reflection wasn't a rifle sight. It resolved itself into the thick lenses of a pair of spectacles, and whomever they belonged to was staring toward Ashe. It wasn't conclusive evidence he was VC, but the muzzle of the AK pointing out through the leaves was more than conclusive.

Like he'd suspected, it was an ambush. There was no way to know how many men were waiting for them, but when he fired a shot, it would alert Dorsey and Batista, give them a warning, and a chance to take cover.

He put the AR-15 to his shoulder, took aim on the left lens, and squeezed the trigger. The report of the bullet was muffled by the jungle foliage, although still audible some distance away. The guy who'd been hiding in what he guessed was a spider hole wouldn't have heard it, not before he died. He fired from inside ten meters, and the time it took for the bullet to fly that distance was infinitesimal. The lens fractured into shards of glass, spattered with blood from where the bullet had entered his eye, and he didn't cry out. Just fell back into the hole he'd been hiding in, and all hell erupted.

Unbeknown to Farrell, the man he'd just shot was the son

of the local VC commander. He wasn't alone, and the other hostiles waiting in ambush opened up. Most had their rifles set to full auto, and a storm of bullets ripped through the jungle toward him, forcing him to lie flat as they ripped overhead. He heard Dorsey's shout from some distance away, giving Batista an order. He had no time to worry about Dorsey and Batista.

They appeared, leaping from their hiding places, rifles at the hip and racing toward him. An older man was in the lead, his face set in a furious expression, and he was screaming something. It wasn't a dinner invitation. Unless he wanted to eat Farrell for his dinner, so he gathered he'd pissed him off. Not that he gave a damn. The job was to kill the enemy. So he started killing.

First, he picked off the older guy, the man who looked as pissed as if he'd put a bullet into Ho Chi Minh. Although the word was the supreme Communist overlord was sick with coronary trouble in Hanoi. Not the best place in the world to undergo serious heart surgery. The guy went down, and a dozen pajama-clad men leaped over his body and kept running toward him.

He flicked the selector to full auto and squeezed the trigger. The long burst emptied the magazine and knocked down four men. It was enough to make the others think twice. They slowed and scattered, and he noticed something strange, a man dressed differently, like a civilian administrator, white shirt and stained, loose, white cotton pants.

What's he doing with them? Time to think about that later.

For now, he gave his attention back to the nearest hostile. A man racing toward him, just five meters away like he fancied his chances. Probably he suspected Farrell was out of bullets and would need to switch magazines, which would give him an opening. He was right, except for the Colt in the shoulder holster, and he snatched it out, popping three bullets into the guy's belly before he was able to draw a bead on him.

The Viet flung up his hands and fell, no more than a meter before he reached Farrell, and he lay on his back, eyes staring up at the sky. Or where the sky would've been if not for the dense jungle canopy. The guy's face was still fixed in a rictus of hatred.

Two more Viets had charged out from cover. Probably they'd realized he was one man and fancied their chances. They jumped up suddenly, less than ten meters from where he lay, charging forward with the muzzles of their AKs spitting fire. Muzzles with bayonets fixed, and there was no doubt they wanted to spit him on the sharp points. Five bullets were left in the eight-round magazine of the Colt, and they wouldn't be enough. Firing a handgun from a prone position at two men flitting between the trees, there were no guarantees.

But the Colt was all he had ready to shoot. He squeezed the trigger repeatedly. One round took a charging man in the left shoulder. He was so mad he barely blinked and still came on. Another tore into the belly of the other man, and he checked, with blood spraying from an appalling belly wound. He fell to his knees but kept coming, crawling toward him like a rabid dog. And the Colt was empty. For a fraction of a second Farrell was caught wrong-footed. Two weapons, two magazines, both empty. Which to reload first?

David Ashe solved the problem. He raced toward him, firing from the hip, spraying bullets every which way. The first man to go down was the guy still standing. Ashe's burst ripped into his head and splattered the trees with blood and brains. The other guy still crawled toward him, like some primordial creature from a horror flick. One hand clutched his bayonet-tipped AK-47 and the other his belly. Strings of intestine were slithering onto the ground, and he was doing his best to hold them back.

The agony would have been terrible, but he was determined not to give up. Farrell was aware of the long bayonet coming closer. Close enough to do serious damage, but the Viet had little strength left, and he grabbed the muzzle behind the bayonet and pulled it out of his hand. An unearthly shriek echoed through the jungle. Farrell got back to his feet, reversed his grip on the rifle, and smashed the heavy hardwood stock over the wounded man's head. The noise stopped, then started again, and he smashed it again and again until he heard the distinctive 'crack' of the skull as it split. At last, the noise stopped.

He knelt to check the body to make sure, but there was no question. His brains were soaking into the soil, fertilizer for the exotic plant life that choked almost every part of South Vietnam. He smashed the rifle against a tree trunk to put it out of commission, reloaded his weapons, and sucked in a few deep breaths.

"That was close," he heard Ashe's voice from behind.

"Too close. Thanks for the assist."

"Any time, buddy. We'd better find Clarence and Pablo, see what they're up to."

They pushed through the thick foliage toward the village, and when they entered, it was deserted. The rest of the VCs had no stomach for the fight and had scattered, but there was no sign of Dorsey and Batista. They went from hut to hut, pushed inside the biggest hut in the center of the village, and they were there. Stabbing the dirt floor with their combat knives.

Clarence looked up. "We heard shooting. How did you get on?"

"While you were digging for buried treasure, we knocked down a few VCs. Like they pay us for."

He took out a small notebook. "How many can I make it?"

"Between us, we killed six."

"I'll make that twenty-six, that's a good body count. Have you checked out the surrounding area, to see if there's anymore? No? Check the rest of the huts first, and when you're done, circle and make sure we're clear. Any sign of Duy Tan?"

He thought back to the civilian. He'd stood out because he was older, and he remembered how he'd been better dressed than the average rural Viet peasant.

"It may have been him, but he got away."

Dorsey grunted. "Too bad, it looks like we missed him. We'll fire the village, so it'll slow down his tax collecting and whoring days for the near future."

Farrell stared at him for several seconds, finding it hard to believe. "Shouldn't we go after him?"

"Me and Batista are busy. If you want to go chasing around the jungle, knock yourself out, but don't get your head blown off. By the way, you don't need to worry about your share, if we find the money, we'll split it four ways."

He fought to hold back his rising anger. "You know Duy Tan will just start again, extorting taxes by day from peasants who can't afford them, and by night whoring their daughters to the Vietcong."

He nodded. "Ain't that a fact? Maybe we can persuade the

CIA to put a bigger price on his head, make it worthwhile to go after him. Go check out those huts, and stop being a wise guy."

He felt weary, a hundred-years-old. This was the Vietnam War in a microcosm. Everything wrong was happening right here, in this village. Duy Tan was a serious menace, giving support to the Vietcong and abusing young women, turning them into whores. He had to be stopped. CIA had paid Clarence's team to go this village and stop him. Yet here they were scrabbling in the dirt searching for loot.

He muttered, "I'll check around."

Ashe was waiting for him outside. He jerked a thumb toward the doorway. "They're in there."

He grimaced. "I can guess what they're up to."

"Yeah. Clarence said to check out the rest of the huts."

The two men walked from hut to hut. Poorly maintained, crudely built, and holes in the roofs where howling winds had swept away the palm leaves they used for thatch. Leaving a squalid miasma on the floor, a mixture of dirt and animal droppings. There were no animals. There were no peasants. At least they'd had the sense to get out, although he reflected their chances of evading the Communists weren't good.

They entered the last hut on the edge of the village, just another stinking, single room. Gloomy, empty, and he was about to leave when something made him stop. He'd a seen a shape crouched in a dark corner, a person. Maybe a body, maybe a hostile, and he brought up his rifle.

"Who's there? We're American soldiers. Show yourself or we start shooting."

The shape moved, and it was a body. Not a corpse, but a live person, small, less than five feet, a young woman. She crawled toward them and slowly got to her feet. She was a pitiful sight, her face covered in blood, her clothing ripped and muddy, and her eyes dulled with what appeared to be pain, or maybe hunger. Perhaps both. Yet beneath the grime, the blood and bruises, the glow of a young, pretty girl couldn't help but show through.

"Do you speak English?"

"Yes, I understand English."

"Who are you?"

"Who am I?" The voice had a musical tone, and once it would have been pleasing to the ears. Except now it was bitter, rasping. As if the world she'd known had turned on her, savage and cruel.

"My name is Tam Linh. I was the village schoolteacher. Now," she gestured out the doorway to the flames that were licking at the adjoining huts, "Now, there is no village, no people, no children. I have nothing. I am nobody."

He couldn't help but feel sympathy for her, and he assisted her off the floor and outside into the sunlight. He estimated her age at somewhere between twenty and twenty-five. Although a casual glance would have put her nearer forty.

"Miss, if we can help in any way, just say the word."

"I need no help. I told you, I am nobody."

He gave her a candy bar from his pack and offered her his canteen for her to sip some water. She nodded her thanks, and he wanted to do something to help at least one victim of the war. Except there was nothing he could do. They were a CIA hit team, Phoenix Program, and all they brought to this place was more death.

"I'm sorry."

"It is not your fault. It's them. The Vietcong, and Duy Tan, who brought them here and gave them our young women to rape and brutalize."

"That's why we came. For Duy Tan."

She suddenly came to life, her head jerked up, and her eyes sparked fire. "You came for Duy Tan? Is he dead?"

"He got away." He decided he had nothing to lose, and he asked her the question, "Do you have any idea where he may have gone?"

"Yes, there is a series of tunnels about twenty kilometers from here. That is where he takes the girls, his underground brothel, so the Communists can abuse them without fear of discovery."

"Can you give directions to this place? Does it have a name?"

"The nearest village is called Dong Thau, but the entrance to the tunnel system is hidden. You'd never find it."

He looked at Ashe and frowned. "Too bad, that means the bastard will get away."

Before he could reply, she said, "I can show you where it is."

He shook his head. "Miss, you're in a bad way. I doubt you'd make the first twenty meters, let alone twenty kilometers. We'll pass it back to our people, and maybe they can send more men to beat the bushes and find this place."

"I can make it." Her voice had become hard-edged, fierce with determination, like a carbon steel blade. She'd been through a lot, her home village had been through a lot, and she blamed Duy Tan for pretty much all of it, "I will guide you there, provided you promise to kill him."

He wondered if she'd been one of Duy Tan's whores, but it wasn't the kind of question you put to a girl in trouble. He looked up at Ashe. "What do you think? Would Dorsey go for it?"

The voice came from twenty meters away. "No, he fucking wouldn't." The big man was standing in front of a burning hut, and some trick of the light made it look like he was part of the flames, like some creature from hell. A vision of flame and smoke as he emerged from the fiery depths into the real world, "Are you out of your mind? We came here to do a job. We missed him. It's over, and we're going home."

Batista strolled up behind him, grinning like a man who'd just won the lottery. He was carrying a bulging leather satchel, and Farrell opined they'd found the money. He squinted at the girl. "Hey, buddy, did you find yourself a boom-boom girl? She should clean up okay. Maybe we can have some fun before we go back."

Abruptly, he felt rage. Rage for the waste, for the pointless deaths, for the abuse of innocent Vietnamese, and the callous intent of Batista to rape this young woman who'd suffered so much. "Negative. We came here to locate Duy Tan. This girl is a survivor, and she can lead us to him."

The Cuban's sneer widened. "Forget her. She's just a lying Viet, they all are. Only good for one thing, brothel meat."

He lost it then, walked up to him, bunched his fist, and let fly a hard punch that caught him on the chin. Batista went backward, hit the ground, and he was already clawing at his Colt. Dorsey stopped him by putting a foot on his arm and pinning it to the ground.

"Don't take it too hard, Pablo. Let him play Boy Scouts

with the whore, and he won't last the day."

He gave Farrell a hard look. "You want to go after him, fine by me. We're heading back. We have business to take care of." He grinned, "Banking, stuff like that. Ashe, do you want to get your head blown off, or are you coming back with us?"

"I reckon I'll go with Farrell. If there's a chance of finding Tan, I'd like to put him in the ground."

"Suit yourself. We're heading to Bien Hoa. We'll wait for forty-eight hours, and if you're not back, I'll report you as missing in action." He started to walk away, paused, and looked back, "Presumed dead."

Farrell watched them leave and glanced at Ashe. "How much trouble do you reckon he'll cause?"

"Take no notice of Clarence. He's a bag of wind. When we get back, all sins will be forgiven."

He somehow doubted it, but he didn't reply. They waited for the rest of the late afternoon and through the evening until darkness cloaked the countryside. All they could see were pinpricks of light from the nearby town. It was time to move out under cover of the darkness. The killing time had arrived.

Chapter Three

Dorsey and Batista retraced their steps, heading back to Binh Long and the Huey that would convey them to Bien Hoa. If Farrell and Ashe had been able to overhear their conversation, Dave Ashe may have taken a different view of their prospects for the near future.

He looked at Batista. "I heard from my brother Melvin, and he's recovering fast. He should be able to rejoin the unit in the next three to four weeks."

"Assuming there's a vacancy. What if Farrell makes it back?"

He shrugged. "What if he does? I can get him transferred." He chuckled, "Preferably somewhere hot like Cu Chi. Maybe they could use him as a tunnel rat."

Batista still looked doubtful. "If he locates Duy Tan and brings him back, it may not be that simple. He'll earn enough brownie points to make him Curtis' blue-eyed boy. He may want him to stay."

He sighed. "Look, Pablo, I'll say this once. I agreed to Farrell joining this team to keep Melvin's place warm. The moment he's out of the hospital, he comes back to the unit. There won't be a problem."

"But, if Farrell…"

"Forget Farrell. Bottom line, he'll be dead."

"How?"

He gave him a cold smile. "Don't worry about it, he's history. When Farrell goes home, he'll travel in an aluminum box in the cargo hold."

* * *

Twenty kilometers was a hard enough hike in open territory, but through the dank, dripping jungles of South Vietnam, every step was torture. Under constant attack from a vicious enemy, but it wasn't the Communists. After the scrap in the village, they had yet to encounter further Vietcong. The enemy was wildlife, insects, snakes, rodents, and with no way of knowing which were poisonous and which weren't, they had to assume they were all a threat.

The humidity was off the scale, and before they'd covered the first thousand meters, they were dripping with sweat. The temperature rose, until the combination of heat and humidity reduced their pace to a slow plod. Frequently stopping to check for leeches on their legs, and having to remove them with the growing tip of a cigarette. Edging past snakes dangling from branches that overhung the narrow track, and if the insects didn't attack, their imagination ran riot until it felt almost as bad.

Insects crawled inside his pants, past beneath his shorts, and they explored the area around his groin. Ashe and Farrell frequently had to stop and check while Linh turned her back. They unfastened belts, unbuttoned pants, and checked inside their shorts. Most times there were no insects, just a crawling sensation that sapped at a man's imagination. At times Farrell wished they would run into the enemy, somebody real to fight, not fucking insects, or a nameless dark shadow that scarred a man's psyche.

He glanced at Linh. "Don't tell me it'll be like this all the way to Dong Thau?"

She nodded gravely. "Yes, it is thick jungle all the way. But that is good, no?" She brightened, and for the first time gave him a weak smile, "There is another path, but it is well used by the Vietcong. This way they won't know we're coming."

He muttered, "Right now, I'd prefer a frontal attack on Hanoi." But he kept his voice low, and she didn't hear. They rested, squatting but not daring to sit on the ground for fear of being attacked by battalions of poisonous creatures. After ten minutes they went on, and he began to wonder if he'd made the wrong call. Every step was torture, and one thing he knew for sure was they'd be in no condition to fight when they got there.

If Duy Tan was hiding inside his underground brothel, protected by the enemy, he couldn't see how in hell they'd get to him. Several times he thought of giving up.

Maybe Clarence was right. Maybe I shouldn't have pushed ahead with this stupid idea. Shouldn't have put Ashe at risk, and definitely shouldn't have put Linh at risk.

Then again, something kept him going. An idea in the back of his mind he'd lived with for several months. Ever since the murder of his brother showed so many things that were wrong with the way they were fighting the war in Vietnam. And one was the attitude of men like Clarence Dorsey and Pablo Batista, men who enriched themselves by chasing loot and avoiding contact with the enemy when things got hot.

That was the way the ARVN fought, or at least a lot of them did. Turning Search and Destroy missions into Search and Evade. Selling their weapons, officers looting their men's wages, and what was the result? The Communists were gaining ground, and if the ARVN and men like Dorsey and Batista didn't do their jobs, they'd continue to gain ground. He wasn't convinced about the Phoenix Program, but at least the intention was to seek out and kill traitors. Men who'd betrayed their country and sent many of their countrymen to their deaths. Killing men who deserved to die didn't seem so bad.

It started to rain. When it rained in Vietnam, it was biblical. The heavens opened and dumped what seemed like an ocean over a man's head. It was so heavy and so powerful they couldn't go on and had to take shelter. The rain kicked up a dense fog, and it became impossible to follow the trail. It was like walking through a waterfall, and they halted under the spreading leaves of a huge palm tree that protected them from at least some of the deluge like a huge umbrella.

Ashe attempted to check their back trail in case they'd been followed, but he was blinded by the storm that had, in any case, obliterated all trace of their passing, so he gave up and rejoined them. "If anybody followed us in this, they're welcome. Shit, I hate this fucking country."

Linh gave him a questioning glance. "If you hate it so much, why are you here?"

His eyebrows rose and he grinned. "Why? One word, money, CIA pays me ten times what I earned as a soldier, and I like to gamble. I've also got a girlfriend, so I'd like to buy a house one day."

Farrell looked at him in surprise. He'd never talked about a girl, and now he'd spelled-out his plans for the future; a real future, not playing with death in the dripping jungles of South Vietnam, fighting the weather, the insects, and the enemy.

"What's she like?" Farrell asked, "I guess she's looking forward to you coming home."

"Nope. I am home."

"I don't get it."

"She's Vietnamese, her name is Huong."

"Pink rose," Linh murmured, "Huong means pink rose."

"That's right. She lives in Saigon with her parents. We'd like set up home together, but they won't allow it. They insist she has to stay home and help them run the family business. If I have enough money, I'll buy a bungalow outside the city, and hopefully I can change their minds."

Linh looked amused. "You hate this country, yet you plan to set up home with a Vietnamese girl and live here?"

"Huong refuses to leave, so I don't have a choice."

"You must love her a lot."

After a pause, he said, "Yeah, I do."

Farrell was fascinated to hear Ashe unwinding about his plans to set up home with a Vietnamese girl, and he pitied Linh. She would've had similar hopes and dreams. Maybe she'd had a boyfriend, even a fiancé, until the Communists came. It was as if she read his thoughts.

"He's dead. They killed him."

"I'm sorry."

"Yes. Thank you."

They sheltered beneath the tree, and if at first the hammering rain had eased the misery of their sweating bodies, they began to suffer the opposite. Cold. Their clothes were soaked, and with no escape, no way to get dry, they began to shiver. This wasn't his first experience of monsoon rain, but before he'd been part of a larger unit, a platoon or a company, and with backup. With a waterproof poncho to ward off some of the rain, with a truck or a helicopter waiting to take them back to a base where they could take a warm shower, dry out and eat hot chow. For the first time, he understood what he'd undertaken. They were on their own. Isolated, cut off. And surrounded by an enemy waiting to kill them the moment they showed their faces. In the cell, at least he had Colin. And there were no insects. No rain. And no VC.

Once again, he wondered if he'd made a bad call, but it was too late. They were committed, and they had to go on. Eventually, the rain eased to a steady downpour, and they could continue. Pushing through the dripping wet foliage, their minds numb, their bodies numb, and all that counted was taking the next step without falling over. Knowing if they did fall, they'd never get up.

It was late afternoon when he pushed aside a branch hung with thick foliage, and he was looking across a wide stretch of open ground interspersed with elephant grass. Opposite lay the town of Dong Thau. This was no village, but a prosperous collection of brick-built buildings, most constructed in the French colonial style. He estimated it was large enough to house a population of around five thousand, large by the standards of rural South Vietnam, and he watched men and women strolling around, going about their daily business. In this place, their business was war.

Most carried weapons, AK-47s, and there were plenty of black pajamas in evidence. The VC was in control. Unless the locals had taken advantage of a surplus of black fabric, and he doubted there was any surplus of black fabric or anything else in Vietnam. Except of course the main staple. Death. He glanced at Ashe, who was beside him.

"There's no way we can go any closer. We have to wait until nightfall. Linh, where are these tunnels?"

She pointed across the open ground. "You see the elephant grass? There's an entrance in there. There are other entrances, but they're in the jungle on the far side of the town. The one in the elephant grass is the nearest."

"You can find it?"

"I think so, yes."

They spent the afternoon and evening watching the town. Seeing pinpricks of illumination as people switched on electric lights or fired up oil lamps. Darkness threw a cloak over the area, blanketing the ground they had to cross. He looked at Ashe. "You set?"

"Affirmative. What do you plan to do about the girl?"

He looked at her. "Linh? If you can point the way, you can wait here."

In the darkness, he saw her head move from side to side. "That won't work. I cannot explain how to find the entrance. I'll have to come with you. When we drop down into the tunnel, I can direct you to Duy Tan's place where he keeps his girls. It is a short crawl, but the tunnel has several branches, and if you take the wrong one you'll get lost. Or even worse run into the enemy. One more thing, the rifles, you'll have to hide them here. They are useless underground. Too unwieldy."

He didn't like it, Ashe didn't like it, but they agreed. They started walking toward the elephant grass, and everything looked quiet, with no sign of the enemy. They were walking with the dark jungle at their backs. If the enemy appeared in front of them the town would backlight them, and they'd see them in time to drop out of sight. They reached the elephant grass and pushed their way through. The grass was over their heads, and it was like walking through a maze, fronds of grass waving gently on the soft night breeze that'd come up. The rain had stopped, but the ground was still sodden, and their boots sunk deep with every step.

They came on it suddenly. She stopped and pointed at the ground. "It is there."

He looked down, and at first, he saw nothing, until his eyes became accustomed to staring into the darkness, and he could see a faint outline. "This is it?"

She nodded. "It's primarily a ventilation shaft, but they made it wide enough for men to climb out in case they needed to escape in a hurry. It's a squeeze getting in and out, but it can be done."

He worried about her going underground, and he had a question on the tip of his tongue. He wanted to ask but didn't know how. Once again, she read his mind.

"Yes, I was here. But not for the reason you're thinking. One of the girls was injured when a VC beat her up. He broke her arm and injured her eye so badly she lost her vision. When they failed to treat her wounds, she caught an infection that almost killed her. I knew the girl and have an understanding of basic first-aid, so they brought me here, and I treated her with antibiotics and splinted the broken arm. That is how I know the location of this place. I was never a whore."

"I didn't think…"

Her eyes flickered. "Of course you didn't. I'll show you how to get inside."

She scrabbled in the dirt and was about to lift the hatch when Ashe hissed a warning. "Someone's coming. I heard somebody cough. It could be a patrol."

She paused and waited while Farrell sneaked a look through the tall grass, and he saw them, seven or eight men coming toward them. Heading straight for them.

"We need to get out of here, now!" he murmured.

They snaked back the way they'd come until they were safely inside the treeline and retrieved their rifles. The shadowy line of men emerged from the elephant grass. There were twelve men, black outfits, AKs, and the distinctive floppy jungle hats. They didn't speak, walking along in silence, and if a man hadn't coughed, probably as he hawked and spat, they'd have had no warning. They came closer until they were less than fifty meters away, and Farrell tensed, considering whether they should retreat deeper into the jungle.

They didn't come any closer. They stopped, chatted to themselves in soft voices, and Linh interpreted.

"He's here. Duy Tan said they were to maintain extra patrols, and when they were sure the area was clear, to post guards to protect the tunnel. I'm afraid we won't be able to use this entrance." She paused, "Wait, I heard a man say something about checking the edge of the jungle. I recognize his voice. He was the man who injured the girl and almost killed her."

Ashe murmured. "We need to get out of here. They'll be coming this way!"

"Shit!" He shook his head in anger, feeling like he'd made a big mistake. He'd insisted on going after Duy Tan despite Clarence and Pablo giving up, and all he was about to achieve was a big nothing. Yet they were too late to leave. The Viets were twenty meters away, and they had to hear them pushing back into the jungle. He measured distances, measured angles.

There's an alternative to a retreat. It's called an attack.

Ashe understood what he was thinking. "You want to take them on? Even if we kill them all, it won't help us get to Duy Tan. They'll know we're here, and they'll be all over us."

"True, but it'll make me feel better."

He shrugged. "There's a lot of them, and two of us."

"They don't know we're here, so it'll come as a big surprise."

He sighed. "Are you sure about this?"

"Yep. You locked and loaded?"

"Always."

"Wait until we see the whites of their eyes."

Ashe chuckled and eased back the cocking handle. Farrell crouched down on the edge of the jungle. They were invisible to the enemy.

"Wait for me to shoot first."

Ashe gave a soft grunt by way of acknowledgment. Farrell selected full auto, took up first pressure on the trigger, and sighted on the man in the lead.

Linh suddenly jerked in surprise. "It's him, the one who almost killed the girl," she whispered in his ear, "Nguyen

Chieu."

He was two meters away, a mere seven feet when Farrell took careful aim and opened fire. The first few bullets ripped into Chieu, and he moved the barrel from side to side, spraying bullets to sweep across the rest of the Viets. Ashe's rifle opened up a split second later, and the result was carnage. The VCs were caught out in the open and unprepared. Not expecting to come under attack. They died.

Farrell slammed in a fresh magazine, and already half the enemy was dead or dying, the rest floundering in chaos and confusion. He and Ashe emptied magazine after magazine until a single man was left alive. He was sprinting away like a hare, and he should have let him go. He didn't let him go. Something welled up inside him. They'd killed or seriously wounded eleven men, eleven VCs, the nasty little shits who abused women, who'd murdered his brother, and he wanted this last man. Wanted him dead. Didn't want him to escape, he wanted a clean sweep, and he chased him down. Racing across the open ground, and they were in the elephant grass.

He couldn't see him, but he could hear him. Hear the soft patter of his rubber sandals as he ran; hear his body brushing through the long grass. Farrell picked up speed and got close enough to hear the rasp of his breath as he raced to get away. He didn't get away. Farrell got close enough to snatch out his Colt and put a bullet in the center of his back. The running man pitched forward and lay on the ground, moaning in pain. He put the muzzle of the pistol to his head and squeezed the trigger a second time. The last shot sounded louder, the kill shot, the peal of the death knell for an enemy.

He stood over the body breathing hard and heard

footsteps behind him. He whirled, and Ashe appeared through the long grass, with Linh behind him.

"What happened?"

"What happened? I killed him."

"Paul, those shots just woke up every VC in the area. They'll come crawling out of the woodwork like lice." He stopped speaking suddenly and listened, "Too late, they're on the way. We need to get back into the jungle, and if we're lucky, and I mean really lucky, we might just get away. Somehow, I doubt it."

The voices, orders, and shouts of command were everywhere. He glanced back, and he knew they weren't going to make it. Before they reached the treeline, they'd be all over them.

Ashe grunted. "We need to get going, and I mean now! Although I doubt we'll make it. There're too many of them."

Farrell didn't move. "If we head for the jungle, that's the way they'll expect us to go."

"Shit, man, there's no other way. Are you coming, or do you want to die here?"

"Neither. We should go in the opposite direction. Head toward the town and look for the tunnel entrance. Hit the deck and crawl through the grass."

Ashe muttered, "This is crazy," as they dived to the ground and started crawling. In the darkness, in the long, elephant grass, they'd be invisible, hidden from the enemy gaze, but not invisible. All it took was one foot to land in the wrong place, one pair of eyes to glance down; one voice to shout a warning, and it was all over.

It was an eerie, creepy feeling, with enemy fighters all

around them, the noise of their sandaled feet as they raced past, and once, a man's sandal brushed the fabric of Farrell's leather flight jacket. In his haste and eagerness to chase down the fugitives, he didn't stop to see what he'd touched, and he ran on. Their footsteps and voices reached the treeline and disappeared inside.

They waited several minutes, and Linh said, "I think they've gone. Won't they be back when they fail to pick up our trail?"

He nodded. "You're right. Let's go, but keep your heads down."

They ran doubled over, listening for the faintest sound that could be another VC. They heard nothing.

He looked at Linh. "I think we're in the clear. Can you find the hatch?"

"Follow me."

She walked unerringly through the grass as if she had some inbuilt radar. He couldn't work out how she could see the way, yet she did. Several seconds later, he worked it out. She wasn't using her eyes. She was using her nose. A faint odor came to him. He'd smelled that stink before, and men had told him where it came from, what it was. A tunnel. The stink of urine, of human waste, of too many men and women confined underground for too long. The stink of disease or rotting flesh, the tunnels were breeding grounds for infection.

Abruptly she pointed down at the ground. "This is it."

He recognized the faint outline and knelt to open it. They'd disguised it with a thin covering of loose earth. He dug into the earth with his knife, exposed the outlines of the hatch, and pulled it open. The stench that wafted up was appalling, and the thought of going down into that black darkness even more so. But they had no choice. Duy Tan was down there, and they hadn't come all this way to give up and go back. Even if they could go back, which he doubted. The jungle was alive with Vietcong, and there was nowhere else to go.

The town of Dong Thau wasn't an option. The place was alive with Vietcong. Once again he wondered if he'd made a mistake persuading them to come here. Maybe they should've left when they had the chance, maybe he shouldn't have fired the shots that killed the VC, but that was then, and this was now. The guy was dead, Charlie was all around them, and they were about to descend into a black pit. There'd be more VCs down there, and if Linh was right, so would Duy Tan. If everything went well, they could slip underground, nail the bastard, and slip away. On the other hand, things may not go well.

Who am I kidding? The odds against us getting out are close to zero.

"I'll go first," she whispered. Before he could object, she climbed nimbly into the shaft and dropped down. She disappeared into the darkness, and he was sure she'd plunged to her death, but her muted voice came up from the depths.

"It's about two meters, a short drop, and it slopes down to the main level, which is about five meters underground."

"On the way." He dropped into the shaft, keeping his knees bent to absorb the shock of the fall, but like she'd said, it was no more than two meters, and he stood next to her in the darkness, "We need to move out of the way for Ashe."

They moved aside as David Ashe dropped down next to them.

This way," she whispered.

His eyes were growing accustomed to the darkness, which

wasn't total. A faint light came from further inside the tunnel system. She dropped to all fours and crawled along the tunnel, and he followed, with Ashe bringing up the rear. It descended steeply, until after what seemed like an eternity of crawling through the semi-darkness the roof became higher, and they were able to stand and walk doubled over.

"It's not too far."

They continued walking. She was so short she didn't need to stoop, and she walked confidently ahead until she stopped at an opening in the side of the tunnel. She kept her voice to a low murmur.

"This is the entrance to Duy Tan's brothel. He occupies the outer room, and he has a cot where he sleeps, usually with the girl of his choice. A doorway on the other side leads to the brothel, which is around four meters square."

"How many girls does he keep in there?"

"Ten or twelve."

It was said in a casual tone, but he was appalled. A muddy space, thirteen feet by thirteen feet, occupied by ten or twelve girls, and when their clients arrived, there'd be the same number of men rutting and humping. He visualized the Ninth Circle of Hell from Dante's Inferno. The one reserved for those guilty of treachery. The Vietcong who abused and raped deserved nothing less. But the girls crammed inside the tiny, miasmic space were guilty of nothing more than being young and pretty. And Vietnamese.

He put an arm on her shoulder. "Hold it. I'll take it from here."

Farrell edged forward and poked his head through the tattered curtain that hid the interior. He could see a room lit by a flickering oil lamp, but it was empty. Duy Tan wasn't there. He felt a tremendous disappointment, but before he could work out their next move, he heard voices from further along the tunnel, and a second later Linh and Ashe darted inside.

"Someone's coming. We need to find somewhere to hide."

"In here."

Linh pointed to a doorway on the other side of the space, protected by another ragged piece of cloth. She pushed it aside, and they heard her murmuring to somebody inside. Both men had their Colts out, cocked and ready to fire, and they pushed through the curtain after her. He'd pictured the Ninth Circle of Hell, but if there'd been a tenth, this would be it, a cramped, dark space, occupied by ten young women. They stared at him and Ashe, their expressions terrified. Their thin ao dais were ragged and stained, their faces bruised and dirty, and he felt a tremendous surge of pity for what they'd gone through.

Linh was whispering urgently to them, apparently telling them to be silent, and a moment later they heard two men enter the outer room. They were chatting to each other in amicable tones like they were enjoying a pleasant stroll in the countryside. Not negotiating the narrow claustrophobic passageways of a dark, fetid pit. Not looking for a slave girl to rape and abuse.

He put his mouth close to her ear and whispered, "Is he out there?"

"No. Customers."

In an instinctive move, they both gripped the barrels of their Colts so they could use the butts like clubs, for a single shot in this place would be the end. There'd be no escape. They stood out of sight on either side of the doorway. Tense and waiting.

The two VCs weren't expecting trouble. They pushed through the tattered curtain into the tiny, dark space, and looked surprised when they saw the girls staring at them. Not in fear, not resigned or beaten into abject terror. Ten young women stared at the VCs, and their smiles dissolved. They disappeared when the steel butts of two Colt M1911s cracked over their skulls, and they dropped to the floor.

They knelt close to their victims, ready to deliver the coup de grace. Inside this tunnel complex, there could be no second chances, no prisoners, no mercy. This was the war the Vietcong had brought to South Vietnam, and this was the war they had to fight, the Communist way, the brutal way, on their terms. They were about to smash the Colts over their heads and finish them when a silent horde of young women pushed forward. Farrell was shoved aside, and the girls fell on the two VCs. Hammering at them, beating at them with their fists, with their nails, with their teeth, and it lasted for several minutes. When they stood back, the men were heaps of bloody rags. Not unlike the girls they'd treated so badly, except they were dead.

He coughed quietly to attract Linh's attention. "We should've kept one alive to question him about Tan." He shrugged, "I guess it's too late for that now. If he's not here, where would he be?"

"I…"

She paused. Someone had entered the outer room, and too late, several of the girls pushed past to grab him, wanting to mete out the same punishment as they'd given the VCs. But they were too slow. They'd been imprisoned and brutalized for too long in a cramped space underground. Duy Tan saw them and moved as fast as a rattlesnake. He darted back out into the tunnel, and they heard his footsteps on the mud floor, racing deeper into the underground warren. He was shouting a warning, screaming in alarm.

They'd lost him, but it was too late to shed any tears. "We need to get out of here," he snapped, "Linh, get them moving."

Ashe stared at him. "You're bringing them with us?"

"What do you think will happen when they see the bodies of those two men they killed? They'll cut them into little pieces and boil them alive. Linh, tell them to head for the entrance. Ashe, stay right behind them. I'll cover your backs."

He followed them, regretting the absence of his AR-15 he'd left on the surface. All he had was the Colt, but then again, if things developed into a firefight, he doubted an assault rifle would make any difference. This was tunnel fighting, and the normal rules didn't, couldn't apply. This was a primordial struggle of beast against beast, and the best weapon to fight with was the most bitter cruelty a man could summon. He followed them as they raced along the tunnel, and he was almost too late. Voices were coming up behind him. He estimated four men.

He waited, back pressed against the tunnel side. In the darkness, the way to kill a man with a gun was to be so close you could almost touch him with the muzzle to make sure you had a solid target. So he waited. They bounded around the corner oblivious to the threat lurking in the darkness. They came into sight, short, like most Vietnamese, so they didn't have to stoop. They reached him, and he pounced. Pressed the gun against the leading man and squeezed the trigger. The force of the bullet slammed the Viet back into the comrade behind him.

A spray of blood and brains announced his death before he hit the earth floor, and the other three men stopped. He ran on and found Ashe and Linh waiting with the girls. Two were lying on the tunnel floor.

She gave him an anxious glance. "They can't make it. They've been imprisoned for so long and so badly treated, they're very sick. I'm sorry, they can't walk any further."

"Shit."

In the distance, back down the tunnel, he heard them. They were coming, the murmur of voices from a distance, the faint patter of feet on soft earth, and he had to make a decision. Try to make the tunnel exit or to fight, kill as many as possible and make the bastards realize if they got any closer, they'd make them pay a heavy price in blood. While they were licking their wounds, maybe they'd have a chance to escape. It was a no-go. This place was like an ant nest, crawling with poisonous, black-clad insects. Armed with AK-47s, explosives, and if they took a wrong turn, there'd be an unknown number of traps. Tripwires connected to hand grenades. Pits filled with poisonous punji stakes.

They couldn't run, couldn't get out in time, which meant they needed a third option, and it came to him suddenly.

"Get back! Back to the brothel!"

Ashe and Linh stared at him in horror. "You can't be serious!"

"We don't have a choice. We can't run, we can't fight, and so we have to hide. Move it!"

They raced back to the entrance to the brothel, through the room used by Duy Tan, and into the stinking, cloying space where the girls had spent so many weeks brutalized, raped, and abused. They huddled in corners, and most were shaking in terror. He didn't blame them. But they'd be shaking in a lot more terror if the VCs got their hands on them again. They heard them coming closer. He and Ashe covered the doorway, Colts pointed toward the ragged curtain, waiting for the first of the VCs to charge in. Waiting to sell their lives dearly, a last-ditch stand. They tensed when footsteps entered the outer room. Waiting for the moment when it was all about to end.

They left. More men ran along the tunnel, and still they waited. After a few minutes, they heard footsteps in the outer room. A man had entered, and one man they could handle. They stood either side of the doorway out of sight, waiting for the moment. It came, the curtain moved, and he looked inside the brothel to check on the girls. Duy Tan.

Farrell threw out a hand, grabbed hold of his shirtfront, and dragged him inside. He opened his mouth to voice the beginnings of a squeal of fright, but he hammered his Colt over the man's head, tapped him again for good measure, and held him down to physically prevent the girls from ripping into their tormentor.

"Cut it out! Linh, explain to them they have to stay silent. Don't make a sound, don't move, don't even breathe. If we're going to get out of this, the enemy must believe we've escaped. If they hear us, we're screwed."

She spoke to them in rapid Vietnamese, and they quietened, although he cautioned himself to keep an eye on them. Given half a chance, he knew they'd ignore his warning and rip into Tan, making enough noise to rouse the Viets. He solved the problem by sitting on him, so they couldn't get close without dragging him off. More footsteps rushed past, men running toward the exit. None entered the brothel.

Maybe it doesn't open for business until later. As long as the bastards aren't queuing up outside we might stand a chance.

They waited for two hours, and he estimated it was daylight on the surface. The Vietcong worked opposite hours to most people in South Vietnam. They awoke in the night, like vampires, emerging to drink the blood of their victims. In the day they returned to their dark places, like this one. To eat and sleep and listen to indoctrination speeches from their Hanoi masters. He gave them another hour until everything in the tunnel was still.

Like the grave. If we're lucky, it won't be our grave.

He spoke softly. "It's time to leave, let's go. Not a sound."

Cash nodded toward Duy Tan, who was stirring. "What about him? It would be quickest and quietest to cut his throat."

"I'm taking him back."

"You what? Our orders are to kill him."

"Fuck the orders. I want to prove we got him, and the only proof is to take him back alive. Forget carrying a body. He can walk."

"Clarence won't like it. The idea of the Phoenix Program is to knock off these bastards, not bring back prisoners."

"I don't give a shit what he likes or doesn't like. Clarence and Pablo were happy to grab his stash instead of going after him. That's not the way I operate, never did."

Ashe was still shaking his head in astonishment. "Paul, whatever is eating you, you got this all wrong. Clarence will eat you alive. And Curtis won't like it, he'll go ape."

"Fuck 'em all. Let's go."

He slammed the butt of his Colt against Tan's head once again. Not enough to knock him out, he wanted him mobile, but enough to set him straight. Behave, or else. Ashe tied a gag around his mouth and fastened his wrists behind his back with a length of communication wire. He put his head out in the tunnel to look and listen. His eyes had become accustomed to the gloom, and he was able to see enough to know it was clear. He heard nothing, and he gestured for them to follow.

They made it to the exit hatch, although they had to assist the weaker of the girls because they couldn't make it on their own. They climbed out into the open, and it was broad daylight. The immediate area was also clear of hostiles, and all they met were the normal sounds of the jungle. The buzz of insects, the soft patter of small animals roaming through the thick foliage, the whistle and the chirp of birds. In the distance, the thump of rotor blades played the music of Vietnam, flights of Hueys heading back and forth to deliver more troops into the bloody maw of the current battle.

High in the sky clusters of contrails, B-52 bombers flying north. On their way to deliver huge quantities of ordnance on the heads of the enemy, another operation against an increasingly confident and aggressive enemy. Sometimes, they'd bomb suspected locations of Vietcong tunnel systems, and he reminded himself they'd just emerged from such a place. He grunted at them to move fast before they fell victim to USAF bombs. They made improvised gurneys for the sickest two girls and started walking away, heading for Bien Hoa. He wanted to see Clarence's face when they arrived with Duy Tan.

They were less than one thousand meters from the tunnel entrance when his worst fears were realized. Ordnance fell from the sky, and it was too close for comfort.

Did we get out of that hole just in time to become targets for our own bombs? Shit, if the enemy doesn't get us, our own guys will finish the job.

Vietnam. Fuck it.

Chapter Four

The bombing lasted for what felt like hours but was probably no more than a matter of minutes. They survived, more by luck than judgment, lying flat on the jungle floor as a constant, unending series of explosions shook the earth. The soft, muddy ground absorbed most of the earthquake-like shock waves, and the tangle of vines and trees screened them from the worse of the hot blasts of fire.

When the aircraft flew away, they were still alive, unscathed by a several million dollar value bomb load, paid for by the American taxpayer. He guessed they'd missed the tunnels they'd recently escaped from, and he made a note to inform them about the correct coordinates when they got back. They walked away, heading for Bien Hoa. It took them all that day and most of the night. They arrived early the next day, tired, starving, and their skin bitten raw by insects.

The guards didn't want to admit them, especially the Viets,

but Ashe had previously served with one of the sentries, and he persuaded the guy to put a call through to the head of the Phoenix Program, Charles Curtis. It took them a half-hour to rouse him from his bed, but he authorized them to let them inside. Their priority was food, so they headed for the cookhouse. The guards had notified Clarence, who'd arrived the previous day. He strolled into the mess tent just as they were wolfing down second helpings, washed down by mugs of steaming hot coffee.

His face was set in his customary sneer. "So you made it back. I guess you never found the target. A waste of fucking time."

Farrell jerked a thumb at the ground. Dorsey hadn't noticed the Vietnamese lying at their feet, gagged and trussed. "We brought him back, Clarence. Why don't you say hello?"

He stared at the body in disbelief. "You humped that body back here? Why for Christ's sake?"

"He's not dead."

"He's not what?"

"He's not dead. He's alive."

His expression changed to astonishment. His skin paled. A moment before the pallor turned to red. "There's no way, Farrell. Our orders are to kill him."

"Yeah, but you didn't kill him, did you, Clarence? You grabbed his loot and took off."

"Fuck you, asshole, that's a lie. We took important documents to give to Curtis in Saigon. And I can tell you he ain't gonna be pleased when you bring Duy Tan back. No fucking way."

He stalked away, and they continued eating every scrap of

food the cooks could provide. Afterward, they strolled outside, watching the activities inside the vast air base. Fighter-bombers and helicopters taking off and landing, men rushing to refuel and rearm, the entire base had greeted the dawn with furious activity. Then again, this was Vietnam, and something big was always going on. The previous year, the Tet Offensive had come as a big surprise. Maybe this year it would be worse.

Batista stalked up to them. Like his boss, he hadn't arrived to swap pleasantries. "We're leaving midday tomorrow. Clarence fixed up a ride on a Huey heading for Tan Son Nhut. He said to make sure you dump the prisoner with the MPs so they can lock him away overnight. Don't forget, midday."

"We'll be there."

He strolled away, and Farrell began looking for someplace to get some sleep after their long ordeal. A harassed lieutenant pointed to an empty tent they could use. "Make sure you're out of here first thing tomorrow. There'll be more men coming in, and they'll need to use it. By the way, Vietnamese civilians using American military facilities is against regulations. So make sure those people stay out of sight."

"Fuck regulations," he murmured to himself, "Haven't they been through enough?"

The tent was large enough for four men, and they had eleven girls to shelter, including Linh. They took Duy Tan to the MPs, and he and Ashe slept out in the open, praying it wouldn't rain. It didn't, but bugs attacked them, and aircraft and helicopters taking off and landing kept up a constant cacophony. Just when they were about to doze off to sleep, yet another shattering roar would shake the ground as an aircraft zoomed into the sky, spreading a cloud of burned, stinking kerosene.

In the early morning, they shook themselves awake, shaking off the dew that had soaked through their clothing. The rain held off, the sun burned through the mist, and their clothes steamed as they dried in the welcome warmth of the new day. The girls emerged from the tent, and he and Ashe strolled over to the cookhouse to scrounge up some food.

They managed to fill their pockets with hot rolls and piled plates high with enough to feed a platoon. When they got back, the girls were ravenous, and they fell on the food, while Farrell and Ashe returned for second helpings. While they drank coffee they watched the bustling activity around the base. Jeeps buzzing from place to place, tankers servicing aircraft with vital supplies of aviation fuel, and uniforms everywhere, like swarms of ants in a kaleidoscope of seemingly aimless movement. A convoy headed out through the gates, trucks loaded with infantry preceded by a Bradley M113. Yet more aircraft and helicopters came and went. Mostly helicopters, and whoever named the Vietnam War the 'Helicopter War' had chosen well.

Their clothing dried, their bellies were full, and they went looking for Clarence. It was early, not yet 10.00, but he wanted to ensure the arrangements still stood. Clarence was nowhere to be seen, and neither was Pablo. Neither was Duy Tan. Farrell had a bad feeling, and he and Ashe went to the guardroom and went inside. A noncom looked up when they entered. "Make it quick, I'm busy."

"We brought in a prisoner last night, a Vietnamese, Duy Tan."

The Sergeant nodded without interest. "So what?"

"We'll be leaving soon, so we'll take him now so we're ready to go."

He gave them an odd look. "What the hell are you talking about? They came and took him a couple of hours ago. How come you didn't know?"

Maybe it's okay, just a foul-up.

"That's okay, they'll have taken him to the helicopter to get ready for the trip to Saigon. Don't worry about it."

The man returned a level stare. "Since when did I worry about a fucking Viet?"

Great.

They left and walked over to the helicopter stand, looking for Clarence and Pablo.

"Maybe they're planning on leaving early," Ashe opined.

"Maybe." He doubted it. He had an idea, and it was nothing good.

* * *

Duy Tan felt terror like he'd never felt terror before. Pablo Batista held him in the doorway of the Huey, facedown, so he could see the ocean of green jungle below. They were flying at ten thousand feet, and Clarence wanted the guy to understand it was a long way down, a very long way down.

"I want a name, a location, and a description, Tan. The guy in charge, who is he? Who's running the Vietcong insurgency in the Iron Triangle, the guy who calls the shots? Spit it out, tell me what I want to know, and I'll tell Pablo to let you back into the cabin."

He was shaking in terror, fighting to get back into the cabin, but Batista held him immobile.

"If I knew I'd tell you," he screamed, "I'd tell you

everything, but I don't know."

"Suit yourself. Batista, toss him out."

"No! No." The scream was louder, louder than the roar of the turboshaft engine, "I give you the information."

"Sure you will. You've made the right decision. First, the name, who is he?"

It came out bit by bit. Tran Quang was a senior commissar appointed, or maybe anointed, by Hanoi. He operated from a camouflaged headquarters somewhere outside Dalat, fifty klicks west of Cam Ranh Bay, the site of a sprawling U.S. base. Batista had to push the Viet further out into the void when he began to have second thoughts and faltered, but they got what they wanted. They had it all, the name, location, and the description.

Dorsey questioned him for several minutes more, but they were nearing Saigon, and it was time to say goodbye. He nodded to Batista. "Okay, we're done with him. Let him go."

Tan gave him a grateful look. "Thank you, thank you. I promise I will do everything I can to help you."

"Sure you will," Clarence grinned, "Here's the thing, the more Communists we kill, the quicker we can win this war and go home. So what we want you to do is die."

He nodded to Batista, who gave a hard shove. He struggled, teetering in the open doorway for several seconds, battling to get a handhold, and he managed to get his fingers around the edge of the door. The Cuban drew out his combat knife in a swift, flowing motion and sliced into the fingers. The blade was razor-sharp, and Tan wailed a final scream of terror and despair as he fell out into the void. Casually, Batista kicked the bloody fingers out the door to tumble after the body.

He grinned. "If he survives he can go looking for them."

"We'll wish him good luck with that. Now we have something worthwhile to give to Curtis. We eliminated the target and got valuable information. I'd call that a win-win."

"What about Farrell? He's a fucking Boy Scout. The chances are he'll blab to Curtis, which could make things awkward. We could have some explaining to do."

"I'll take care of Curtis. When we bring back a good result, he'll put Farrell down as a troublemaker if he complains. Don't worry about it. He's not long for my unit. Melvin is due back soon, and he can transfer someplace else. Assuming he's still alive."

"You really think…"

"I know. Trust me."

* * *

The journey back to Saigon was a nightmare. Phoenix had arranged the helicopter to transport personnel back to Tan Son Nhut, and Clarence and Batista had taken it. They weren't about to fix another. His requests to use the radio to contact Curtis were refused. He was CIA, which made him a civilian, and the military had little time for CIA, blaming them for so many things that had gone wrong in this benighted country.

In the end, they managed to hitch a ride from a friendly soldier driving an empty supply truck heading back to the capital. Farrell assumed he was inclined to help fellow Americans when he saw him and Ashe until the truth dawned. He couldn't give a shit about fellow Americans, but when he saw a gaggle of pretty girls, even if they did look a bit beaten up, he was sold. He also insisted three of the prettiest traveled with him in the cab.

During the journey, Farrell thought about how he'd deal with Charles Curtis. He didn't anticipate any problems, for Duy Tan would be able to confirm his story. The truck driver drove them into the center of Saigon and left the girls with Linh to organize accommodation in a hostel where she knew the owner, and he fixed up to meet two of the girls the following night. They drove on to Tan Son Nhut and the beginning of the new nightmare.

He'd expected trouble. After all, Dorsey and Batista were sure to tell it differently, until Curtis spoke to Duy Tan and heard the truth.

He banged on the office door and walked inside. He hadn't expected Dorsey and Batista to be with him, although afterward realized he'd walked straight into an ambush.

He looked at Curtis. "I guess you know about Duy Tan."

"As much as I need to know. You did well, all of you. I sent out a team to get a result, and that's what you brought back, a result. And now we have a new target."

"Where is he?"

"Where is who?"

"Tan."

"Tan? What about him? He's dead. Past history."

He glanced at Dorsey. "Clarence, what kind of a game are you playing? You took him from Bien Hoa, so what have you done with him?"

The familiar sneer was there. "What have I done? I followed orders, Farrell. Like you should've. They sent us to locate and kill a traitor, and that's what we did. Before we finished him, we persuaded him to part with valuable intelligence. You should've stayed with me and Pablo."

He shook his head in disbelief. "He's dead?"

The sneer became a triumphant grin. "They don't come any deader."

He looked at Curtis. "I don't know what he's been telling you, but it's bullshit. These two men ran after they'd found Duy Tan's horde of cash, leaving me and Ashe to finish the mission. We've been through hell, crawling around Vietcong tunnels. We found him and brought him back to Bien Hoa. Now this bastard is saying we ran. It's not true. Total bullshit."

Clarence chuckled. "It's you who's talking bullshit, Farrell. You got a yellow streak running down your back, and I don't believe there's any place for a man like you in this outfit."

He bunched a fist and was about to swing, but Ashe grabbed him from behind and held him back. "Hold it, hitting him won't do any good." He looked at Curtis. "What he says is true, Sir. It was these two cowards who ran."

Batista and Dorsey assumed phony looks of outrage, threatening any man who dared to suggest they were cowards. Curtis listened for a minute and slammed his fist down on the desk. "Shut the fuck up! All of you!"

They quietened, and he gave each of them a ferocious glare. "I don't know who's telling the truth, and frankly, I don't give a shit. My job is to make sure you get a result. You got a result, and that's all that counts. I have plenty of targets, a long list of names, and I want you to stop this crap and work together. You're a team, not a bunch of street gangsters." He looked at Farrell. "I'm disappointed in you. I looked at your records from the last time you in Vietnam, and I thought you were better than this."

He didn't reply. There was nothing he could say, not a single damn thing. He waited while Curtis spelled out what he had planned. They were to work as a team, and he had another assignment lined up.

"There're two men I want taken out, both believed to be in the area of Ben Cat. The first is Vo Kiet, who is an official of the government of the South Vietnamese government. He's employed to tour rural areas and report back to Saigon on how they can implement land reforms. It's part of the government plan to counter Communist promises to give land to the peasants, which we know are a crock of shit."

"What's he done?" Ashe grunted.

"He uses his job roaming around the countryside to identify targets for Vietcong hit squads, mainly village elders who're opposed to the Communists. After he leaves a village, Charlie moves in and murders the target. Then they replace him with one of their stooges. Vo Kiet has to go down, although finding him could be tricky because he moves around so much."

"And the other," Farrell asked.

"Xuan Dieu. He was in charge of an irrigation scheme in the Delta, designed to improve water supplies for peasant farmers. He uses his job to pass intelligence about our troop movements to the enemy, and as a result, we've lost too many soldiers to ambushes. When he realized we were onto him, he disappeared. We believe he's hiding somewhere inside the Triangle."

"The Iron Triangle?"

"What other triangle is there? More VCs and North Vietnamese soldiers hiding out in that place than you can shake a stick at. You're aware of President Nixon's efforts to bring the war to an end? Any chance of getting the North Vietnamese to the negotiating table depends on removing men like Kiet and Dieu so they realize the gloves are off and we're playing hardball."

"You haven't mentioned Quang," Dorsey murmured.

He nodded thoughtfully. "Yeah, Tran Quang, we don't know where he is, but he's right at the top of the target list. Before he died, Duy Tan gave Clarence the name of Tran Quang. He's Hanoi's number one man in the Vietcong, and he also has a lot of clout with the People's Army. If he calls in a battalion of troops to support the VC, they send them. He's that important. Problem is, he's a hard man to track down. We'll keep looking while you men go after Kiet and Dieu. Remove them from the equation, and by that time, hopefully, we'll know where to look for Quang. That's all. You may as well go and get cleaned up. You've had a hard time, so take a couple of days before you go after Dieu and Kiet. Dorsey, stay behind, there're a couple of things I need to run past you."

They left, and Batista went off without a word. Farrell wondered what was being discussed in the office between Dorsey and Curtis. He suspected it wasn't anything good.

* * *

"I don't trust him, and the sooner we get Melvin back the better."

Curtis nodded. "Clarence, I know how you feel about your brother, but my hands are tied. There are contractual agreements I have to adhere to, and they must be honored. I can transfer Melvin to a different unit when he recovers, and I know he'll make out okay. It'll make things difficult if I have to change those arrangements."

He scowled. "I don't give a shit about making your life difficult. He's a troublemaker. He makes up the numbers, that's about all he's useful for. I want him out."

He looked thoughtful. "What exactly went on with Duy Tan? How did it happen?"

"I told you. We located him and brought him back to Bien Hoa so we could give him a flying lesson on the way back to Saigon. Throw him out the door of the Huey, and nobody would be any the wiser. I could've put a bullet in him, but why waste bullets? Besides, Batista had him hanging out the door, and he gave us Quang. What's the problem, Mr. Curtis? You said we'd done well when we got back. Put him down and brought back valuable intelligence."

"Sure, sure. Except Farrell and Ashe recall things differently. They say you ran, leaving them to pick up Duy Tan and bring him back to Bien Hoa."

"Farrell's full of piss and wind. He's a waste of time, a liar, and a coward. You shouldn't take notice of anything he says."

"What about Ashe? He's always been reliable. Maybe I should terminate his contract."

"Maybe." A cunning expression came over his face, "There could be a use for Farrell. We could send him to find Quang."

"I thought you said he was a waste of time."

"Hear me out. We know finding Quang will be next to impossible. The guy moves around like a ghost. Why not let him find us? What I mean is find Farrell, and that snot-nosed buddy of his, Ashe."

Curtis gave him a doubtful look. "Are you suggesting what I think you're suggesting?"

He grinned. "When you're hunting a tiger, you stake out bait, a sacrificial goat. What I'm saying is we let the enemy know their target is Tran Quang. It'll shake his feathers, and as soon as he moves his location, we'll be there. Waiting."

"You'd let them die?"

"I'd let Farrell die. Maybe we can set Ashe straight if he survives, but Farrell goes. Isn't he worth sacrificing to get Quang?"

Curtis didn't look too happy. "I'm not too sure, Clarence. Sacrificing one of our own. It's not ethical." He thought for a few seconds more and shrugged, "Then again, if there's no other way, it could be for the best. Fix it up."

Dorsey strolled away; satisfied he'd got what he wanted. All he needed was to make it happen.

But why wait for Tran Quang? I could get word to Kiet and Dieu, let them know a certain Boy Scout's gunning for them. They'll be waiting for him when he gets close. Farrell will be out of my hair, Melvin will come back, and things will go back the way they were. As for Ashe, if he survives, he'll have to learn to keep his mouth shut.

* * *

He and Ashe left the base and strolled to the bungalow. Farrell took a hot shower while Ashe rummaged for the ingredients to make a meal. He came up with steaks and pre-frozen French fries. Farrell emerged in clean clothes, and they seated themselves on opposite sides of the small table. Maybe things weren't that bad.

They made small talk, and he learned more about David Ashe. About his service in Vietnam, and how he'd vowed never to return, until CIA offered to fill his boots, or rather his offshore untaxable bank account, with more cash than he'd ever dreamed of when he was in uniform.

"I wasn't sure about joining an assassination program, but the men we take out are the worst of the worst. Traitors and scum, murderers, responsible for killing thousands of Vietnamese civilians, murdered because they don't like the Communists. Leaving behind families, wives, and children, to fend for themselves. I've seen enough weeping, wailing women and children to last a lifetime, so I got down to work."

Farrell finished the last chunk of steak, chewing thoughtfully. "Money talks. It helps."

"You signed up for Phoenix. Wasn't that your motivation?"

He shook his head and explained about the murder of his brother, and how he'd wound up in prison. Doing the same job as Phoenix, without the pay and benefits.

"I had to either take this on or spend the next few years rotting in a cell. There's another reason. Curtis told me he'd get me a name so I'd have a chance to settle the score."

"You believed him?"

"Maybe, maybe not, but while I'm here I'll have a better chance of finding the guy who gave the order to kill him. Dammit, Dave, they butchered him while he was on a medical mission to save the life of a pregnant Vietnamese. When I do…" He drew the edge of his hand across his throat, "He goes down. All the way."

They cleared the dishes into the sink and spent the day

relaxing, swapping war stories, and catching up on more sleep. In the early evening, Ashe found a bottle of booze he'd stashed in the closet. Whiskey, but it wasn't Scotch. Suntory, Japanese. Dave filled two glasses, and they toasted each other. The booze was surprisingly good.

Ashe suddenly made an abrupt suggestion. "Why don't we head into the city, see how the girls are doing?"

It sounded like a good idea. "I'll pick up the tab for the taxi."

"No need. A fighter jock was going home and selling his car, so I bought his car cheap. I'll get cleaned up and we'll head on in."

They strolled around the back of the bungalow, and the bright red Pontiac GTO was parked under a carport next to the boundary wall. It had seen better days, for sure, and it looked like the fighter jock had given it some brutal treatment before he sold it on, but when Ashe started the engine the throaty roar suggested it hadn't lost any of its potential for brute force power. He drove skillfully, weaving through slower-moving traffic, and managed to avoid colliding with water buffalo that had wandered onto the highway. A bit further, a flock of chickens was pecking at the stubble that'd sprouted on the carriageway. They scuttled out of the way fast when they saw him coming, clucking with anger at the rude intrusion on their feast.

He squealed to a halt outside the hostel, which had once been a hotel. The reason it had ceased to be a hotel was obvious. The owners had failed to keep pace with the dilapidation, and several of the balconies hung down at drunken angles, victims to wet and dry rot, and the pests that chomped on everything they could find to eat. Inside the building, a hatchet-faced

Vietnamese woman gave them a look harder than stainless steel.

"No men! Go away."

Farrell gave her a winning smile. "We brought in some girls yesterday…" He realized he didn't know her full name, "Uh, Linh and some other girls."

She glared back at him. "Prostitutes."

"Well, uh, no. They had a hard time, is all."

She snorted. "They went out. Stupid. Bar across road, Jade Palace."

He thanked her, and they left, walking across the street to the dubiously named Jade Palace. There was no jade and no palace in evidence. The place was a shithole, with loud Western rock music bellowing from a sound system inside to accompany the stench of cheap perfume and unwashed bodies. They walked through the Western-style batwing doors into a cacophony of earsplitting violence. The Rolling Stones were thundering out 'Paint it Black,' so loud there was no chance of carrying on anything like a conversation. Not that most people appeared to be interested in talking. They were drinking beer from bottles dripping with condensation. Those who weren't, held bottles of spirits by the neck, glugging them straight down.

A few couples gyrated on the tiny dance floor, and in dark corners, some were locked together so close it would've been against the law in a public place. Not that they seemed troubled, a few were openly humping, in one case laying on a table. Nobody took any notice.

He spotted Linh and the girls in the far corner of the room, and they strolled over. He had to shout to make himself heard. "Having fun?"

She gave him a tight-lipped greeting. "Not really, but the

place is cheap, and it's close to the hostel."

"Why don't we go outside for a chat? You can tell me how things are."

She nodded eagerly, climbed to her feet, and shouted something to the girls. They left Ashe trying to make a shouted conversation over the noise.

"How's the hostel?"

She frowned. "Better than a Vietcong tunnel, but not by much. They don't charge, which helps."

"Free?"

"None of us have any money, and it's run by a Catholic charity set up to help fallen women."

Fallen women.

He didn't comment. "I get the picture. What're your long-term plans?"

A shrug. "I don't have any. Maybe I can find work as a teacher in Saigon, although it won't be easy. My documents were all destroyed during a previous raid on the village, and I have no way of proving anything. My identity, my qualifications, nothing. I'll try to get replacements, but it won't be easy."

"I can help out with a few dollars."

She gave him an emphatic shake of the head "Paul, you've done too much already. I could not accept. Don't worry, somehow I'll make out. There're other jobs I can do. It's a question of looking around. Bar work, cleaning." She smiled, "Exotic dancing, there's a big demand in Saigon."

"I bet there is, but I'd give the exotic dancing a miss if I were you."

She smiled, and for a fleeting instant, she looked pretty and carefree. "I was joking."

"Yeah, I get it. I'll look around, and if I find anything, I'll let you know."

She thanked him and suggested they went back inside. "Otherwise, they'll think we're up to something."

They strolled back, and for a moment he considered how much he'd liked to have got up to something, got to know this girl better. But he dismissed the thought. He'd saved her from a Vietcong hell, and the idea he could stick around just to collect a reward left a bad taste. They spent some time chatting to the girls, or rather Dave Ashe chatted to the girls while Linh translated. He noticed several of the customers were snorting coke, and he felt uncomfortable. The old familiar yearning to fill his nostrils with the white powder and get the familiar buzz; a feeling of power and energy, of escape from everything bad about the world in which he lived. He fought down the urge, but it was hard. They left and drove back to the bungalow. Ashe dragged out a recent acquisition, a videotape of The Good, the Bad, and the Ugly. They watched gunslinger Clint Eastwood go head-to-head with bounty hunter Lee Van Cleef as they hunted for treasure buried in a cemetery. Or something like that.

The movie finished, and in the silence, he sipped more of Ashe's Japanese whiskey. "That shootout at the end, I wish it was always that easy," he mused.

"Nothing's easy in Vietnam."

"I guess not. About these two targets, Dieu and Kiet. What do you know?"

"Not much. The word is they're based close to Ben Cat, although they operate in a wide area, traveling around, identifying targets for the Communist kill teams."

"Like us."

Ashe reacted violently. "We're not like them, not in a million years. What we do is righteous. The men we target are murderers. We bring justice to them and their victims' families. We're nothing like them," he ended, his voice filled with anger. Then he calmed, "Sorry, I guess I got carried away."

"No sweat."

Two days later, they were on the road to Ben Cat. They were squeezed into an M151 MUTT jeep, the radio antenna poking up into the sky, and their gear packed around them. Clarence insisted they take a detour to Bien Hoa, where he aimed to collect a recent intelligence report that might give them a clue as to Vo Kiet's current whereabouts.

"As you know, he passes the names of leaders loyal to South Vietnam back to his Vietcong bosses, who send in a few men to slice and dice them. He uses the radio to stay in contact, and we have assets in place to listen in. If he's filed a recent report, we'll have a good idea where to look. Ben Cat is a big area, so we need somewhere to start."

It sounded like a plan. The journey was just twenty klicks, and they reached the sprawling air base inside a half-hour. Clarence went looking for the intelligence officer. Batista stayed with the jeep, while Farrell and Ashe climbed out to stretch their legs. Ashe went off to find the PX and buy some smokes, while Farrell went for a stroll. He felt edgy, which was no surprise. The familiar urge was coursing through his veins. He was still thinking about the bar awash with drugs where they'd met Linh and girls. Thinking about the coke, and he knew on a base this size he wouldn't have to go far to find one of the local pushers to sell him a hit for a few dollars.

Is that what I'm doing? Looking for cocaine? Maybe. But it's not gonna happen. It can't happen.

He walked out to the flightline and watched the ground crews working on the fighter-bombers parked at the side of the tarmac. The nearest was a pair of F-100 Super Sabres. Probably they were preparing them for their next Wild Weasel mission, flak and radar suppression for high and low-level bombers. The ground crews go his attention, especially a couple of guys who were smoking, against all regulations when surrounded by the stink of aviation fuel. It wasn't Virginia tobacco. The fragrant scent of marijuana drifted toward him, carried on the wind, and served as a further reminder of the addiction that'd brought about his downfall.

He'd have given anything to wander over and talk to them about parting with some grass. But like that time in the bar, when he'd fought back the desperate need to stuff his nose with coke, he resisted the urge. If he started, he'd never stop. He watched them for a while longer, his emotions raging. They gave him hard stares, as if he was a plainclothes cop checking them out. He gave them a friendly wave to reassure them and turned away. As he did so, the earth moved. A salvo of heavy shells had slammed into the ground nearby and erupted in a tornado of high-explosive, smoke, and flame.

He'd seen it before. The Communists used Soviet 130mm M-46 towed field guns, and they packed a powerful shell. With a range upward of fifteen klicks, they could standoff and shell a target at long distances. Hitch up to the towing vehicles when they were done, and drive away before counter-battery fire and fighter-bombers had time to react. He looked to the northwest, where the shells were coming from, in time to see a new salvo arriving. The low trajectory suggested the distance wasn't anything like fifteen klicks, more like five, which meant somewhere on the opposite side of the Dong Nai River. Close enough.

He was still jittery, still preoccupied with the drugs his body needed, and as if his body was answering the call, a drug poured through his system. But this time it was adrenaline, spiking his metabolism, powering him into action, as powerful as a cocaine high. He started to run, sprinting back to the MUTT, and there was no sign of Batista. Ashe was leaning against the vehicle, a burning cigarette held halfway to his mouth as if he'd been about to take a drag when the shells hit.

He looked at Farrell as he ran up. "What's the deal?"

"What's the deal? The bastards are trying to kill us. I'm going after them."

The cigarette dropped from his hand. "Paul, you can't be serious. There's a battery of enemy artillery out there somewhere, heavy artillery. There could be forty or fifty VCs with trucks, artillery pieces, and more assault rifles than you can shake a stick at. You know the way this works. They shoot and scoot. If we keep our heads down for a few minutes more, they'll be gone."

"The hell with letting them get away! Dave, I gotta do this. If I can find them, I can pinpoint them for the fighter jocks."

"You're crazy. Are you on something?"

He was crazy. That was true. Crazy for drugs, and the adrenaline that'd spiked in his body had come as a relief, a way to take his mind off the desperate need for a fix. All he knew was he needed to keep moving to stop his body from torturing him. There was a good incentive to move. More salvos of heavy shells arrived, churning up fountains of dirt and flame. Smoke hung over the base, and men ran everywhere like ants. Engines were firing up, and within minutes aircraft and helicopters would be in the air, seeking out the enemy artillery battery.

They'd be wasting their time. The VC weren't stupid, and they'd have an escape plan lined up. He didn't want them to escape. He had a mission, a chance to take his mind off the terrible craving that possessed him day and night, body and soul. Waiting to trip him up in a single unguarded moment. The sentries tried to flag him down as he roared out through the gates. He ignored them, heading northwest for the bridge over the Dong Nai River.

If I'm fast, really fast, I might just locate them before they take off. Call in the gunships and roast their asses!

"If you take the curves any faster, the jeep will overturn."

He hadn't realized Ashe was with him, and he glanced aside. He wasn't on his own, and he needed him. Couldn't do it on his own; "Fire up that radio. We're gonna need it!"

"You got it."

Within minutes they were approaching the bridge, and he sped across, astonished by what he was looking at. The Viets were so confident, they'd set up a battery of three big artillery pieces in plain sight on the opposite bank of the Dong Nai. He made it halfway across when the guns bellowed again, sending three more heavy shells into the Bien Hoa Air Base. It was their last salvo. Men rushed to hitch the guns to the heavy trucks backed up and waiting to take them in tow.

"Call it in. If they move fast, they can get them all."

Ashe was already on the radio, talking to Bien Hoa, and they were giving him grief.

"The stupid bastards don't believe me. They've got their

fucking heads up their asses."

"For Chrissake, tell them if they miss this opportunity somebody can forget their future chance of promotion."

He grimaced and spoke into the handset. It took several minutes to persuade them. They'd probably made a call to the CIA Station in Saigon to confirm he was who he said he was. Eventually, they took it seriously. He didn't need to give them any coordinates.

"I told the stupid bastards they'll find them next to the Dong Nai Bridge on the west bank, and to get the lead out or they'll miss the party."

He flung down the handset in disgust. "They said they're gonna move. Finally. It'll have to be fast, or they'll be too late."

He grunted. "Same old story, too little, too late."

He drove off the bridge, keeping the gas pedal pressed to the floorboards. Three heavy trucks moved slowly, overloaded with troops and towing three heavy guns. They weren't about to move fast. He took a parallel street, matching their speed, and every few minutes saw them drive past an intersection, keeping to the riverbank until they unexpectedly turned inward toward the city of Thuan An. When they reached the twisting, densely packed streets, they could easily disappear. They'd have an escape route prepared long in advance, and very soon aircraft would be overhead, searching for them. And finding nothing.

He reached an intersection and turned toward the convoy just as the last truck rolled past. Startled soldiers stared down at the jeep. They weren't in uniform but were unmistakably military. Ashe had an AR-15 in his hands, and in case they were in doubt about their intentions, he threw it to his shoulder and fired a short burst at the rearmost vehicle. Men returned fire, but most bullets pattered harmlessly into the surrounding buildings. Some found softer targets. The streets were crowded, and people screamed, panicked, or writhed in agony after they'd been hit. The VCs had never been too picky about collateral damage.

Ashe fired again, this time emptying a full magazine into the troops crammed into the rear of the truck, and a man took several bullets that threw him into the street. His body thrashed in agony, spraying blood on the ground. If he wasn't already dead, he was when Farrell drove over him. It wasn't deliberate. He was unable to avoid him without hitting people scattering every which way. Then again, the guy was a goner, and he'd been spraying bullets indiscriminately into the crowds of civilians. Some people deserved everything they got.

Sooner or later they'd get lucky, and he dropped back fifty meters to avoid the automatic fire. All they needed was to keep them in sight, and the trick was not to get too close. More rifle fire came from the rearmost truck, and he had to swerve the jeep from side to side to avoid giving them a stable target. Their shooting was crap. They were firing from the rear of the big, Soviet trucks with iron-hard suspension that jolted every time they hit a bump in the tarmac, and this being Vietnam, there were more bumps than on a Coney Island carnival ride.

"Where the hell are those aircraft?" he snarled at Ashe, "Call them again. Tell them they'll lose them if they don't hurry."

He knew they'd be heading for somewhere they could hide. Not into the jungle, they were too far away. Driving into the center of the city, it had to be something else, an empty warehouse, even a derelict factory or apartment block with space to squeeze the trucks inside. Yet they knew they were being followed, and he wondered how they planned to shake off the tail. Probably working out how to kill them.

He got the answer a few seconds later. The soldiers in the rearmost truck moved aside, and two men pushed forward a wheel-mounted machine gun, an antique Soviet Maxim. The design may have been sixty years out of date, but it could still spew out six hundred 7.62mm rounds every minute, while the gunner crouched behind the thick steel shield, protected from incoming fire. They'd used them in World War I, in World War II, the North Koreans in the Korean War, and the Russians generously supplied them to their Communist buddies in North Vietnam.

"Shit!"

The gun barrel angled toward them, and he had to wrench the wheel hard over. The jeep took the turn on two wheels as he drove into a side street, avoiding the hurricane of machine gun bullets. He turned into a parallel street and swung back to locate the towed artillery.

"Don't get too close to that machine gun," Ashe warned, "There's something to be said about following them from a distance."

He didn't answer. They'd reached the street where they'd last seen the trucks, and they'd disappeared. Pedestrians had flattened themselves against sides of the buildings to steer clear of the gunfire, and vehicles had pulled into the curb to give the Vietcong trucks space to get past. But they'd gone. Vanished.

"Where are they?" he snarled, "They can't have just disappeared. I'll circle the block. They're here somewhere."

Ashe raised the handset as a call came in and talked to a man on the other end. Simultaneously, a pair of F-100 Super

Sabres roared overhead. Probably the same two they'd seen with ground crews preparing them for takeoff. "They want to know the enemy's current location. What do I tell them?"

"Tell them to give us another couple of minutes. They can't have gone far."

He relayed the message, put down the handset, and began to reload his AR-15. Farrell drove up the next street, took a right, another right, and they were back where they'd started. They weren't there. They'd disappeared. Vanished off the face of the earth, or at least vanished off the city streets.

Where the hell are they?

Ashe took another call on the radio. "They're getting impatient. Maybe they think we never saw them and we made it up."

"Do they think we made up the shells that landed on the air base? Keep looking. They're here somewhere."

He drove past several pagodas. A collection of buildings with gilded roofs, and it wasn't difficult to imagine the old days, solemn aristocrats in their long robes strolling around, attended by servants and fluttering maids tripping daintily in their ao dais. Except this wasn't a history lesson, and he concentrated on searching for the towed artillery.

Where are they? Inside a building, for sure, but which building? None of them are big enough. Except for the pagoda, and that's ridiculous. Insane. Or is it?

He stood on the brake and slid the jeep into a one hundred and eighty-degree turn. "They're inside the pagoda. Call it in."

Ashe looked at him, aghast. "You're kidding! That place is a museum. It's several hundred-years-old, maybe a thousand. We can't tell them to bomb an ancient building."

"Dave, you were Air Cav, and you've seen the kind of tricks they get up to. Didn't you ever see them hide troops and heavy weapons inside a school or hospital?"

"I guess so. But this is…"

"It's the same thing. Tell them to flatten it!"

"If you're sure."

"It's the only solution. Occam's razor."

"Occam's what?"

"Occam's razor. The simplest explanation is usually the right one."

He still hesitated, and Farrell grabbed the handset. "They're hiding in the ancient pagodas, the biggest one. It's on the northern side of the city."

There was a moment's silence, and the voice that came back sounded as incredulous as Ashe. "I'd need authority to bomb a historical building."

"I'm giving you the authority."

"And who the hell are you?"

"Paul Farrell, I'm with CIA. Deputy Director for Operations."

"You're serious? Okay, Mr. Farrell if you say go ahead, consider it done."

"Do it."

Ashe was looking at him, mouth agape. "You know what you just did? If they find out at Langley, they'll hang you out to dry."

"Only if I'm wrong, Dave."

"You're that sure?"

"Of course."

He wasn't sure, not one hundred percent. Just on a

balance of probabilities, and that was all he had to go on. They watched the Super Sabres swoop down on their first attack run. Bombs fell from the six hardpoints on each aircraft, and the pilots pointed the nose of their aircraft up after release. They were well away when the bombs exploded, and the effect was devastating. The ancient structure, revered by so many Vietnamese over the centuries, an important and major tourist attraction for the city, fell apart.

He stopped the jeep to watch the show, and his entire future depended on whether he'd made the right call. The fighters returned, this time churning up the rubble with their 20mm autocannons, each loaded with two hundred heavy-caliber rounds. When they'd gone past, more of the building had collapsed.

"I don't see them, Paul," he said uneasily.

He was trying to work out how to handle the destruction of an ancient pagoda, a cultural landmark worth millions. Dollars, not dong. If he'd made the wrong call, he was screwed. Well and truly fucked. So far, there was no sign of them.

Ashe muttered, "I think you made a bad call."

Chapter Five

"Wait."

The Super Sabres flew past, performed a flashy 'loop the loop' and roared back for a third attack. This time, they launched missiles, two Sidewinders each. The Sidewinder was an air-to-air missile, not designed for air-to-ground operations. But fitted with infrared guidance systems, the missiles sped unerringly toward the heat of the burning building, and the result was spectacular. A series of vast explosions spewed out smoke and flame, far more than anyone could have expected from four missiles. The kind of explosions that could only be created by the sympathetic detonation of a large quantity of ordnance, like the kind of 130mm shells carried by North Vietnamese heavy artillery.

"I'll be damned," Ashe murmured.

Men were scrambling from the burning wreckage; black pajamas, floppy jungle hats, and rubber sandals, which anybody could've worn, although most didn't, for fear of being linked with the enemy. The AK-47s they carried were the giveaway, and as the wind cleared a break in the smoke and dust, the spectacular results of the attack by the Super Sabres were revealed. Three big 130mm guns, three heavy trucks twisted into scrap, and interspersed between them, bodies, lots of bodies.

In their confusion and terror, the survivors ran every which way, although most headed north. The fighters were waiting to pounce, and after they'd expended the last of their cannon rounds, helicopters arrived from Bien Hoa. Bell Cobra gunships and Hueys with mounted door guns. They lashed the fleeing Vietcong with bullets and rockets, chasing them down and finishing them off. A few, maybe a half-dozen, headed in the opposite direction, straight into the arms, or rather the muzzles, of Farrell and Ashe.

They didn't see them blocking the way, until they squeezed the triggers and fired on full auto. The long bursts of automatic fire put paid to any ideas they had about escaping into the city. The battle was over. Any remaining survivors had disappeared, a hard lesson learned. He started the engine, put the jeep into gear, and drove back to Bien Hoa.

This time, there was no delay at the gates. The word had reached the air base, probably when the aircrews reported what they'd seen. They weren't in uniform, but the sentries stood to attention and gave them crisp salutes. One man shouted, "Fucking A!"

They drove inside and found Dorsey and Batista waiting for them. Clarence didn't share the enthusiasm for what they'd done. He looked pissed.

"Where the hell have you been?"

They had to know. Every man they'd passed had stared at them, and a few had tossed friendly waves.

At least some people appreciate a good turn.

"Sightseeing."

Clarence scowled. "Fuck you, Farrell. Next time you go off with my jeep, you talk to me first. Get out of that seat."

He didn't reply, just climbed into the back. Batista took over, and they drove away, heading for Ben Cat. They drove past the smoking ruins of the pagoda, and once again, Dorsey had to know, but he stared in the opposite direction. The drive to Ben Cat was a tad over twenty-five klicks, and even on poorly maintained roads that didn't deserve the name 'roads' they made it in a half-hour. It was late afternoon, and they had five hours of daylight left before darkness descended. Night, the time when Charlie came out to play.

They stopped outside the main police station, the Vietnamese National Police. About as corrupt a unit as could be found in a country where corruption was as natural as breathing. Where many of their cops were ghosts, fake names on the payroll to fatten the bank accounts of senior officers. For many others, their bosses were frequently north of the 17th Parallel dividing the two Vietnams. In a city called Hanoi.

Clarence jumped out of the jeep, and Batista was about to follow when Farrell put a hand on his shoulder. "That's okay, Pablo, you've done all the driving. Take it easy, I'll go with Clarence."

It wasn't part of the plan, but Farrell was already striding toward the entrance, and with no choice, Dorsey hurried to keep up with him. They were inside for almost an hour, and when they emerged, they were no further forward than when they started. They'd been passed from cop to cop; with a series of oily smirks that told them they were wasting their time. Finally, they were in the office of the colonel in charge of Ben Cat, and he at least had the grace to keep the smirk off his face.

"Vo Kiet? Never heard of him."

They kept straight faces. "He works for the government in Saigon," Dorsey supplied, "He's on the Land Reform Commission. This is the area assigned to him. Colonel, so how about you check your records?"

The neutral expression slipped a fraction. "I told you I'd never heard of him. I'm sorry I can't be of any assistance. If there's anything further I can do…"

Farrell stared back at him. "How about you check your records?" A pause, "Just in case."

He scowled. "I think we're done here. If you have any further questions, you can contact National Police Headquarters in Saigon. Good day, gentlemen."

Fuck you, too.

They left the building, unaware of the cop who'd followed them, standing in the shadows of a doorway opposite, watching.

"What next?" he asked Dorsey.

"Next? I can contact a couple of informants who regularly pass on information to the CIA. I'll talk to them and find out what they know. Me and Pablo will take the jeep. You two can wait around; get yourselves a beer and something to eat. We'll be back in a couple of hours."

Pablo started the engine, and the jeep drove away. They watched them go, and he had a bad feeling about it. "They're up to something. Any ideas?"

Ashe shrugged. "Beats me. We'd better find someplace to

eat."

They didn't have to go far. In the center of the town, there were several bars and small restaurants, and they entered a place that looked sanitary. The beer was cold, they served a halfway edible burger, and the place was clean. If undercover Vietcong ran it, the burger could be poisoned, but on balance they doubted it. They found a table where they could eat facing the door. Ben Cat was not a place to turn your back on the enemy.

They noticed a cop stroll into the restaurant. Cops had to eat, although they hadn't seen doughnuts on the counter. He walked up to their table.

"Do you mind if I join you?"

He was an older man who looked about sixty, which in this country made him around forty. Short, thin, wrinkled, and his head was bald. He still looked fit and capable, like he could handle himself when he tackled the bad guys. Farrell lowered his burger and gave the cop the once-over. His hands were empty of any weapon, and he gestured toward an empty chair.

"Knock yourself out. The beers and the burgers are okay." He took another bite.

"You are looking for Vo Kiet." It wasn't a question.

He nearly choked. "Excuse me?"

"Vo Kiet. He works for the Land Reform Commission in Saigon."

"What do you know about him?"

"He also works for the Communists."

"Tell us something we don't know. Like where is he?"

"You have come here to kill him?"

He thought for a few moments. The honest answer to that question would've been a simple yes. This guy was a cop, and

119

maybe he was one of the few honest cops in South Vietnam. Or maybe he wasn't."

"Maybe we've come to question him about his tax return."

He didn't smile. "I can help you find him."

"You know where he is?"

A pause. "Not exactly, but I know the places he frequents. Not in Ben Cat, but out in the rural areas. He moves around, never sleeps in the same place twice. He knows sooner or later somebody will come for him, and he has an elaborate warning system in place. Men are paid to look out for strangers, and if they see any getting close, Kiet moves on. He will not be an easy man to find. Or to kill."

They were intrigued, and Ashe raised an eyebrow. "Mister, what's your interest?"

"I hate the Communists who're ruining my country."

"Most of the cops in this town wouldn't agree with you. They weren't inclined to help when we asked about Kiet. What's your angle?"

"My son is Vietcong."

What the fuck!

"He works for the enemy? And you expect us to trust you."

"They indoctrinated him with their nonsense about Communism, about Karl Marx, and equality for everybody. After he joined the Vietcong, they posted him to a unit in the area that the Americans call the Iron Triangle. He spends most of his life in the tunnels, and for most of that time he's sick. The last I heard he's not expected to live. Always, it is the foolish young men and women they send into the tunnels. Equality only exists for those at the top. People like Le Duan and Giap."

"And Ho Chi Minh?" Ashe murmured.

"He's dead. When he was alive, he wasn't the worst of the bunch."

"For Hanoi, that's saying something," Farrell grinned, "Okay, tell us who you are. We know you're a cop, that's all we know."

"My name is Dao, Le Dao. I am a senior sergeant in the National Police here in Ben Cat."

"And your interest in Kiet?"

"When my son Le Luc first joined the Vietcong, he discovered Kiet had been diverting money intended to buy land for landless peasants into his private bank account. He's a crook, a common thief. Yet when my son complained, Kiet had him posted to the tunnels at Cu Chi, with orders he must spend most of his time underground. That was eighteen months ago, and he's rarely seen daylight since. When he is not sick, he spends most of his time digging new tunnels. They treat him like a slave, and I fear he will soon be dead."

"How do you know this?"

"A Vietcong deserter brought out a message from Le, begging me for help. So far I haven't had the opportunity to act. Some of my colleagues are Communist sympathizers, and if they knew about the message, they would pass it on to the Vietcong. Luc would be executed."

Farrell nodded. The explanation was believable, in line with the horror Hanoi was inflicting on the South. "And you can help us find Kiet, how?"

"I am a policeman. Despite the corruption in South Vietnam, people still have some respect for the law. I can question informants and check through our files to discover the most recent sightings and figure out a pattern of his movements. A pattern I believe will lead us to him."

"Us?"

"I must come with you. For what he has done to my son, I want his head on a pole in the center of Ben Cat."

He looked at Ashe, who gave a slight nod. "Agreed. Where do we start?"

"I will return to police headquarters before they become suspicious. I took a short break to come out here and talk with you. Today I'm working the late shift through to 22.00, and during the evening our building will be largely deserted. I will spend the time searching out everything we have on Kiet. Tell me where we can meet when I finish work, and I will hand over everything I have."

"We can meet here, just after 22.00." He put out a hand, "And thanks, Dao. Make sure you have a sharpened spike ready."

He returned a grim look. "I will."

He left, and they ordered more beers. Ashe's big worry was how they'd deal with Clarence. "He won't go for it, I know him."

"Then we have to persuade him."

He shook his head vehemently. "You don't understand. He runs a tight ship. At least he thinks he does. He gets away with everything, like the theft of Duy Tan's cash. Clarence aims to exit this war with enough money stashed in his bank account to set him up for life. And I'm talking a lot of money. Millions."

"What about Batista?"

A shrug. "He promised to cut him in for a share, the same as me. Enough to keep him satisfied."

"But you're not satisfied."

The expression on his face was so sincere, Farrell had no reason to disbelieve him.

"Because I believe in what we're doing. Okay, we kill people, but they're righteous kills. If we don't take them out, they'll keep on killing innocent people. Men and women who're trying to make a difference and the Communists hate them. I believe we should concentrate on the assignments Phoenix gives us, and not waste time robbing people. Before you say robbing Duy Tan didn't make a scrap of difference, I promise you he'd have robbed him regardless. It didn't matter a jot whether he was a hostile or a friendly."

He was beginning to understand what made Dave Ashe tick. He was one of those rare people fighting this war, a true believer. He believed it could be won if enough men stood up for what was right. What was that old saying?

'The only thing necessary for the triumph of evil is for good men to do nothing.'

The guy who said that was the English philosopher Edmund Burke, one of the good guys.

They needed to get Clarence and Pablo on side, and he was still thinking about it when Dave checked his watch. They were overdue. They ordered more beers and waited. And waited some more. When they arrived they were two hours late, and they weren't alone. They had company. Two Vietnamese girls and they were young. Very young, and the two Phoenix operators were both very drunk. They staggered into the bar; Dorsey bumped against a table, and sent the place settings flying.

The elderly proprietor came out from behind the counter, shouting angry protests about the wanton damage. Clarence put a huge hand against his chest and pushed, sending him sprawling into the wreckage.

"Fuck off, Grandad, or I'll smash up the rest of your bar. Bring me and my friends some beers, and make it snappy." His eyes fell on Farrell and Ashe, and he grinned. "There's more where these came from, do you want me to give you the address? They're cheap, and you can rent them by the hour, or a big discount if you take them for the whole night. That's what we did."

He shouldn't have replied, and the moment he did, he knew he'd made a mistake.

"Two things, Clarence. First, we're due to go looking for our target. We agreed to approach during the hours of darkness, so they don't know we're coming." He held up a hand as Dorsey opened his mouth to interrupt, "Second, those girls are underage. I don't hold with abusing children. Back home, they call it rape."

He let loose an outraged bellow. "Fuck you, Boy Scout. You don't tell me what to do. I'm in charge of this outfit, unless you've forgotten, and that means what I say goes."

He bunched a huge, meaty fist and swung at him. Paul stepped aside, easily evading the punch, and he went off balance, nearly falling into the pile of broken crockery.

"I'll fucking kill you!" he snarled, as he recovered his balance and tried again. A drunken man makes a lousy fighter, and once again Farrell sidestepped. Dorsey spun half around and fell back to the floor. He lay there, shaking his head in confusion, spitting threats and curses. Farrell glanced at Ashe, who'd taken out his Colt and had it pointed at Batista. Just in case he got any weird ideas.

The girls were regarding the fight with pretended nonchalance. They were probably well used to drunken men fighting each other and figured they were safe from the violence. Until the time came for the men to pay for their services when they'd probably find themselves on the receiving end.

"If I were you, ladies, I'd find yourself some other clients. These guys are trouble."

One shook her head. "Mister, they promise to pay big. We stay."

He'd tried, and it was all he could do. He glanced at Ashe. "I reckon we're done here. Why don't we wait outside until they sober up?"

They left the bar, and when they glanced back inside a few minutes later, everything had returned to normal. The broken crockery on the floor had been swept up, Clarence and Pablo were seated at a table, one hand clutching the neck of a bottle of bourbon, and the other fondling the breasts of the girls they had on their knees. A nervously smiling waitress was bringing heaped plates of food to their table, and he shook his head in exasperation.

"Vietnam. Up is down, and down is up. You think those girls would've taken the chance and left them to it."

Ashe gave a near-perfect imitation of the girl who'd spoken to Farrell. "Mister, they promise to pay big. We stay."

He chuckled, and they strolled across the street to wait for Dao. He arrived a few minutes after 22.00, clutching a plastic briefcase. "I got the latest reports that came in about Kiet's movements."

"How come the cops are monitoring his movements?"

He shrugged. "Our senior officers like to know what he's

up to. That way, they can calculate the size of the bribes."

"It figures. Do we know where he is?"

The answer shot back, and it was the last place they want to go looking. "Cu Chi."

"You're kidding me. Vietcong HQ."

"I'm sorry, that is the information I have. If we are to kill Vo Kiet, we must go to Cu Chi."

"Tell me he's not in the tunnels."

"No, he is in the town."

"Thank the Lord. All we need is for Clarence and Pablo to finish what they're doing and join us."

Ashe rolled his eyes. "They plan to stay the whole night."

"Sure they do, except we don't have the whole night to wait. We'll give them until midnight and pull them out."

"They'll go ape."

"CIA is paying us to locate and take out these men. Not to spend the night with whores. Midnight, that's all they've got."

When they went back inside the bar, the proprietor jerked a thumb at the back room. They walked through the plastic curtained doorway into a kitchen. Dorsey and Batista were half-dressed, lying on the floor, their arms flung around the girls, each of whom was naked.

He tapped Clarence on the shoulder. "We're leaving."

He opened one bleary eye. "Fuck off. I'm not stopping you."

"We have a lead on Kiet. If we leave now we can get him."

"I told you to fuck off."

He walked to the sink, filled a pan with cold water, and threw it over Clarence. Did the same with Pablo, and both men came off the floor like scalded cats, spitting curses and threatening to rip him apart. He ignored them and told the girls to get dressed and leave. They pulled on their clothes and made a fuss about extracting payment from the two clients, who made a fuss about settling the bill. In the end, he managed to negotiate a fee that satisfied neither. They calmed and left the bar. Shortly after, he and Ashe went back outside with the two reluctant and bleary Phoenix operators trailing behind them.

They reached the jeep, and Clarence gazed at the cop who'd changed into civilian clothes. Army surplus pants, held up by a wide leather belt that carried a holstered pistol. Jungle boots and a quilted Chinese jacket completed his ensemble.

"What does he want? A bribe?"

"He's coming with us." Before he could erupt in fury, Farrell explained how Dao could help them.

Clarence wasn't interested. "Forget it. I don't trust Vietnamese cops."

They argued for several minutes until Dao removed a bunch of files from the plastic briefcase he carried under his arm and showed them to Clarence. He didn't understand Vietnamese, and it may as well have been written in Chinese. Dao translated some of it, and he saw sense enough to agree if they were to use the information they contained to track Kiet, they needed Dao.

They climbed into the jeep, and Dao squeezed between Farrell and Ashe. Batista stomped on the gas and drove away with a squeal of tires. They endured a nightmare journey as he deliberately drove over every obstacle he could find, taking every turn on two wheels. Making the point in case they weren't aware that he was pissed at being hauled away from his night of passion. They were aware. They also ignored him as the jeep roared toward Cu Chi. Farrell was wondering about the tunnels, about the rumors they stretched for more than two hundred kilometers. It didn't seem possible unless a man considered how the Communists operated.

They attached little or no value to human life, using persuasion and lies to attract recruits. When persuasion and lies failed, they used threats. When threats failed, they used force. The result was men like Le Dao's son, condemned to suffer and die in the fetid, poisonous insect-ridden darkness. Which meant the tunnel system could be even longer than most estimates. Some believed it extended beneath Cu Chi Base Camp, and if that was hard to believe, others maintained the tunnels stretched beneath Saigon itself.

He believed it was possible. The Egyptians built the pyramids with tens of thousands of slaves. Provided they had sufficient slaves, men could move mountains or dig hundreds of kilometers of tunnels. The Communists had slaves, thousands, hundreds of thousands. Halfway to Cu Chi, he was still wondering how many tunnels lay below the road they were driving over.

It's as if the Vietcong are operating beneath our feet. Eerie.

Dao pulled a document from his plastic briefcase and read it by a tiny penlight. Abruptly, he shouted, "Stop!"

Batista cursed, but he stomped on the brake pedal. Clarence gave Dao a poisonous look.

"What's the deal? If you need the bathroom, you can wait."

"They are here."

They stared into the dark green jungle on either side, as if hostile faces were staring out at them. Involuntarily, they all tensed, waiting for a burst of gunfire to rip into the jeep. "Where?"

"I'm not sure." Clarence snorted, but he went on, "The intelligence points to a newly built base camp in this area. We are in danger of running into an ambush. This was a mistake."

"I don't get it," Clarence grumbled, "How come our intelligence people don't know about it?"

"The colonel in charge of police in Ben Cat is reluctant to pass on information to Saigon."

He cursed and spat over the side of the jeep. "Dao, this sounds like a crock of shit. We should go back, finish what we started." He grinned, "Those girls owe us."

"It states that Vo Kiet is involved in the construction of the base camp, built on land intended to be cleared for the land reform program. I believe he is in the area."

"I don't care if he's under the jeep changing the oil. We're going back."

"Too late."

They glanced at Ashe, who'd been looking behind them, and they swung around to follow his gaze. A bunch of men had materialized from the dark jungle and spread across the road. Batista cursed and trod on the gas pedal. The jeep lurched forward, but he brought it to a halt. Ten men had appeared in front of them, and more were stepping out of the jungle. They were fucked.

Has Dao led us into an ambush? No, he did try to warn us, except it's too late.

Batista, shocked by what they faced, had unconsciously left his foot on the gas pedal. The engine was roaring, although out of gear. Two hours before he'd been lying with a girl in the backroom of a bar, his belly full of booze. Now he faced a horde of VCs. He was staring death in the eyes, and he froze.

Farrell didn't freeze. "Get off the road and drive into the jungle, now!" He'd noticed a narrow gap between the trees.

Is it wide enough for the jeep? Who gives a damn? As long as we're in the cover of the jungle, maybe we'll have a chance.

For a second longer, Batista failed to move, until Clarence screamed at him, "Get this fucking thing moving!"

He slammed the lever into gear and let go the clutch. The jeep kangarooed forward, and by chance the wild gyration saved them. The Viets opened fire, but the jerking motion of the jeep presented them with a difficult target. By the time they'd adjusted their aim the MUTT was into the trees. Foliage scraped the bodywork on both sides, as Batista kept the pedal pressed flat to the floorboards, forcing their way through like toothpaste in a tube.

He collided with trees that were fortunately young enough to have slender, flexible trunks, and the jeep kept moving, even when the thin, whippy branches became entangled with the exhaust muffler. As they sped forward, it ripped it away from the chassis, dragging along behind them. The engine note sounded like they were driving a tank.

He drove like a man possessed for two frantic kilometers, using the beams of the headlamps to pick his way through. They thought they might just make it, until the jeep slammed into a tree with a thicker trunk. This time it didn't surrender. The tree stopped them dead, and Clarence screamed when the collision threw him over the windshield, and he went sprawling onto the jungle floor.

He was unhurt and jumped to his feet, still clutching his

rifle. Farrell, Ashe, and Dao were stunned after they'd been slammed forward into the backs of the front seats. Batista had collided with the steering wheel, and he was favoring what had to be a cracked rib, maybe two or three.

Clarence shouted at them to run. "They'll be right on our tail. We have to keep moving!"

Farrell wasn't so sure. There was no sound of any pursuit. Maybe they'd outrun them, but this was bandit country, with as many VCs as there were woodlice. "Clarence, we need to know where we're going, or we could run headlong into them."

"Farrell, you dumbass, they could be right behind us."

"So why can't we hear them? Clarence, if we abandon the jeep, we abandon our gear, and we abandon the radio."

"What do you want?" he snarled, "Wait for them to kick our asses?"

"Why don't we take a minute and work this out? Maybe we can get the jeep fixed and drive out of here."

"Without a muffler, they'll hear us in Hanoi."

He had a point. But Farrell was reluctant to abandon the jeep just yet. He told them he'd take a minute or two to scout their back trail, and soon he heard them coming and returned to the jeep. "Okay, they're on the way. We have around five minutes."

Clarence grimaced. "Screw you and your crazy ideas, Farrell. We would've been out of here if we hadn't waited. Grab everything you can carry, let's go."

They shouldered their rifles, spare canteens, and stuffed MREs into their packs. Dorsey took a step and froze. "Quiet," he hissed.

The warning was unnecessary. They'd heard voices.

Vietnamese voices, and they were getting closer. It sounded like a skirmish line, men spread out, beating the bushes, and in a few minutes, they'd find them. Clarence started to move, taking a step into the thick, foliage, and stopped when Batista muttered urgently, "I can't move. I'm in agony!"

He scowled. "You stupid bastard, you're gonna get us all killed."

Farrell lifted him into his arms, but Pablo voiced a long, low scream. Ashe clamped a hand over his mouth and hissed, "Shut it, or you'll get us all killed."

They should've died. The Vietcong had to find them. There was no way they could miss a crashed jeep stuck in their own backyard.

Chapter Six

The rain saved them. Farrell vowed never again to complain about the rain that fell like the Niagara Falls over South Vietnam. Although the tree canopy afforded them some protection, the deluge crashed down on the jungle. Torrents of water found their way between the thick leaves to crash down over their heads. It was so heavy they had to take cover in the lee of the jeep to avoid suffering what felt like drowning.

"It's like waterboarding," Clarence grunted, "Now I know what it feels like."

"You've done that?"

"Sure I have. It works well."

"I'll take your word for it."

"I thought I heard something." Dao got to his feet, despite the torrential rain crashing over them like liquid artillery fire, and peered out from behind the nearest tree. Moments later he was back, "They went past. I don't believe they saw us. They're having as much trouble with the rain as we are."

"I hope the fucking weasels drown," Clarence grunted.

"I hope one man drowns. Kiet is with them."

Farrell jerked in surprise. "Did I hear you right? Vo Kiet? The man we came here to kill."

He nodded. "The man I came here to kill. I overheard them talking, and it looks like he's more important than we realized. I believe he's the regional commander for this part of Cu Chi."

"I'll be damned. A pity we missed him."

"We haven't missed him, not yet." Clarence stared at Farrell, his expression hostile, but he didn't say anything, "Now we know where he is, we can follow him and put a bullet in him."

Dorsey snorted. "He's with around forty VCs, and where he's going, there may be more."

"Clarence, we have to nail this guy. I say we go after him."

"Pablo can't travel, and he sure can't fight."

"Why can't he stay here and try to fix the muffler on the jeep? It'll be painful, but it could save our lives. Think about it. We'll still have the radio, so we can call in an extraction."

He saw sense, and they left a complaining Batista with the jeep and set out to follow the VCs. The wheel had turned. The hunters had become the hunted. The intelligence Dao brought out from Ben Cat told of a new base under construction. Where else would Kiet head for? Off the radar, safe from American and ARVN patrols, marauding fighter-bombers, and helicopter gunships.

Dao led the way. This time there'd be no screwing around like before. No prisoners. He'd made a mistake. The guy had deserved to die for his murderous treachery. The Phoenix Program operated with a bunch of cutthroat mercenaries. That's what he'd signed up for, killing the traitors, wherever they could find them. The men they hunted had declared war on their own side. Killing them was like exterminating vermin, except more satisfying.

Clarence stumbled along, bringing up the rear. Still not recovered from the booze he'd imbibed back in Ben Cat. They made good time, despite the rain. The further they penetrated the jungle, the easier the path became to follow. The undergrowth was trampled flat where hundreds of men had passed on their daily toil. Most would have been laborers or more likely slaves. Pressed into service to obey the orders of their masters from Hanoi.

The journey went on for hour after hour, and at times he wondered if they'd missed them, until Dao held up a hand and knelt on the ground. They copied him, and the cop glanced back. "It's three hundred meters ahead."

Farrell saw nothing apart from the rain and wet foliage. "Where?"

"It's well camouflaged, almost invisible, but if you look carefully you'll see it. Straight lines. There are no straight lines in nature."

He looked again, trying to adjust his eyes to squint through the torrential rain, and suddenly he saw it. The clouds had moved, leaving a narrow gap to allow a shaft of moonlight to reflect on what Dao had described. Straight lines. A compound.

Farrell kept his voice to a low murmur. "Give me a minute. I'll take a look. I doubt they'll have sentries out on a night like this."

He crawled forward until he was within one hundred and fifty meters. They'd built a wide compound hacked out from the thick jungle. A roof of camouflage netting hung from the trees like a giant tent, and they'd threaded fresh foliage into the mesh. If they hadn't seen them come this way, they could've walked straight past and never seen it.

He lay in a pool of water six inches deep and recalled his vow. Never object to the rain that'd saved their lives.

Next time I do this, I'll bring a rubber boat.

He waited for another shaft of moonlight to light up the scene, but it didn't happen. He was about to crawl back when he saw something, and he paused. If they were going to nail Kiet, they'd need to spot him without being seen. He'd found what he was looking for.

Poking out through the overhead camouflage they'd built a watchtower in the upper branches of a tall tree, a narrow, railed platform. Designed for a sentry to keep an eye out for enemy patrols, it afforded a good view over the entire compound, a place to see and not be seen. He crawled back and described what he'd seen.

Clarence was unconvinced. "How does that help us?"

"I'll go back and climb the watchtower."

"Yeah, right. And?"

It was the growing need inside him that made him spit it out, the need for coke to feed the whining, insistent voice in his head. And if he didn't have coke, he'd settle for the adrenaline rush and blood, Kiet's blood. He'd do it for his brother. "When I see him, I'll put a bullet in him."

They were aghast. Clarence shook his head. "Pal, the moment you pull the trigger, they'll be all over you. You'd be signing your death warrant. Not that I give a shit, but this place will be like a hornets' nest."

"Not if I do it right. I'll figure out how to send a signal for you to pepper the place with gunfire like it's an attack. You might kill even some of them. They won't pick out a single gunshot in the middle of a heap more gunshots. I'll take him down and join you back at the jeep."

He stared at him in astonishment. "That's it? That's your plan?"

"Not quite. Dao, I need you with me. Curtis showed me the photo they have on file, but I'm not sure I can recognize him."

"I can recognize him. But I would like to take the shot."

"Whatever. We're gonna have one chance of this, and that's to take him at daybreak when there's just enough light to spot the target. But before they're all awake. When the camp starts to stir. Catch them napping."

"I understand."

"Clarence, Ashe, make sure you're there for us."

Ashe nodded. "Roger that."

"When we're ready to start shooting, I'll break off a small branch and let it drop."

"Got it."

They crept forward through the rain, and it had become heavier. They reached the almost invisible perimeter fence of the compound and the tree that was the base of the watchtower. The structure was twenty meters high, almost reaching the camouflage canopy. They saw no ladder.

"How do we get up?"

Dao shrugged. "No idea. But we'll have to get past the

fence to find out."

The idea of entering a compound crawling with VCs didn't appeal, but with no choice, they crawled through wide gaps in the fence, constructed from interlaced bamboos. There was enough room for a man to wriggle through. Inside, the camp was quiet. Lashed by the rain, nobody gave any sign of wanting to greet the dawn. They reached the tree, and they'd hammered long steel nails, making pegs in the trunk to use for steps.

Dao was behind him, and they climbed from peg to peg to the enclosure at the top. They had a view over the entire compound, and he pulled a small branch from an overhanging tree to use as a signal for Clarence and Dave to start shooting. Now came the hard part. Waiting.

He prayed for the rain to continue, a screen of wet mist to keep them hidden. Once again, he wasn't sure he'd made the right call.

Was I crazy, entering a Vietcong base camp? Probably, but I haven't figured out another way.

Before dawn, the camp started to stir. Men were walking around, partly protected from the rain with improvised ponchos made from what looked like plastic garbage bags. They visited the latrine pit, and several men approached an open-sided hut that looked like the cookhouse.

"Paul, this was a good plan," Dao said suddenly, "We are sure to see him and kill him."

"I'm glad you think so."

"Except I don't know how you plan to deal with a sentry, should they send one up here."

"Let's just hope they don't think it's necessary."

He returned a doubtful look. If a man did climb up, they'd have a single option. Kill him. He drew his combat knife, ready to slit his throat the moment his head came into view. It wouldn't fool them for long, but they didn't need long. Just enough time to spot Kiet, give the signal for the shooting to start, and pop a bullet in him. They'd be away, while the VCs charged in the opposite direction. From where they believed the attack had come. As plans went, it might even work.

Dao whispered urgently. "They appear to think it's necessary. A man is heading this way. I believe he may be coming up."

Shit.

He flattened himself on the platform, next to the narrow opening where the guy would appear. He gripped the damp hilt of his knife. Waiting for the moment when a head popped into view, neck exposed, and he'd sliced the blade across the guy's throat. Before he fell he'd reach down and pull the bleeding, dying body onto the platform. The tree trunk shook slightly as he climbed, and Farrell had to force himself to be patient. Not peek over the top and show himself, and he noticed Dao with his gun out. Just in case.

But it wasn't an automatic like they issued to the National Police. This was a Soviet-built Nagant Model 1895, a copy of the Belgian Nagant revolver. Big, and with a reputation for rugged reliability, it was also very heavy. The cop was waiting to back him up, to slam the steel butt onto the guy's head if things went wrong.

The head came into view. First, a soft jungle hat, and the eyes appeared. In the rain and half-darkness, he didn't see them, and he rose in front of them to climb out onto the platform.

Farrell reached over, knocked off the jungle hat, and grabbed the guy by his greasy, lank hair. His grip almost slipped before he slashed down with the knife. One cut wasn't enough, although blood poured from the wound in copious amounts. He slashed again, and again, and it took five cuts before the guy stopped struggling. All the while, he was hissing a mantra beneath his breath.

Die, you bastard! Why won't you just die?

He almost dropped him, which would've ended everything. They wouldn't take too kindly to the body of one of their own crashing to the ground in front of their eyes, but just as the wet blood almost caused his grip to fail, Dao reached down and grabbed him by the collar. Together they hauled him onto the tiny platform. They didn't need to check the body for signs of life. He was as dead as they come, although his heart blood was soaking into the timbers.

Farrell was breathing heavily, and he nodded his thanks to Dao.

"I nearly lost him."

"But you didn't. Paul, Kiet could appear at any moment. As soon as I see him, give the signal, I take the shot, and we get out fast."

You don't say.

They scanned the compound, squinting to make out the movement below in the dim light and the hammering rain. Occasionally, a man would emerge from a primitive hut, walk across to what they assumed was the latrine, and walk back. Still no sign of Kiet. Dawn broke, and they shrank back out of sight as more men appeared. The minutes ticked past, and he had a feeling he'd made the worst call of his life. If Kiet didn't appear in the next few minutes, the entire compound would be awake, men bustling around as they went about their daily chores. The diversion should give them a chance to escape, but there were always unknown factors. And there was Clarence.

There were also the half-dozen men who pushed aside the primitive gate and walked into the jungle. Heading in the direction of the jeep, probably sent out to check they hadn't missed anything. When they made their escape, it could be one problem too many.

He was beginning to think Kiet had slipped away in the night when Dao touched him on the shoulder. "I see him. Emerging from the larger hut in the center of the compound, walking toward the latrine."

He didn't resemble the picture Charles Curtis had shown him back in Saigon. The picture would have been taken several years before when he joined the Land Reform Program. He'd grown older and thinner. If this went the way they'd planned, he wouldn't grow any older. Farrell had a clearer shot than Dao, and he told him he'd handle it. The cop frowned but nodded his agreement. The trick was to put the bastard down. Paul cautioned himself to make the shot good. He'd get one chance at this, and only one.

"Paul," Dao whispered urgently, "Someone else is coming up. It has to be now."

"No sweat. Take care of him while I do this. Although when the shooting starts, I'm guessing he'll get back down."

He lined up his sights on Kiet, deciding to go for the chest, the larger target. A headshot would be more certain, but if he missed, he may not get a second chance. He aligned the iron sights on the Vietnamese traitor and took up first pressure on the trigger. "Dao, drop the branch."

A moment later, "It's done."

In the next few seconds, the plan unraveled. Dorsey and Ashe started shooting, firing short bursts into the compound, and sending the enemy into turmoil. They were running every which way, and he saw the target run, away from the bullets. He squeezed off a shot that went unnoticed in the storm of gunfire hitting the compound. It missed. Kiet climbed through the bamboo fence, and he was getting away. With a muttered curse he shinned down the tree, hit the ground, and clambered through the fence to chase him down. Dao, his big revolver held ready, was close behind.

They chased him into the jungle, and he ran like a hare, but they were closing on him. They heard his footsteps pounding across the jungle floor, and they caught glimpses of his clothing. He darted through narrow gaps in the foliage, squeezing between bushes, vaulting over tangles of vines, and they hurtled after him. Until they were close enough for a shot, and he brought up his rifle ready to fire a short burst. And stopped.

Kiet had run into the arms of the half-dozen Vietcong they'd seen earlier heading out from the compound. Now they were facing seven hostiles, instead of one. He didn't hesitate, flipped the selector to full auto, and cut loose with a long burst. Spraying bullets into the surprised enemy, and three men went down. The rest brought up their rifles to return fire, but Dao was a man on a mission. He kept running toward them, bringing up the big Nagant, and opening fire. The 'boom' of each shot was loud, and he aimed well, taking down two more hostiles. The last man sprinted away, with Kiet trying to keep up.

They went after him, and this time the traitor wasn't so lucky. His foot caught in a vine, tumbling him to the ground. Dao reached him, and he didn't hesitate.

"Vo Kiet, you've been tried, found guilty, and the sentence is death."

The man looked up at him. "No, no, you don't understand. I need…"

He didn't discover what he needed. He let him have two bullets in the chest, and at least one tore into his heart. In seconds the life went out of his eyes. Farrell had left him to handle it, chasing after the surviving Cong, and he found him shivering behind a small stand of trees. Farrell stood over him, looking down at the cowering man. He stared down at the ragged, emaciated man, another victim of Communist propaganda. A man who'd believed the crap about free land, about democracy, about a better deal from a benign Communist government. He almost felt pity. Almost. A second later he killed him.

Dao walked back through the bushes, reloading his revolver. "He's dead."

"We're done. It's time to get back to the jeep and get out of here."

They made it back, often having to crawl on their bellies to avoid vengeful VCs scouring the area, looking for the intruders who'd invaded the compound they'd so carefully and secretly constructed in the middle of the jungle. Frequently, they had to lie flat on the soft, stinking mud until VCs had gone past. Then they'd continue their long, slow crawl until they reached the place they'd left Batista. Except when they reached the spot where they'd left him and the jeep, there was no sign of either.

And no sign of Dorsey or Ashe.

"We'll circle the area. We must be looking in the wrong place."

There was no sign of hostiles, and they were able to get to their feet and start beating the bushes. How hard could it be, looking for an M151 jeep? Then a voice suddenly hissed, "Over here."

It was Ashe, and he jerked his gaze around. He still couldn't see him.

"Where are you?"

"You're looking in the right place. You can't see us."

He saw movement and to his astonishment, he was looking at Ashe's grinning face.

"It was Batista who did this. He camouflaged the jeep by weaving thin branches and fastening them around the bodywork with vines. He's made it invisible. Why don't you come on in?"

Hardly believing what he was seeing, he climbed through the foliage, and he was staring at the MUTT. Clarence was seated in the passenger seat, and Batista the driver's seat.

Ashe grinned. "What do you think? Pablo has a serious talent."

"It's amazing."

"Ain't it just? What about Vo Kiet?"

"He's supping with the devil. Pablo, I forgot to ask, how're the ribs?"

A grimace. "Too fucking painful, but while you guys were out there, I thought I'd do something to take my mind off it. That's why the camouflage. Now you're back, I need a medevac. Can we fix up to get me out of here?"

"The muffler is u/s, so we can't use the jeep. If we walk

out, we could run into the enemy. They're crawling all over this place. We need to wait until the heat dies down. After the attack, they're sure to break camp and move someplace else. It'll take them a few hours, but if we keep our heads down, we should be safe. Say, we still have the radio, so I'll call Curtis, give him an update."

Farrell switched on and pulled on the headphones. It took him several minutes to find a usable frequency, and several minutes more for them to call Curtis to the radio room, but eventually, he heard the familiar voice. That was all he heard. Clarence snatched the headset away from him.

"Yessir, we got him. Don't worry. Xuan Dieu is next. When we get back, we can figure out where to go looking for him, but in the meantime, Batista is hurt. Yeah, cracked ribs. How bad? Painful, but not fatal, he's had worse. "

Batista grumbled it was more than painful. It was agonizing. "Tell him to fix up a medevac."

Clarence ignored him. "The jeep is u/s, so we need transport out of here. The place is crawling with VCs, so if you could send in a Huey with a gunship escort to pick us up, we'd be obliged."

He listened for several seconds more. "How secure are we?" He chuckled, "Batista did a good job of camouflaging the jeep, and it's almost invisible from anything more than a couple of meters. Yeah, stupid bastards don't know we're still here. They don't even know what hit them. If they saw anything, all they saw were civilians, and only from a distance in poor visibility." He chuckled again, "I guess so, it could easily have been a bunch of pissed-off locals with a grudge about something. Christ knows, there're plenty of grudges against the

Vietcong. What was that? You want us to stay?"

He listened for a few minutes more and ended the call. His face was white. "He wants us to stay."

"Until nightfall?" Ashe asked, "Not a good plan, Charlie comes out to play at night."

"He wants us to stay for several days, maybe even a week. He said if we're so well hidden, we're in a good position to observe the enemy without them knowing we're here. We have a radio, we have food and water, and we have weapons and ammunition, so he said to hunker down and call in sitreps every twelve hours."

Batista was wide-eyed. "You're kidding me! If we stay here we're dead."

He shrugged. Clarence may have been a thoroughgoing bastard, a real son of a bitch, but he was no coward. "Maybe, maybe not. He does have a point. We're on the edge of the Iron Triangle, a unique position to feed information about Charlie's movements. It's intelligence there're desperate for, so he jumped at the opportunity."

"Jumped at the opportunity to feed us to the wolves. Clarence, this isn't what we signed up for. We're Phoenix Program, not a recce patrol."

"We're what Charles Curtis says we are. Unless you can find something in the contracts we signed that says different."

Batista spat on the ground, climbed out of the jeep, wincing with the pain of his cracked ribs, and went to poke around outside. Farrell looked at Clarence. "He has a point. The guy's hurt."

"I don't give a shit. I give the orders around here, and if Curtis says we're staying, we're staying."

"How much did he offer you? You wouldn't have agreed so easily if there was nothing in it for you."

He flushed red, although whether with anger or embarrassment it was hard to say.

"Fuck you. I earn my pay, Farrell, so make sure you earn yours, that's all you need to worry about. You may as well know there was something else. Curtis believes Dieu is in the Triangle, and if we see him we may get the chance to put a bullet in him. They'll build a new compound, that's for sure, but it's unlikely to be more than four or five klicks from the one we found. Once we have a location, we can radio Saigon, and they'll arrange to pay them a visit." He grinned, "We're back in business."

"A visit?"

"A B-52 visit. Once they have the exact location, they'll bomb the shit out of it."

"As long as we're out of here when it happens. The bomb aimers aren't always as accurate as people believe."

"Scared?" he sneered.

"Of several tons of bombs falling on my head? Yeah, I'm scared."

He grunted. "We'll be out of here before it happens. When you've had some chow, you can take Ashe and your cop friend back to the compound and keep an eye on them, see what they're up to. They won't waste any time moving their equipment to the new location, and I want to know where that is. We also need to keep an eye out for Dieu."

They helped themselves to MREs stored in the jeep. There was no way they could heat any food, so they ate leathery meal bars washed down with bottled water. When they were done, they camouflaged themselves, using leaves and thin branches fastened outside their clothing, and sticks of greasepaint to hide their exposed skin. Dao was enthusiastic about going with them. He'd seen Vo Kiet go down, but there was something else he wanted, and the truth dawned on Farrell. They were on the edge of the Triangle, and he believed his son could be somewhere close.

Is that his plan, to inflict as much damage as possible on the Communists, and to find his son?

He couldn't blame him. Knowing that if his son stayed with the Vietcong he was a dead man. There was no guarantee he'd agree to desert the Communists, and the question was how much of a true Communist was he? His father would have to confront him to get the answer. Probably after a long period inside the Cu Chi tunnels, most of it spent in hard, manual labor, ridden with frequent bouts of sickness, his belief in the cause would have evaporated.

They set out to return to the compound. As they left, he could have sworn he heard a faint burst of static, like somebody switching on the radio to make another call, and he idly wondered about Clarence's agenda. Then he put it out of his mind, and they crept through the undergrowth, looking every which way for the enemy. Although covered in foliage, they looked like three small trees moving through the jungle. Several times they heard a noise in the distance, and it had to be the enemy. Each time they froze, melting into the bushes so a man would almost have to bump into them to know they were there.

The compound was a hive of activity. Men were running around like ants, taking down buildings, and some removing radio equipment and cooking utensils, tables, and tin plates from inside. Carrying them away, heading south, deeper into the

Triangle. They watched for almost three hours without the enemy seeing them, and they had what they'd come for. Most of them had gone, the compound stripped like locusts had attacked it.

"They're on the move, so we can follow them, see where they're going."

Ashe returned a grim smile. "Yeah, I'd like to see the Air Force send them a few juicy bombs for a Christmas present."

"Ashe, it isn't Christmas. Besides, they're Communists, they don't celebrate Christmas."

"In that case they deserve to get hit. Bastards. As long as they bomb the new compound, it won't do any good hitting this one, it's empty."

They rose from cover and were about to follow the last of the VCs when they heard a droning noise in the distance. It was faint, like aircraft flying high, very high. Farrell made out patches of sky now they'd removed the camouflage. Several clusters of contrails were visible, each consisting of eight plumes that marked the progress of the B-52 bombers.

Ashe followed his gaze. "Some poor bastards are about to get it. I'm glad it's not us."

He nodded. "Me, too. Let's go."

He took one step and paused, looking up again when he heard the whistling and saw dark shapes falling from the underbellies of the heavy bombers. A moment later realization hit him like an arrow in the heart. They were directly overhead, and somebody had fucked up. They were bombing an almost empty compound. Almost empty, but for the three Phoenix operators watching in horror as several tons of high-explosive came closer.

The whistling sound was louder. They were seconds away from oblivion.

Ashe bellowed, "Fuck this!"

Dao mumbled something that sounded like a prayer to the gods of his ancestors.

Farrell shouted, "Run!"

Chapter Seven

Five kilometers away Tran Quang heard the crash of exploding bombs. They'd prepared this base over a network of tunnels, both old and new. Tunnels stocked with ordnance, weapons and ammunition, food, and rudimentary medical supplies for the lucky few. The underground facilities sheltered them from bombs and artillery. They also gave them a hidden base from which to launch operations against American and ARVN troops.

He was a veteran of frequent bombing by accursed American aircraft. His first inclination was to order his people to take cover in the tunnels. His second was to wait. After the bombing of his home in Hanoi, when he'd been trapped for so long in the basement with the body of his dead wife, he hated the prospect of spending any time underground. He suffered from acute claustrophobia and had frequent nightmares of being trapped underground in the darkness. A fact he kept hidden from his men. As the Senior Political Commissar inside the Iron Triangle, appointed by Hanoi, he was careful not to show fear.

His men were like wolves. If they thought he was afraid, they'd denounce him, and he'd find himself suddenly recalled to Hanoi. Accused of cowardice, and handed another assignment. Probably digging the hated tunnels, as a punishment for failing to display the necessary qualities of courage and determination to his men.

His second inclination proved to be correct, for the bombs were falling several kilometers away, somewhere in the area of the base they'd just dismantled. He glanced at Xuan Dieu, the man he'd put in command of the new base.

"The fools, they're bombing empty jungle. Make sure they do not discover this location. Hanoi would not be pleased."

Dieu nodded. "I will keep men on patrol day and night, and make sure the enemy to not get near."

"Good. There's something else, Dieu. Those men who attacked our base and killed Kiet weren't Americans or ARVN. I believe they were CIA mercenaries. You've heard of the Phoenix Program?"

"I've heard of it, but how could you know they carried out the attack?"

"I have my sources, who tell me the target was Vo Kiet."

"You're sure?"

"Yes. Comrade Dieu, I discovered they have a target list, and your name is on it. You cannot go back to running your irrigation project for the Saigon government. They know you are one of us, and the moment you show your face they'll place you under arrest and likely sentence you to death."

He paled. Xuan Dieu had enjoyed the considerable

prestige his work gave him. Skilled work, designing and implementing irrigation schemes. Work that allowed him to travel around, and he'd pass on information about what he'd seen to the Vietcong. He wasn't as committed to Communism as some. He'd studied at the university in Hue, and he enjoyed his work. The prestigious appointment had also given him high status in a country where most people were illiterate peasants.

It had never occurred to him he'd have to give up his job, or his fine salary, which allowed him to keep up a high standard. His fiancée lived in Saigon, and they planned to be married the following year. He'd been saving money for a bungalow in the suburbs, in a safe area away from the war. Waiting for the time when the Communists ruled the country, and people could live in peace and freedom. Although he knew that day would be a long time in the future.

Quang was staring at him intently. "Is there a problem, Comrade Dieu?"

He gulped. Tran Quang was not a man to whom you could confess misgivings about the Cause. Anything less than one hundred percent dedication was grounds for punishment. He pictured himself as a porter, carrying heavy loads along the Ho Chi Minh Trail, and he shuddered. He'd seen men who'd been pressed into service as porters, and they became half-starved skeletons. Flogged when they faltered, and when they were unable to work, sick, and frequently close to death, they left them where they fell.

"No problem, Comrade Quang. Of course, I will remain here and follow your orders." He had a sudden thought, "What other names are on that list?"

He saw the flicker in the other man's eyes, and he knew

everything he needed to know. "You are on it?"

A pause. "Not that it's any of your business, but yes, the CIA regards me as a high-value target. Their Phoenix Program is dangerous."

Dieu nodded. "I will be careful, Comrade."

"You'd better be. Comrade, I want you to go back to the base we evacuated and see if anything valuable is left after the bombing. Take a man with you in case you need to send a message back for more men." He glanced around and saw a laborer struggling to carry a heavy wooden case. He looked ill, barely able to manage the load, "You! What's your name?"

"Le Luc, Commissar."

"You are ill?"

He opened his mouth to reply, and Dieu notice he'd lost all of his teeth. His skin was deeply lined and wrinkled; yet he had to be less than thirty years of age. "I was in the tunnels. A digger."

That explained everything. "Go with Comrade Dieu and obey his orders. Hurry, man."

He put down the case and overbalanced, he was so weak. But he managed to regain his balance, and he joined Dieu. The two men left, following the route back to the previous base. They didn't talk. Luc was too ill to speak and had to use all his energy just to keep walking. Dieu was using his energy to think hard.

Is it true they would arrest me if I return to my work? Perhaps, but perhaps not. My fiancée will be bereft if I never return, and I'd miss working for the government as an engineer. Although I wouldn't miss my work for the Vietcong, that's for sure.

Most men were hungry, sick, and miserable. He didn't

want to be here. He wanted things to be the way they were, and for the first time, he regretted his decision to give his allegiance to the Communists.

* * *

They sprinted through the jungle, pushing their way through thick tangles of vines, ignoring cuts and abrasions, leaping over fallen logs until they reached a stream. Farrell shouted, "Get in the water!"

They plunged into the fetid, stinking stream that was around eighteen inches deep, and they were just in time. Bombs were exploding around them, and many struck the recently vacated base. But not all, and a bomb exploded a mere fifty meters away. The earth shook so much it tossed them clean out of the water, and they splashed back down into the stream as the vibrations subsided. Fires raged everywhere, smoke blanketed the area so it was hard to breathe. Pressed down in the stinking water, he had to put his head up between explosions to suck in breaths, and the air was hot, thick with smoke. Each time he breathed, he choked as he filled his lungs and put his head back under the surface.

The bombing went on forever. When the B-52s finally flew away, they remained in the water, just in case they weren't done and they came back. After a half-hour, they climbed onto the bank, dripping with water, and were shocked by the furious force of the enormous detonations. The jungle had become a wasteland of broken trees, torn up branches, and the bodies of dead animals and birds. There were also a few bodies of the remaining VCs who'd been clearing the last of their equipment.

The compound had disappeared, like the jungle around it.

It was hard to envisage how this place had until recently been alive with VCs going about their daily tasks. With living accommodation, a cookhouse, storage facilities, a primitive perimeter fence. All gone.

Ashe frowned. "I'll say this, when those bomber boys do a job, they make it good."

He frowned. "They've been hitting Hanoi, and so far it hasn't persuaded them to throw in the towel."

"The Commies are stupid."

"Stupid, maybe. But they're also dangerous. Remember, we haven't beaten them yet."

He gave him a look. "You think they could win?"

"Ask me in five years. Right now, I'd say the jury's out."

Outside the blast area, Dao found the trail, easy to follow after hundreds of feet had flattened the foliage. Within days the fast-growing undergrowth in South Vietnam would have hidden everything, but mere hours had elapsed, and following the beaten path presented no difficulties. They were confident they wouldn't encounter any hostiles after the massive bombing when Farrell heard something.

He stopped and signaled for them to drop out of sight. They melted into the bushes and waited while two men walked past in silence. The one in the lead looked familiar, and Farrell had a feeling he'd seen his face before. Like a photo attached to the target list. He didn't recognize the man behind. He was gaunt, his legs bent at both knees as if he'd suffered from rickets, the disease that affected the bones. They waited until they'd disappeared, and when they got up to resume walking, Dao was ashen.

He looked at Farrell. "It's Luc. My son."

"You're sure?"

"Why would I not recognize my son? It's him. The other man is Xuan Dieu."

"Dieu, our next target?"

"Yes, it is him. I must follow them and rescue my son."

It was a bad idea. "Dao, that's not gonna happen, not right now. First, we have to locate the new base they'll have started constructing. Then we go back, and Clarence will call in the location. Then, we can look for your son, and we'll take care of Dieu at the same time."

They argued, and the cop became upset, but eventually, he saw sense. Especially when Farrell pointed out unloading more bombs on the new base would send a world of pain to the Vietcong, payback for what they'd done to his son. He relented. They walked on through the silent jungle. No birds sang in the trees, no insects buzzed and chirruped in the bushes, no small animals trotted unseen in the thick foliage. There was nothing. Silence.

It was like walking through a graveyard. The area was a graveyard, where every living thing had been pulverized out of existence by the enormous weight of bombs that fell from the sky. Dao was lost in thought, shocked at suddenly seeing his son and shocked by his appalling appearance. The poor guy had watched a living corpse walk past him, barely recognizable. It no surprise all he'd wanted was to rush to help him. Instead, he had let his suffering continue.

At least they had a line on Xuan Dieu. Farrell was confident they'd get him, and soon. They stopped when they reached a clearing they'd hacked out of the jungle. Laborers were working like beavers, cutting trees, and removing the stumps and loose branches. Others were already rigging the camouflage nets overhead, to make the project invisible from the sky. It was remarkable, a testament to the legions of slaves they'd coerced into working for them. There was little doubt by the following day they'd be back in business, unless the B-52s had the location and paid them a repeat visit.

He took a compass bearing, circled to take a second bearing, and rejoined Ashe. "We've seen enough. Now we need to get back so Clarence can call this in. The bombers will wipe this place off the face of the earth."

"No."

They both looked at Dao. "What's the problem?"

"My son. He is sure to return here soon, and he cannot survive a bombing such as we saw earlier."

He was right. Farrell had grown to like the old cop from Ben Cat. He deserved better than helping to bomb the place where he'd just found his son.

We have to do something, but the situation's complicated. The bombing has to go ahead, no question. We can't leave such a juicy target untouched, can't allow the Viets to use the place to help them kill friendly soldiers. There's a solution, and that's to get Luc out. And put a bullet in Dieu at the same time. Simple. All we have to do is retrace our steps and we'll find them.

Ashe could read what he was thinking, and he nodded. "Let's do it, get him out."

They started back, following the path to reach the area devastated by the bombs. The destroyed compound was empty. The jungle silent, refusing to give up its secrets, and it was like they'd dematerialized into the devastated land. A place created by high-explosives, a place of broken bodies, broken trees, and broken branches. But no Luc and no Dieu.

He looked at Dao. "I don't know where they are, but we have to get back and call in the location of the new base. When we're done, we'll look for them. My friend, we'll find him."

He didn't look convinced, but he didn't have much choice. They started back to find the jeep. Once again they almost missed it, until he saw movement, a head poking out beneath a wide leaf, and he recognized Clarence. They'd found them.

Batista was sitting in the driver's seat. Clarence confronted them, looking uncomfortable. "What happened? I thought you got caught up in the bombing. I was worried."

Sure you were.

"They hit the wrong target. I guess they didn't know the VCs had just vacated the compound. Clarence, why did they attack now? They almost got us killed."

He looked away. "I don't know why they went in early. You were lucky to survive."

"Ain't that a fact?"

He gave him the coordinates of the compound under construction, and he called it in. While he was on the radio, Farrell debated telling him about Luc. Clarence wasn't the kind of guy to look favorably on any Vietnamese, North or South. On the other hand, Dao had become an invaluable part of the squad. That had to count for something. In the end, he decided for all his oddball behavior, he'd do the right thing.

He took it well and even patted Dao on the arm. "We'll do everything possible to keep your son safe."

Farrell wasn't so sure. "Clarence, we need to agree on a timescale. At least a couple of days to do the job we came here to do and kill Dieu. After that, they can bomb the crap out of the place."

He nodded. "Don't worry. I'll call them again and stipulate we need more time before they go in. How about that?"

"Okay."

Clarence fired up the radio again, and he listened to one side of the conversation. He heard nothing untoward.

When the bombs started to fall, I wondered if Clarence had double-crossed us. But why would he deliberately kill his squad? Only a psycho would do that.

They unpackaged more MREs and tried to enjoy yet another unappetizing meal. He ached for decent hot food; an ache he knew would go unsatisfied for a good long time. They were exhausted, as much from the shock of the bombing as lack of sleep, and they lay on the waterproof and bugproof ponchos they'd taken from the jeep to rest. He tried to get some sleep. Within minutes he was dreaming. Dreaming he was in a faraway place, a better place. Not a place like this, little better than his cold cell at Leavenworth.

During his sleep, he dreamed about his brother, murdered in South Vietnam. He also thought about his downfall after killing a guy who turned out to be a cop's son with connections inside the Saigon government. This Southeast Asian hell was at the back of all of it, and he was unaware he tossed and turned, his mind in a furious turmoil. Part of that turmoil was remembering the familiar yearning, the desperate need for cocaine to help him forget the demons. When he opened his eyes, he suddenly realized Clarence was staring at him with a gaze so malevolent it felt like he wanted to kill him.

Why? Okay, I took his injured brother's place in the squad, but it's too extreme to think he wants me dead just for that. Only a total nutjob would want that. CIA wouldn't employ such a man, would they?

He ignored him, got to his feet, and went to find something to eat. The MREs were running low, and as he helped himself from the dwindling stocks, Clarence wandered over. The malevolence had vanished, and he looked almost normal.

"I talked to Curtis while you were asleep. He insists we stay for the time being. We're in a perfect place to strike at the enemy, deep inside the territory they control. Or believe they control. We've heard men walking through in the north and heading toward that new base. Probably they're intending to launch a new offensive real soon. Another Tet, an all-out push to drive to Saigon."

He munched on a high-protein bar that tasted like pressed sawdust.

Who the hell invented these things? And did they ever sample them before they unleashed them on an unsuspecting military?

After a sip of water, he looked at Clarence. "They could easily stumble on this place by accident. What exactly does he want us to do while we stick our necks out?"

"He said he wants us to do the job they pay us for. Take out South Vietnamese traitors and target the guys in charge. Communist bigshots. Give it a few days, then we pull out."

Farrell held up the remains of the meal bar, the bit he couldn't finish. "We're almost out of food."

"Charlie has food. We'll take it off him."

"Charlie's food stinks."

"It's better than going hungry."

"That's debatable, Clarence."

He outlined more of the plan. They'd stake out the beaten

paths and take down likely targets as they arrived, either alone or in small groups.

He wasn't impressed. "How many of these bigshots walk through the jungle alone? They're not that stupid."

A shrug. "There'll be enough for us to cut a few notches into our gun butts."

"Hasn't it occurred to you the moment we start shooting, they'll know we're here, and they'll beat the bushes until they find us?"

He grinned. "That's why I stashed two of these in the jeep." He produced a strange-looking pistol that looked like the kind of toy a kid would use for plinking at targets in the backyard, "It's called a High Standard HDM. OSS developed them during World War II. It's a .22 caliber and almost silent. They won't hear any shooting. And we can chalk up a big body count to keep Charles Curtis happy."

"What about Dieu?"

A shrug. "We'll get him. He can't stay inside that compound forever. When he comes out, his ass is ours. If he doesn't come out, he'll be inside when the bombs hit."

It sounded like a plan until Dao brought up a major flaw. "My son is in the compound."

"Yeah, well, if we can we'll try to get him out before all hell breaks loose."

The cop wore a strange expression, and it wasn't hard to work out what was going on inside his head. He was going after Luc, and there wasn't a damn thing they could do to stop him slipping away during the night and go after him. If he got caught, they could torture him and make him give them up. In which case they could expect a visit from their friendly local Vietcong.

Besides, all it took was one failed ambush, and they'd be onto them like a pack of bloodhounds.

Clarence shrugged. "We start tomorrow." He looked at Farrell. "After dark I want you to scout between here and the base, pinpoint the best ambush sites."

"I will go with him," Dao said quietly.

"Suit yourself." He chuckled, "You're a cop. Maybe you can make some arrests." Dao didn't reply, "Maybe not, but you can make yourself useful and carry any food you happen to come across. Vietnamese make the best porters. You guys were born to fetch and carry."

Nobody smiled. Farrell began to check out his gear for the coming night, and when he was done, he settled down to catch up on some Zs. He didn't think he'd sleep, despite his exhaustion. The desperate urge had resurfaced, here of all places. He tried to doze, but his agonized brain told him to get a fix at any price.

Eventually, he gave up. His body was wound up like a bowstring, and he attempted to loosen up with simple calisthenics. Dorsey and Batista watched him with amused smiles, and he suspected they knew exactly what he was going through. A moment later, they confirmed his suspicion.

Batista lit a joint, and the fragrant odor of Mary Jane wafted around their tiny encampment. He wanted to warn them if the enemy were close they could smell it, but he didn't warn them. He wanted a toke. Needed it. It wasn't coke, but it was a drug to numb the mind, to take away the pain. He was desperate, yet he fought the urge. Knowing a single drag on that joint would bring it all back.

"You want to join us?"

Batista was holding out the joint, inviting him to partake. He didn't reply at first and almost rushed over, grabbed it out of his hand, and sucked in the soothing sweetness of the cannabis. He'd taken a single step before he realized what he was doing. It was almost like a magnetic force dragging him toward that inviting substance that would solve all of his problems at a stroke. He resisted the urge, grabbing hold of the jeep to use it as an anchor against the voice that was calling for him. Like a science fiction tractor beam, and almost as irresistible.

"No." The moment that word came out of his mouth he knew it wasn't convincing. They'd sensed his need, like predators sniffing out their next prey.

"It'll help you relax," Clarence chuckled.

"I don't think so. I'm going out there to take a look around."

"Are you sure? It's still light out there."

"I'll stay in the shadows."

Ashe got to his feet to go with him, but he shook his head. "I can manage."

He left their improvised camp, and he wasn't going for a look around. He knew where he was going, toward the new Vietcong base. Before he made it halfway he heard voices close by. The enemy, and he should've let them pass. He was carrying his rifle, but a single shot from an AR-15 would bring the enemy down on his head, like the Four Horsemen of the Apocalypse. He ducked down into thick foliage, making himself invisible, and waited for them to come.

Like Clarence had said, they were coming in from the north, and to his astonishment, an officer of the People's Army of Vietnam stepped into view. A full Colonel, identified by two stripes and three stars on his yellow shoulder boards. Three men walked ahead of him, all People's Army, enlisted men, they'd be his escort. The Colonel was an older man, maybe in his late forties, walking slower than the soldiers, and he'd fallen back.

Farrell regretted not bringing the silenced pistol. He could've taken him almost without making a sound and slipped away before they knew what'd happened. Too bad, he didn't have the HDM. But he did have something even more silent. He slid out his combat knife, a Ka-Bar. Adopted by the United States Marine Corps in early World War II, the knife was as effective for silent killing now as it had been back then.

He knew he shouldn't do it. Knew the Colonel only need manage to shout a warning if he fluffed the approach, and the three soldiers would be on him like dogs on a bone. Yet he needed to do it. His body was still in turmoil, wracked by the desperate need for the drug, for any drug, and he craved action almost as much as a chemical high. Anything to take his mind off that terrible urge. This guy was going down.

He laid his rifle on the ground and waited at the edge of the bushes while the three enlisted men pushed ahead. Twenty meters back along the path the Colonel followed, his face flushed and sweating from the intense humidity. He gripped his knife, ungripped it, wiped his hand on his pants to dry the sweat, and took a firm hold of the hilt. He balanced on the balls of his feet, kneeling like a sprinter on his starting blocks, waiting for the moment, and when it came he jumped.

His left hand reached out to clamp over the man's mouth, and he brought the knife around to stab into his chest. The officer jerked in surprise, tried to move away, but he had a hard grip over the mouth, holding on in desperation. Desperation, because the point of the blade had struck something hard in the man's tunic pocket, probably a cigarette case. Whatever it'd struck, it wasn't going any further, and he jerked it back to stab again. Fighting to hold the struggling man, who fought back desperately, doing his best to wrench the hand from his mouth.

His hand was slipping off the guy's sweaty skin. He couldn't hold on much longer, and he made a final, last-ditch attempt to finish him. Stabbed up with the knife, aiming the point of the blade into the one area that presented a target. Beneath his chin, and he pushed up hard into the soft flesh. It went in, and he squirmed even more. Fought like a crazy man, but he was weakening, his blood spurting from his ruined throat. Farrell pushed up harder until the squirming stopped. A last breath hissed out from his ruined throat, as a gush of blood poured from the gaping wound. Like a tap had been opened.

He didn't have any time to waste, and he started to drag the guy into the bushes. If they knew what'd happened, they'd hunt him down, bring in more men, and they wouldn't give up until they'd found him. A search could uncover the jeep, which would mean death for Clarence, Ashe, Dao, and Batista. He pulled the body into thick foliage and covered it with leaves and fallen branches. It was the best he could do in a hurry, and he rushed back out to the path to cover the blood that had soaked into the ground.

When he reached the spot where he'd stabbed him, he thought he must've made a mistake. There was no sign of the place where a man had been killed, and he looked left and right to work out how he'd missed it.

Dao suddenly appeared. "I covered the evidence."

He was grateful, but he shouldn't have been there. "I said

166

I'd be okay."

"Nonetheless, I am here if you need help."

"We need to get off the path. They'll be back when the Colonel fails to show."

They threaded their way through the bushes, making sure not to leave any tracks the Viets could follow. Until they got to the spot where he'd hidden the body, and Dao nodded approvingly. "With luck, they won't find it for a long time. Perhaps never."

"That's the idea. Dao, I know why you've come, but we can't go near the compound. He'll have to take his chances."

His eyes misted over. "He is my son, my only son. I can't leave him in this place."

He sighed. "Dao, I'll do my best for you. If we can get him out, we will, but not if it costs us our lives. Why don't you head back to the jeep, pick up one of those HDM pistols, and come back after dark? Maybe find Luc and get him out."

"You are not coming back with me?"

"I need to be on my own."

The old cop's eyes regarded him for several seconds. "Is it heroin?"

He shouldn't have been surprised. A veteran cop would've seen the signs a hundred times. "Something like that."

"I noticed you battling with some inner demon, something that was eating you up inside. It's usually drugs."

For some strange reason, he liked Dao, and he decided to level with him. He told him about Mark, and how he'd taken the drugs to ease the pain. How while he was out of his head he'd gunned down a Viet responsible for carrying out civilian atrocities in a peasant village. Atrocities like the one that caused the death of his brother. How after the guy's father, a senior police officer, complained, they gave him a prison sentence. He described his time in Leavenworth, and how Charles Curtis had offered him a job with Phoenix. "That's it, the whole story and this is where I ended up. Back in Vietnam."

"You're still fighting the addiction."

He didn't answer. He didn't need to. It was that obvious. A moment later they ducked low. The three enlisted men were beating the bushes, looking for their Colonel. Their voices were excited but tinged with panic. Which was no surprise. They'd been detailed to escort a senior officer, and they'd lost him. Their bosses wouldn't be impressed. The punishment would be severe, probably final.

The soldiers were getting closer. Farrell had his rifle ready to start shooting if they came across them, and Dao had his ancient Nagant pistol cocked and ready. They could deal with them, no question. But the moment they squeezed the triggers, all hell would break loose. The search drifted away, and they thought they were safe, as the Viets fanned out in the direction of the jeep. It was unlikely they'd find it, and all Farrell and Dao had to do was wait.

It wasn't going to be enough. They started to come back, deeper in the bushes of the jungle, and if they stayed on the same route, they'd walked right into them.

Dao murmured, "A few minutes and they'll be on top of us."

He was right, and yet there was no obvious solution. Farrell was inclined to think they'd have no choice but to start shooting when they stumbled on their hiding place. Dao wore a fixed, grim expression. They could take down the three soldiers, but they'd have no choice but to run to avoid the men pouring out from the compound to chase down and kill the intruders. They would die, which would end any chance of rescue for Le Luc.

He kept his voice to a low murmur. "We have to take them. We don't have a choice. As soon as they go down, we make a run for it, back to the jeep. We'll have to evacuate, so that's the end for Luc, I'm sorry."

It's my fault. If I hadn't killed the Colonel, the soldiers wouldn't be beating the bushes.

Dao looked more miserable than ever, and he knew he was saying goodbye to his son. Luc's last chance was vanishing, and there was nothing he could do about it.

He took a glance in the opposite direction, to make sure there weren't more soldiers coming in from the compound, and the jungle was quiet, empty. He looked back to gauge the amount of time they had left and looked back in the direction of the compound. His brain was working through the permutations.

What is it, two klicks? What if we run into more North Vietnamese soldiers or Vietcong? What if we don't run into them? What if we stay here and kill those men? Yet they're looking for a live senior officer, not a corpse.

"Dao, we may be able to miss them, but we'd have to head toward the new compound. If we go now, I reckon we can avoid them."

"But…"

"Let's go."

He snaked on his belly out of the tangle of foliage, keeping pressed to the ground, careful to make no sound, to break no dried twigs, or disturb a small animal or bird. He didn't hear

Dao, but when he risked a quick look around, he was two meters back. Silently working his way through the tangle of vines and creepers, and ten meters back, the nearest soldier.

For a second he had a clear line of sight to Farrell and Dao, and if he looked up and peered through the gloom, he'd have to see them. He didn't look up. Instead, he was looking down, searching for the officer. He moved off at a ninety-degree angle, looking away, and they continued crawling along the ground. After an hour of crawling through the tangles of creepers and vines, brushing against centipedes and other insects, he called a halt. The new compound was right in front of them.

He was about to stand for a better look when he heard boots pounding behind him, one of the soldiers racing back to the compound. Probably this man had decided to admit the truth, that they'd lost the officer, and call for help. The man disappeared out of sight, and they waited a while longer. A mistake. More troops and VCs rushed out from the compound to beat the bushes. And they were heading toward them to start the sweep.

He'd made the worst possible call, and he looked at Dao. "I'm sorry. We're fucked."

Chapter Eight

They weren't fucked. An officer, maybe a commissar, shouted orders, and the men formed into squads, jogging back along the trail to search in the last place he'd been seen. They'd have a chance if they could get back to the jeep. They started working their way back, and several times had to hide deep inside thorny, almost impenetrable bushes. Feeling all kinds of bugs and insects crawling over them, unable to move as VCs prodded and probed inside the foliage.

As they got closer, they smeared mud over their faces to cover their skin, but it wasn't enough. A face pulled aside a branch and peered in at their hiding place. He didn't see them, not at first. Squinting to look through the gloom, he had to see them, sing out a shout of recognition, and they'd descend on them in a savage horde filled with murderous fury.

He gripped his knife, changed his mind, dropped it, reached up, and gripped the guy's collar. Pulled hard, dragging him off balance into the bush, and clamped a hand over his mouth.

"Dao, finish him!" he hissed.

The guy was fighting back hard to free himself when Dao attempted to club him with the big Nagant revolver. It would have been enough, but the guy was thrashing around so much he missed the blow. The Viet scrabbled to lever away the hand clamped over his mouth, and Farrell fought back to stop him. He struck out, a fist slammed into his face, he hit him again, and he had to take the lumps. At last, he managed to jab a knee into his belly, which caused him to jerk in surprise. The violent movement stopped.

Farrell kept the one hand clamped over the mouth, let go of the hand still holding his collar, and smashed a punch into his nose. He heard the crunch of breaking bone, and the guy groaned through the hand covering his mouth. He brought up the hands attempting to protect his stomach, trying again to wrench away the hand over his mouth. Farrell slammed the knee into his belly again. And again. He groaned even more, but the sound was still too low to carry outside the bushes.

Dao tried again to use his Nagant as a club and caught him a glancing blow on the side of his head. The guy was weakening fast, but not fast enough. He used the last of his waning strength to attempt to break free, and shoved Farrell off him. The Viet was still fighting like hell, and he had to finish this fast before his hand slipped, and he bellowed a warning. He rolled to one side, and he was lying on something hard, the combat knife he'd dropped. He put a hand underneath him, gripped the hilt, and pulled it out and over the Viet's upper body, ready to stab down.

He was aiming to bring it under his chin to slice through

the throat, but the guy saw it at the last moment and made a huge effort to protect his throat and duck away. The blade missed the throat, but by ducking all he'd done was expose the upper part of his head, and the point stabbed into his left eye. But not deep enough, and he writhed even more. In desperation, Farrell pulled the knife back out and stabbed in again, but this time with every ounce of his strength, and it went in deep. A torrent of blood and mucus, mixed in with brain matter poured out from the terrible wound. The Viet gasped a final time, his body jerked, and he lay dead.

Dao was watching, the gun held ready to hit him again, but when he saw it was unnecessary, he looked out through the bushes to check for any Viets taking an interest.

"We're clear. Nobody heard anything."

"They'll miss him."

"I don't think so. Desertions are a big problem for the Vietcong, and men go absent all the time. I doubt they'll miss him. Not senior officers, but there's a good chance they won't find him. The jungle hides the Vietcong, but it also hides dead bodies. I doubt they'll ever find them."

He nodded, still breathing heavily after such a close call. The search had widened, and they didn't seem to have missed the dead man. They crawled along the jungle floor, keeping their heads low, making for the jeep.

When they got back, Clarence gave them a cold stare. "We heard the fuss, what happened?"

"Nothing we couldn't handle." He told him about the officer, and about the man they'd killed.

Clarence shrugged. "You can cut a couple more notches on your rifle. I have to call in, and I'll tell Curtis we're building a good body count."

He grabbed an MRE and a bottle of water and stretched out on the ground on a poncho to protect him from the insects. Clarence radioed in and engaged in a murmured conversation with Curtis, but he didn't hear any of it. The reaction from what they'd done had left him exhausted, and he fell asleep immediately.

When he awoke, something had changed. Batista had taken out a sharpening stone and was honing the blade of his knife. Not a conventional combat knife, but a long, thin stiletto with an ornately decorated blade. Clarence and Ashe had stripped both High Standard HDM suppressed pistols, laying out the components on the hood of the jeep as they cleaned and checked each one. He watched them remove the bullets from the ten-round magazines and re-insert them. Something was up.

He stretched and got to his feet. Ashe looked around. "Did you enjoy your rest?"

It was light already. "How long did I sleep?"

"About five hours."

He wasn't surprised, and he felt better. "What gives with the guns? Who're you going to kill?"

Clarence glanced over and grinned. "Anybody and everybody, pal. I talked to Curtis, explained our situation, and told him what we'd done. He was so impressed he told us to hang in here for a few days, until they send in the bombers to take out that new compound. In the meantime, he wants us to earn our pay. We're gonna sneak out each day and pick off targets of opportunity."

"We're staying?"

"Right. We'll split into teams of two. Two men stay here

while the other two go looking for Mr. Charles and do some killing. Curtis says it's time we produced results. Like that senior officer you killed, that went down well when I told him. Farrell, make no mistake, we're an assassination squad. Which means we assassinate the enemy."

He wasn't impressed. The idea had good points and bad points, but they'd come here to cross names off the kill list, and one of those names was Xuan Dieu. He was inside that compound, and the more men they found and killed, the more likely they'd latch onto what was going on. Dieu would run before the bombers struck.

He ran it past Clarence, but he wasn't interested. "Quite frankly, I couldn't give a shit who we kill, as long as we kill Viets." Dao shifted uncomfortably, but he didn't seem to notice, "Maybe we'll get lucky and get Dieu, or maybe another squad will nail his ass to a barn door. Maybe the bombers. What the hell difference does it make?"

It made all the difference, but he knew it was useless to argue. Dieu was a facilitator of death, and if he went down, there'd be fewer killings. Especially if his death demoralized a few men to desert. There was only one solution, locate him over the next few days, and put him in the ground. In the meantime, he had to go along with the new order from Curtis and from Saigon.

They started work that day, and at first it went well, so well he wondered if he'd been wrong. Their hideout in the middle of the jungle the enemy believed they controlled was undiscovered. When he set out for the first combat patrol with Ashe and Dao, they hacked into a Vietcong squad like bolts of lightning.

Four men were approaching from the north, each wearing

the uniform of the People's Army, including the iconic pith helmets. Three were enlisted men, the other a lieutenant. Their AKs were slung nonchalantly over their shoulders like they didn't have a care in the world, and they were chatting and laughing with each other. Why wouldn't they? This was friendly territory, their territory, controlled by the Vietcong. There shouldn't have been any enemies closer than twenty klicks.

Apart from the enemies above, and some cast nervous glances up through the tree canopy as Hueys clattered overhead, conveying troops to and from some distant location. They paused, waiting, but the helicopters went past, and they chuckled to each other in relief. A man took out a pack of cigarettes and passed them around, and they lit up. They were standing bunched together on the narrow path that led to the new compound, in no hurry to arrive and start work.

Which was fine by the three men waiting in ambush a few meters away. They needed them to resume walking and get closer. Farrell was behind a fallen tree, clutching the HDM, with Dao alongside him. Ashe was hidden inside a clump of bushes, the second HDM in his hand. He'd persuaded Dao to keep his Nagant holstered. The hand cannon would make so much noise they'd hear it as far as the DMZ, and he agreed to use his knife.

He murmured, "Don't move until I take the first shot."

"Do not fear. I will not."

They started walking again, getting closer. He waited until the leading man was three meters away to squeeze the trigger, and the HDM thumped out a single shot. The man went down with a bullet through his heart. A split second later Ashe fired, and the man bringing up the rear followed the first victim to hell. The two in the center looked around in confusion. There'd been no noise, and at first, they didn't seem alarmed. These jungles were infested with deadly snakes and insects, and death was the constant companion of every man who ventured through this dark, dank region.

Farrell fired again, another man went down, and Ashe put a bullet into the last soldier, a lieutenant. The bullet struck him close to the center of the chest, and it should've taken him in the heart. He should have been dead, but he'd moved at the last moment, and the bullet missed his heart, leaving him alive. He had no doubts about what had happened. Snakes and poisonous insects didn't carry guns. He unslung his rifle and searched the jungle gloom, looking for the source of the bullets. For something to shoot back at.

His back was to Dao, and the Vietnamese darted out, blade in hand and death in his heart. Farrell recalled the hatred this man had for the Communists, for what they'd done to his son and his country. He wanted vengeance. The lieutenant started to turn, and Dao launched himself, knife arm outstretched, the other reaching for the throat. But the officer twisted at the last moment, and Dao sailed past him, slumping on the ground.

He brought his rifle around to take the shot, and Farrell snapped off a further bullet with the HDM. It didn't fire. The weapon had a reputation for unreliability, and it lived up to that reputation. Ashe didn't have a clear field of fire, and it was down to him. The Vietnamese cop was about to die, and the sound of the shot would bring all kinds of shit down on their heads. He leaped forward; instinctively reaching for the Colt he still carried in the shoulder holster, forgetting for a moment he couldn't use it.

The hostile heard him and swung around. Saw the round-eye coming at him and jerked the muzzle of the rifle away from Dao toward Farrell. They were within microseconds of everything coming to an end until Dao managed to grab the guy's ankles and pulled him over. With a cry he fell, losing his grip on the AK-47. It was the opening Farrell needed.

He jumped on him, and while he scrabbled to recover his rifle, he slammed the Colt over his head. He turned to fight him off, and he hit him again, and again. Yet the guy was strong, and the blows had little effect. He hammered a fist back at Farrell, who rocked with the force of the punch, but he slammed back a harder blow with the Colt. The Viet officer carried a pistol in a holster on his belt. A pistol he was reaching for.

Ashe ran toward them, trying to get in a shot with the HDM. Dao had got to his feet, knife in hand, and was also looking for an opening to use it. He had to give them that opening, and he absorbed the next punch that almost took his head off, allowing him to roll with the guy on top of him. The Viet's lips widened in a sneer until he understood the roll had been deliberate, and he was exposed to the two men he hadn't realized were close.

Ashe's pistol spat out a bullet, and Dao's knife went where he aimed it, into the officer's kidneys. As he opened his mouth to scream in agony, Dao put his hand behind the man's neck and held it, wiping the blade across. Warm blood gushed out over Farrell, and the weight of the PAVN officer became limp and heavy. He got to his feet and nodded his thanks. "That was close."

Ashe frowned. "It could've gone bad. I'd get that pistol looked at. You don't want that to happen too often, not around here."

"Amen to that."

They dragged the bodies away, hid them in deep jungle, and retraced their steps to the jeep. Batista grinned at the state of him, covered in drying blood, but Clarence ignored it. He was interested in one thing. "What's the body count?"

He wrote in his small notebook and stuffed it back into the pocket of his shirt. None of them had any illusions he was multiplying the body count by a large factor, probably ten. None gave a damn. The mission was becoming increasingly dangerous with each day that went by, and they had several close calls. Yet by the third day, they were still undiscovered. Ashe and Farrell set out with Dao on yet another sweep to look for new targets.

They found targets. They also found Le Luc. He sensed rather than saw Dao stiffen, and he dropped to the ground. "What is it?"

"It's my son, it's him."

Three men were coming toward them, heading in the direction of the wrecked compound. Presumably checking for something they'd left behind, or maybe they were suspicious about the number of men failing to arrive from the North. They stopped on the path, staring down at something. At first, looked like they'd seen something suspicious. Something they'd missed, like blood on the ground or a piece of dropped equipment. It wasn't.

The two VCs said something to Luc, and he nodded a dull acknowledgment. Farrell was appalled. He resembled a collection of bones covered in skin, and he coughed constantly like he was sick. He carried a shovel, and he buried it in the earth where they pointed. He dug for almost an hour while the two men watched and smoked. When he was done, they shoved him to one side and sent him sprawling. One man unstrapped his pack and removed a bundle of wooden stakes.

He looked at Ashe. "The motherfuckers, it's a punji trap. Poison stakes. They must suspect something, and they're setting a trap. They probably think the locals are responsible. Not soldiers, because there'd be shooting, and they'd have a backup. Like Hueys and fighter-bombers."

"This is my chance," Dao breathed, "Let me have a silenced pistol. I'll take them both and free my son."

He shook his head. There was no way to get close enough to be sure to make the shots count. "Dao, it's not gonna happen, not today. If anything goes wrong, they'll start shooting, and they'll be all over us like wild dogs."

"I must get him away from those men." His jaw was set in dogged determination; "I will not leave him here. If necessary, I will use my knife."

He swapped glances with Ashe, and there was no way they could persuade him to give it a miss. He didn't blame him. It was his son, and he'd feel the same way.

"Okay, we'll do this together. Dao, I want you to show yourself, draw them in close. You're a Viet, so they won't notice anything strange when they see you. You can tell them you were out foraging for food."

"Very well."

He stepped out into the open, and they flung themselves down ready to take the shot. Farrell had the barrel of the HDM resting in the notch of a tree branch. Ashe lay prone, his pistol in the crook of his arm. Dao strolled toward the VCs, and at first, they didn't see him. They were busy pushing the punji stakes into the earth, and Luc still lay sprawled on the ground, probably grateful for the rest.

The soldiers finished pushing the stakes into the hole and began covering it with thin branches and plant debris. They got to their feet and jerked suddenly as they realized a stranger had appeared on the path. A Vietnamese civilian, and after a brief hesitation, they called out a challenge. He replied in a nervous, hesitant tone, and both men relaxed.

They hadn't noticed the Nagant and assumed he was unarmed. They barked an order, but Dao kept walking toward them, hands outstretched, palms up. 'I come in peace.'

They looked at each other and chuckled. They were going to have some fun with this ignorant peasant, and maybe he had something worth stealing. They walked toward him, and with no obvious threat, their rifles were slung on their shoulders.

Too bad, whatever they planned, it isn't going to happen.

Two silenced pistols spat almost in the same instant. Two Communists bit the dust, and they lay on their backs, blood pouring from their ruined chests. No mistakes this time, no near misses, and no jammed weapons. Two single shots into the heart of each man.

They helped Luc to his feet, and for several seconds he was too weak and dazed to understand what was going on. Until he noticed Dao, and his expression broadened into astonishment. The two men met, holding each other, gabbling in Vietnamese. Farrell stood back, astonished by how much worse the young man looked close-up. Like they'd just released him from a German concentration camp at the end of World War II. His clothing was ragged, and the bones of his face made him appear skull-like.

They gave it a few minutes, and he interrupted their greetings. "We need to hide those two bodies deep in the jungle and get back to the jeep. My guess is those men are gonna be missed."

They dragged them into the bush, and like they'd done with the others, dug shallow graves. Before they buried them, Farrell searched both men, looking for documents or anything useful. He found more than he expected. A clear plastic baggie, and he didn't need to know what was inside, cocaine. Something inside flared, the old, desperate need. He should've tossed it away, emptied the baggie onto the ground, but he didn't. Some instinct made him tuck it into his pocket. He couldn't explain the reason, but since when had the desperate, crying need of an addict needed an explanation? It came from deep inside, a substance that had taken away his free will and almost turned him into a slave.

I won't snort it. So why did I take it? Maybe because I need to challenge myself, to prove that I don't need the stuff. That has to be it.

They covered up the bodies and made their way back to the jeep. Clarence wasn't impressed when he saw Luc. "Who is this guy?"

"Dao's son." He explained about the punji trap they were digging, and how they'd killed the two men with the HDMs.

"You stupid sonofabitch!" he snarled at Farrell, "They're not gonna believe those guys vaporized into thin air. They'll come looking, and they're already suspicious. We…" He paused. In the distance, they heard a loud whistle, the kind they use for sport, or to control large bodies of men, "Shit, that's done it. They know we're here. They must've found the bodies, and now they're out looking for the men who killed them. Do you know what that means? They're looking for us. You dumb motherfucker, you should've left it alone."

"Clarence, look at the guy. How could we leave him? The poor bastard doesn't have long to live. They're starving him, treating him like a slave."

A shrug. "Not my problem, pal."

"You're all heart, Clarence."

"Fuck you. Batista, keep an eye out for what's going on out there. If they get close, we'll have to make a run for it."

He fired up the radio and called Saigon. They connected him with Curtis, and he explained what'd happened. "No, we didn't get Dieu, and that's down to Farrell. You need to bring forward the bombing raid, plaster the place with high-explosive. Finish it with napalm, and a dose of Agent Orange for dessert. Put this place beyond use." A pause while he listened, "Sure, sure, I know Dieu is important. Get those bombers in the air. We're getting out. Yeah, yeah, I'll radio in when we're ready for exfil."

He slammed the handset down. "Farrell, Ashe, get ready to leave. We'll be traveling fast and light, so just enough ammunition, food, and water for the rest of the day."

Luc was trying to say something. Dao listened to him and gestured for their attention. "You must hear him out. He has something important to say."

"Not now, we're busy!" Clarence snarled.

He started to stuff spare magazines into the pockets of his jacket when Batista reappeared. "We don't have long. They're spread out in a long skirmish line, beating the bushes. They have to find this place."

He nodded. "Get your gear. We're leaving."

Pablo looked dubious. "Clarence, we're gonna have to break the Olympic record if we're gonna make it. They'll see us when we leave, close in, and cut us off."

He cursed. "Forget the packs. If we don't move now, they'll blast our asses. All of you, out of here!"

Batista grunted. "It's a no go, Clarence. They're too close. We're screwed."

"Fuck! What the hell are we gonna do?"

"We take the jeep."

He glared at Farrell. "Are you serious? Without a muffler, they'll hear it all over the Triangle."

"What difference does it make? Like Pablo said, the moment we show ourselves they'll start shooting. If we make some noise, so what? If we're in the jeep, we can outrun them."

His eyes filled with indecision, and Farrell decided for him. "Pablo, start the jeep. Dao, you and Luc get in the back. Ashe, Clarence, clear the camouflage so we can drive out."

He shot him a venomous look. "What're you gonna do?"

"I'm gonna try to hold them while he drives the jeep out."

He checked for a full magazine and squeezed out through the camouflage. He was behind a tree, and it didn't look like they'd seen him. They were close, much too close, less than fifty meters away. A moment later the jungle reverberated to the roar of the jeep engine. The VCs responded fast, starting to run, while Clarence and Ashe worked frantically to clear a gap for Pablo to drive out.

It still wasn't wide enough, but he drove forward, smashing through the remainder of the branches, and the two men vaulted into the vehicle as it shot forward. The enemy still hadn't started shooting, too shocked and surprised by the sudden appearance of an American military jeep. Astounded it had materialized in the middle of the jungle they confidently believed they owned. He added to their shock by throwing the rifle to his shoulder and cutting loose, spraying bullets into the advancing men.

Batista drove past, narrowly missing running him down, and accelerated away. Farrell ran to catch up, and he almost didn't make it. He made a despairing grab for the rear of the bodywork. Dao and Ashe reached out and dragged him inside onto the crowded rear seat. A few bullets whistled around them, and then long bursts of automatic fire lanced toward them.

They came from all around, from behind, and from the flanks. Like Batista had said, they'd advanced the skirmish line like the horns of a bull. Now they'd found who'd been killing their men, they weren't about to let them get away. He reloaded, switched to burst mode, and sniped at the targets on the right flank as the jeep rushed away. Clarence opened fire, Ashe shot at the encroaching men on the left flank, and Dao added the Nagant's distinctive and loud bellow to their concentrated fire. The jungle came alive with the higher-pitched cracks of the AR-15s and the loud chatter of crude but effective AK-47s.

They weren't going to make it. The enemy was closing in, and Batista couldn't get up enough speed as he threaded along the narrow track. Sometimes bouncing off trees, sometimes driving over them, and once, he picked a fight with the wrong tree, and almost overturned the jeep when it refused to bend. The VCs sensed the advantage and were getting even closer. They managed to block the path and cut them off.

Clarence shouted, "Dammit, we're fucked. There's no way out!"

Farrell glanced around, and he was right. They'd cut them off, and there was no way through. This time they were fucked.

Chapter Nine

They shouldn't have survived. Somehow they did. Farrell worked out they had a single chance, to ignore the rear and the flanks and concentrate everything to the front. He shouted to them, and they responded, turning to train their guns to the front. They opened fire, sending out sheets of bullets, and most hostiles dived for cover. Three men braver than the others refused to duck, continuing to fire their AKs at the jeep. They took them down with a storm of automatic fire, supplemented by Dao's Nagant.

Now the enemy knew they had a real fight on their hands, and these civilian intruders in the military jeep had shown they packed a punch. They were wary about taking chances. A few took potshots at them as they roared past, but they were poorly aimed and half-hearted. Pablo pushed the jeep to the limit, hacking and smashing his way through the thick foliage, keeping the gas pedal pressed to the floorboards until the firing died away. They were out of immediate danger, and they reached the highway that led to Saigon.

He threw a right, pushing the speed to the limits. The roar of the engine was a deafening roar of thunder, but nobody objected. They'd got away without a scratch, and who could complain? Eventually, Clarence told him to slow.

"We've left them behind, Pablo. We'll stop and take a break. Jesus Christ, that was a close one."

They climbed out of the jeep to stretch their legs, except Dao and Luc. Farrell glanced back at them, and his eyes narrowed. Dao's shirt was covered in blood, and he lay slumped on the seat while Luc tried to comfort him.

"What's up?"

His eyes were filled with grief. "He took a bullet. I think it's bad."

He got back into the jeep and knelt next to him. A jolt of anguish tore through him. This man had become a friend and had saved his life. Somehow, he'd assumed he would always be around, indestructible, one of the few good men in South Vietnam. Now this. "Dao, my friend, how is it?"

He managed a faint smile. "My son is free. I can die a happy man."

"No, you're not gonna die. We'll get you to a hospital, and they'll treat your wound."

He shook his head. "I don't think so." He coughed, and blood sprayed from his mouth, "I am bleeding inside. There is nothing they can do. Please, listen to what my son has to say. It is important."

"Later. What matters is getting you to a hospital."

"No. No hospital, it will make no difference. Listen to

Luc."

Reluctantly, he gave in. Dao was probably right about dying. Although he was determined he'd do everything for him when they got back. He looked at the younger man, and already Luc looked better. Rescue from slavery and death was a surefire way to lift a man's spirits. "I'm listening."

"Quang."

"Uh-huh. Who is he?"

"I talked with my father, and he told me your mission is to kill South Vietnamese traitors. Men who have sold their allegiance to the Communists."

"Like you did, Luc?"

A look of shame came over his face. "You must understand I had no idea what they were like. I discovered too late they are animals."

"I won't argue with that. Okay, tell me about this Quang."

"His name is Tran Quang. He is the senior political commissar for this region. As well as having overall control over the Vietcong, he recruits and controls South Vietnamese traitors. He's merciless, and if the men under his command do not beat their captives, people loyal to the Republic of South Vietnam, the punishments are severe. For every cruelty inflicted by the Vietcong, he will inflict scores more. He is determined to rule over the region with a reign of terror. You are searching for Dieu, and people say he washes his hands in the blood of his victims. But Quang is worse. He is the man who drives them."

"We know about him. Where is he?"

"Here, the region you call the Iron Triangle."

He shrugged. "It's a big place, Luc. Finding one man would be like looking for a needle in a haystack."

"Perhaps not. I know of a base they have constructed five klicks north of Ben Co, built above a network of tunnels. He is there. At least, he was until recently."

"Tran Quang?" They looked around, and Clarence was standing behind them, listening. He looked contemptuous. "He's here, Tran Quang?"

"Maybe not, but you should call it in, it could be important."

"I'll mention it next time I radio Curtis."

"Best to do it now. We could run into trouble, and we may not get the chance."

Because we'd be dead.

"I said no!" he snarled, "Get in the jeep. We're moving out."

He vaulted into the passenger seat, but Ashe stayed where he was. "He has a point, Clarence. How long would it take to call Curtis? A few minutes?"

"And if the guy's lying? Don't forget, he's Vietcong."

"He was Vietcong. And if he's lying, Curtis can work it out for himself, process the name through the CIA intelligence databases, and see what comes up."

He looked at Batista. "Start the engine, we're leaving."

He didn't start the engine. "He could be right. I reckon you should call it in. If it's true we'd look good in Curtis' eyes. Who knows, we may get a bonus."

He sighed heavily. " If it means that much to you, I'll do it."

He switched on the radio and got through to Curtis again. This time, the connection was fast, and he passed on what Luc had said. When he mentioned the name Tran Quang, Curtis must've reacted, because Clarence's eyebrows shot up. He listened for several minutes, argued for several minutes more, and ended the call. He looked pissed.

"They want us to go to Ben Co and check it out."

Batista grimaced. "That's crazy. We have a jeep they'll hear coming from ten klicks away, and we're low on food, water, and ammunition. There's no way."

"You haven't heard the rest of it. They're sending a Huey with fresh supplies. We'll abandon the jeep, and they'll put us next to the bank of the Song Sai Gon River, that's about three klicks from Ben Co. We hike in and check it out. The area is all thick jungle, and there's no way overhead reconnaissance can pick it up from the air. We give him accurate coordinates so they can send in the bombers."

"Did you tell him about the tunnels? When they hear the bombers coming, they'll disappear into the tunnels, and it's all for nothing."

"I couldn't give a shit. I passed on the information like you wanted and look what happened. Dropped us in the crapper."

He was getting immune to Clarence's insults, and they'd started to bounce off. "What do we do right now?"

"He said to wait, and the Huey will be along inside of an hour. Pablo, drive the jeep off the road into the jungle."

Clarence was incandescent with anger, and maybe he had a point. They weren't Army. They worked for CIA. Sending them on a reconnaissance patrol wasn't what they paid them for. Their job was to sneak up on South Vietnamese traitors, kill them, and get out. He had a feeling something was going on, and it was nothing good.

Forty minutes later, they heard the distinctive roar of a

Huey getting closer. Clarence sent up a signal flare, and it dropped in for a landing fifty meters from where they waited. They ran toward it, Ashe and Farrell carrying Dao, who was weakening fast. Luc ran behind them, and there was something different about him. He'd straightened, grown. Not the shambling, half-starved slave he'd been when they first saw him. He was still a mass of bones covered in thinly stretched flesh, but his eyes had cleared, and he looked like a man who'd suddenly found his mission in life.

He also had a gun. He'd removed Dao's holster and strapped on the big Nagant.

Why would he need a hand cannon when he's accompanying his father to the hospital? True, he wants payback for what they did to him, but I'm not sure it's a good idea. The guy's still barely strong enough to walk, let alone carry, aim, and fire a heavy revolver.

They boarded the helicopter for the short journey to the south bank of the Song Sai Gon River. No more than five minutes, but for Dao, it was a lifetime. He died two minutes after they took off. A gush of blood poured from his mouth and puddled on the aluminum floor. Luc cradled the body of his father, and despite the habitual Vietnamese custom of not showing emotion, his shoulders heaved, and he sobbed in his agonized grief.

Farrell felt like he'd lost a friend. He'd got close to him in the short time they'd been together. Dao had been an honorable, decent man, who'd risked everything to save his son. It hit him hard.

The crew chief handed them their gear, packs loaded with bottled water, MREs, and most important, plenty of spare mags. He also handed over a radio.

"Curtis said we're to standby until you're ready to return. When you've pinpointed the location, call it in, and we'll get you out. You can bet your bottom dollar the heavies will be ready and waiting."

"B-52s?"

"You betcha. They say the CIA guy running Phoenix almost had a heart attack when he heard the name, Tran Quang. It's a name that's been making bigger and bigger waves just lately, and he's one bad dude. Most times when there's an atrocity, he's behind it. He gives the order, and they go in and butcher everything they can find. He's right at the top of the list."

He meant the kill list. Farrell nodded, the death of Dao had hit him hard, and there was something else. He wasn't happy about the radio. Sure, they had to have a means of communication, but the chances are they'd have to move fast, and carrying a heavy backpack radio into an area thick with hostiles didn't sound like a good idea. Neither did taking Luc along. He was a sick man, and although his lust for vengeance had given him a new lease of life, he was still very weakened by his enslavement. Yet he knew the location, which made him essential.

The helicopter flew low over the jungle canopy. The river appeared, and the pilot swooped down in a gut-lurching descent to put the skids on the ground next to the south bank.

He turned to look at his passengers, staring at them through mirror sunglasses. "You should be okay. Intelligence says the area is clear."

Clarence grunted. "The last thing we need is to find ourselves in a hot zone."

He grinned. "Nah, you're okay. Just don't go near the jungle."

"That's all I need. A wise guy."

"We'll wait for the call."

"You're gonna wait here?"

He grimaced. "You're kidding me. Too many hostiles, anybody would be crazy to stick around."

Thanks a bunch.

They stepped out onto muddy ground close to the river. Clarence raised his arms and stretched to limber up. "Farrell, carry the radio, unless you want to give it to the gook."

He didn't react to yet another insult. He was too preoccupied thinking about his behavior since he'd talked to Curtis.

What's his agenda? There's something he's not telling us. And it's nothing good.

He put his arms through the shoulder straps of the heavy man-portable radio.

Clarence pointed at Luc. "Lead the way, and try not to run into any of your Commie pals."

It was doubtful Luc fully understood his meaning, but he pointed to the north and started walking. At least, he took three steps, which could be called 'started walking.' The noise of the helicopter increased as the pilot powered up to take off, the rotor blades bit the air, and all hell broke loose. Bullets slashed across the open ground, coming from the nearby jungle. He threw himself to the ground, groaning beneath the weight of the heavy radio. Intelligence had been wrong. No surprise there.

No surprise they'd run into a hornets' nest. This was the edge of the Iron Triangle, the nearest point to Saigon, and he had little doubt the enemy was busy extending their tunnels toward the capital. Some rumors maintained tunnels may have burrowed beneath Tan Son Nhut, which seemed unlikely. But however far they'd reached, one thing was certain. They weren't about to allow anybody get close enough to find out.

He searched for targets, but the enemy was hidden inside the treeline, and all he saw was the occasional wink of light as a rifle fired. He fired back, but with little hope of hitting anything. Behind them lay the river, and in front, a remorseless and determined enemy. He glanced around, and the helicopter was in trouble, taking hits to the fuselage. The pilot had slumped over the controls, but the crew chief was attempting to revive him. He came to and nodded he was okay, despite the blood that had soaked his flight suit.

The engine note had slackened when he was hit, but it began to pick up, and they were readying to take off. They had to get out of there, and fast, and that meant the helicopter. He ignored the incoming fire and catapulted to his feet, running toward the helicopter, struggling beneath the weight of the radio. He was just in time. The skids wobbled as the aircraft began to take off, and he dived into the cabin and pulled himself forward to the cockpit.

"You have to wait. If you leave them here they'll die."

The pilot turned a face to him that was white with pain, and more than a hefty dose of fear. "Mister, if we stay here we'll all die. We're getting out of here!"

"No!" He pulled the Colt from the shoulder holster and pointed it at his head, ignoring the appalled look from the co-pilot, "Put this thing back down, or it'll be the last time you ever pilot a helicopter."

"You can't threaten him!" the co-pilot shouted, and Farrell saw him slide a hand down to his holster.

"Don't even think about it, pal. Pull a gun, and it'll be the last thing you do. Put this thing down, and get the rest of them aboard."

The engine note eased, and the skids settled back on the ground. They were already running for the helicopter. Ashe put an arm behind Luc and propelled him forward, so his feet were almost off the ground. They threw themselves into the cabin, the engine roared at maximum power, and the helicopter leaped into the air. The enemy was firing furiously, and they began to emerge from the edge of the jungle, enraged the helicopter was getting away.

The VCs didn't have it all their own way. The crew chief squatted behind the machine gun and squeezed the trigger, and with so many bullets he was sure to hit something. With no shortage of ammunition, he hosed down the attackers, and as the distance widened, they saw several men go down. The co-pilot was flying the machine, and he didn't waste time trying for height. They zoomed away skimming the grass, flying at maximum speed, and although several bullets zipped through the fuselage, none hit anything vital.

Farrell slumped on the floor of the cabin. He put a hand down and touched something soft. The body of Le Dao, and he jerked his hand away. Remembering how the poor guy had gone through hell to get his son back, only to take a Vietcong bullet in return. Luc was staring fixedly at the body of his father, and when he looked up and his dark eyes met Farrell's, there was something deep inside. Something that wasn't hard to work out, part rage, part agony, and more than ever he wanted payback.

Yet every kilometer they flew further from Ben Co, the more impossible it would be.

They flew directly to Tan Son Nhut, and Curtis was waiting next to the pad. As they climbed out, he confronted Clarence, hands-on-hips, his mouth set in a tight frown of anger.

"You fucked up, Dorsey. A simple recce mission, and now we're further away than we were before from getting Quang. He's pure evil, determined to kill and keep killing, to build a mountain of corpses. And you lost him."

Clarence remonstrated, pointing out it wasn't his fault they were waiting for them, but Curtis was having none of it. They'd missed the location of a man who'd recently appeared at the top of the CIA's most-wanted list, all for nothing.

"We'll find him again," Dorsey grunted.

"When, next week, next month, next year? Ten years? I talked with General Creighton Abrams, told him about your fuck-up, and he agreed to blanket the entire area in a single, massive bombing raid before they have a chance to run. They're preparing the B-52s even as we speak, and this one is going to be big. The fighter-bombers will hit them with a Wild Weasel strike to flatten the defenses before the bombers go in, and when they leave, there'll be nothing left but charcoal."

Clarence grinned. "There you go. Problem solved."

"Dammit!" His voice rose to a bellow, so loud the engineers servicing the Hueys popped their heads out and looked, "The problem isn't solved. Your mission was to pinpoint the location of Tran Quang, and you failed. You also failed to nail Dieu and cross a few other names off the list."

"We didn't fail, Boss. We got some."

"Not the major players, and not Quang. We'll just have to

hope the bombing raid does for him."

"It won't."

He jerked his head around and glared at Farrell. "What makes you so sure?"

"That compound sits on top of a major tunnel complex, and they go deep. The bombs won't reach them. Not unless they score a direct hit, and that's not likely. As soon as they hear the aircraft overhead, they'll disappear underground like water down a drain. All you'll do is flatten a few acres of overgrown real estate. Maybe kill a few VCs if you're lucky, but men like Quang and Dieu, they're survivors. When the dust settles, they'll come back out and start planning the next attack."

Curtis shook his head. "Dammit, this is all I need. What the hell am I going to say to Langley and Abrams? I told them we had Quang bang to rights. If what you say is correct, he'll be sheltering underground. Shit, shit, shit!"

"When do the bombers go in?"

"The Wild Weasel strike is timed for dawn tomorrow when we hope they'll be asleep. An hour later B-52s unload. For what it's worth."

Curtis scowled and stalked away, and Ashe suggested they go to his bungalow. "We can get cleaned up and find a change of clothes. Luc, how about you?"

Before he could answer, Clarence intervened. "No fucking way! He's a Commie, and he comes with us. They'll want to interrogate him."

"Clarence, he's just lost his father, and he gave us intelligence that nearly led us to Quang."

"Sure, almost. And what happened was we ran into an ambush. Big coincidence."

"You can't blame Luc. There's no way he could've told them we were on the way. That was just bad luck."

They argued back, and it got so heated Dorsey pulled a gun, but Ashe grabbed his arm and wrestled it from him. "Put it away, Clarence. We're taking Luc back with us. He's sick, half-starved, and if there's anything you want to ask him, talk with him when he's had some rest and a proper meal."

He relented, and they walked across to Ashe's rented bungalow. He found the makings of a meal, and they seated Luc at the table. Everything put in front of him he wolfed down until the Viet declared he'd had enough. They told him he could sleep on the sofa, and he lay down fully clothed in his rags and promptly fell asleep.

Ashe glanced at him. "This isn't going to work. He stinks. We have to get him cleaned up and find him somewhere else to stay."

"Later. The guy's been through hell."

He looked gloomy, but he nodded his agreement. "We'll talk about it in the morning."

They slept late, and Farrell brewed fresh coffee and walked outside onto the wooden veranda. There were the usual sounds from the airfield, jet engines on test, starting and shutting down. More jet engines starting, the noise increasing to a roar as an aircraft picked up speed along the long runway and roared into the sky. Other fixed-wing aircraft were landing, as well as helicopters, Apache gunships, Hueys, Sikorsky Jolly Greens, and Chinooks.

In the distance, he heard a rumble like thunder. Even from this distance, he heard the B-52s unloading their ordnance over a patch of jungle outside Ben Co, for all the good it did. Sure, they'd kill a few VCs and North Vietnamese regulars. Maybe destroy a few tunnels. They may even locate the compound, and it would disappear in a blaze of smoke and high-explosive fury, but he'd seen the speed they rebuilt them, and it wouldn't slow them down one bit.

He got to thinking. What would slow them down? He didn't have any answers. Until he thought back to the days they'd spent in the jungle south of Ben Cat, hitting the enemy from behind, where they'd least expect it.

How can we get Quang and Dieu when they least expect it?

The answer was intelligence, and that meant a man like Luc who could find the location on the ground. Hit the rats before they scuttled into their holes, especially rats like Dieu. And Quang. Wasn't that the primary mission of the Phoenix Program, to take out traitors like Dieu? And men like Quang, the dark soul of the Communist program. A man whose prime mission was to murder those officials and peasants who refused to submit to Hanoi.

There's one answer. We need Luc.

He listened to the bombing for a while longer until it ended. Smoke was rising in the distance, and he heard the bombers droning overhead, returning to their bases. Probably Guam, a long overwater flight. Leaving behind a jungle wasteland, as well as the bodies of pitifully few enemies.

He couldn't get the thought from his mind. It cycled through his brain like a moving electronic sign, and there had to be a way to get them. He kept returning to the same answer, an insider. Someone who could sneak in and call back the location, but who?

By midday, his reaction to his father's death was hitting

Luc even worse. After the privations he'd suffered he was weak, and even staggered several times as he tried to walk. They had to stop Clarence spiriting him away for a brutal interrogation that could finish him. Find someone to look after him, someone who would be kind and caring. A picture entered his mind, a picture of a pretty Vietnamese girl who'd once been a village schoolteacher. A girl who'd showed exceptional bravery when they rescued the women kidnapped by the Vietcong.

In the early afternoon, they drove into Saigon to talk with Tan Linh. They walked into the hostel, and she was talking with some of the other girls they'd rescued. They were busy, all working hard to clean it up. Instead of the filth and dereliction he'd encountered the first time, the place had taken on a new gleam. Two girls were scrubbing floors, Linh was polishing the huge mirror behind what'd once been the bar, and more girls were washing down the paintwork. They were earning their keep, demonstrating despite appearances they were honest and decent. Not the way the Vietcong had painted them.

She greeted them with enthusiasm, and the girls stopped work and fluttered around them. "Paul, it's good to see you again. You look like you've had a rough time."

"I've known worse."

"Really?"

"No, not really. It was bad, and we lost a good man." He nodded toward Luc, "This man's father. That's why we're here. We'll be going back into the field soon, and he needs looking after. The Vietcong treated him badly."

Her eyes narrowed with concern. "He was a prisoner of the Vietcong?"

"He was a member of the Vietcong. Don't worry, he's

come around to realizing the mistake he made. They killed his father, and they almost killed him. He's on our side, and he needs somebody to take care of him until he's recovered well enough to look after himself."

"Of course we will help him." When she translated the girls nodded their agreement. In less than a minute four girls had grabbed him and taken him away, "They said they'll tidy him up and find somewhere for him to sleep. This place is female only. No men are allowed to stay, but I'll talk to the owner, and we'll fix up a room at the back he can use. Don't worry, we'll take care of him, feed him up and get him new clothes. Within a few days, you won't recognize him."

They chatted for a while longer. She was good people, and the man she finally settled down with would be a lucky man. It wouldn't be him. Sure, she was grateful he'd rescued her, but that wasn't something he'd take advantage of. He wasn't about to enter a relationship with any girl. He reeked of death after he'd agreed to join Phoenix to go after the man responsible for the death of his brother Mark. His chances of survival were close to zero. And there was something else. His addiction. The desperate need, and until he was over it, his life was on hold. No, that wasn't true. His death was on hold, waiting in the wings. Not for much longer.

They left Luc in good hands and strolled around Saigon to see the sites, careful to avoid the pitfalls and traps waiting for the newcomer and the unaware. Like snipers, satchel bombers, grenade attacks. They reached the bungalow just before midnight and turned in. He didn't sleep. His soul cried out for release, demanded he open that baggie he'd taken off the dead VC. It burned a hole in his pocket.

Just one snort, it couldn't do any harm, could it? I've been clean for a long time, so I reckon I can handle it.

He left it alone. He needed sleep, and if he filled his nostrils with the white powder it would keep him awake all night and for most of the next day, and he'd feel like hell. But he didn't sleep, and before dawn he walked outside, prowling up and down the veranda. The sky was clear, and he looked up at the stars. Trying to work out their names, and like always he failed. One star was brighter than the others, and he decided it was Mars. The name was appropriate for Vietnam. The God of War cast its eerie glow over the country.

He went back inside and tried to sleep, but when the first rays of dawn shone through the window he was still wide-awake. He wondered if just a little coke would help see him through the day, but he resisted. Instead, he showered and dressed and joined Ashe in the kitchen. They ate breakfast and strolled over to the air base, hoping to find Clarence and Pablo in the hangar where they stored their gear. They weren't there, and they looked for them in the cafeteria.

They weren't there either. Puzzled, they returned to the hangar, and they were inside. Dorsey tossed him his usual sneering greeting. "What kept you?"

He ignored the jibe. "What's up, Clarence?"

"We're going back."

"Back?"

"Ben Co."

"Clarence, they bombed the crap out of that place, what's to go back for? Unless you want to poke around the tunnels, they're about all that's left."

"Curtis wants us to look for Quang."

"If he's alive, he'll be in the tunnels, and you can forget going down there."

"Not necessarily. Curtis confirmed he hates the tunnels almost as much as he hates us. He was trapped for a long time in the ruins of his bombed-out house in Hanoi. He could be dead, that's a possibility. Either way, we go in, confirm he's dead, and if he isn't, we bury him."

"It's crazy. The chances are we'll run into more trouble than we can handle."

He shrugged. "Those're the orders. We leave in three days, which will give time for the dust and smoke to settle. The latest reconnaissance reports show much of the place is still on fire after the bombing raid. Visibility is close to zero in places, so we need time for it to clear. We're also gonna need a guide now we don't have Luc. Someone familiar with the place like him." He grinned, "You have a couple of days to relax and enjoy yourselves. Why don't you go into the city and visit those whores you brought back? Farrell, as I recall, the schoolteacher was a pretty one. I'm betting she'd be a good fuck."

He felt like punching his teeth down his throat, but he resisted the urge. Like he'd resisted the urge for cocaine, so far. Say no to drugs. And say no to putting Clarence on the floor. No matter how often he'd felt tempted.

With no mission planned for a couple of days, they returned to the bungalow and decided to spend time in the city. They drove in, found a restaurant close to the hostel, and enjoyed a fine lunch. Afterward, they strolled around in the sunshine, looking at the pretty girls. Once they ducked into a doorway when they saw a guy who looked like he was about to toss a grenade. To their considerable relief, it was a false alarm.

A civilian with a pack strapped to his back, and when he delved inside for the contents, he pulled out a pack of sandwiches.

They ate again in the evening, this time a slap-up meal after Ashe reminded him of the paycheck due at the end of the month. They wound up in a bar, watching a floor show performed by dancers with more enthusiasm than skill. But they were young and pretty, so worth a watch. He thought again of Linh and wondered how she was making out. Probably she'd be fine. She was a schoolteacher, fluent in English, and likely to find a position in Saigon without too many problems.

After a hair-raising drive through the streets of the city, they got back to the bungalow and worked their way through a bottle of Scotch. He should've slept, but once again he didn't. Maybe it was too much booze, or maybe something else, the enemy that lived inside him. The enemy words chewed away at him, constantly gnawing at his psyche. Telling him to take out that baggie he kept in his top pocket. One snort and he'd feel better. It was tempting, more than tempting, and once it was almost too much. He got out of bed, delved in his pocket, and stared at the white powder inside the clear plastic for long minutes.

He didn't open it. If he did, that would be the end, and he was likely to go off and do something stupid. Like go looking for Clarence Dorsey and beat the crap out of him. Which would get him precisely nowhere, and the chances were Clarence would make sure he ended up dead in some back alley. In the morning he still felt like hell. He spent the rest of the day lounging around the bungalow, strolling outside for brief periods to get some fresh air to clear his head.

He thought constantly of Dao, a good man. He thought

again of his death so soon after he'd rescued his son, and it was so unfair.

War is unfair, but hell, Dao didn't start it. I didn't start it. I'm just trying to pick up the broken pieces and fit them back together. It's too late for Mark and too late for Dao.

By mid-afternoon, he'd had enough, and he had to do something. Had to answer the questions that'd dogged him ever since Clarence told them they'd be going back. He strolled over to the air base.

Curtis was in his office, and he looked up with an annoyed glance as Farrell pushed the door open. "What do you want? Don't you knock?"

"Not usually. Tell me about this mission, returning to Ben Co."

"I ordered Clarence to brief you, so you should know everything you need to know."

"It stinks."

"Too bad, but that's the job. Was there anything else?"

"There is. You recall when you came to Leavenworth and visited me in my cell?" He nodded, "You said something about tracking down the guy responsible for my brother's death. How about it? Do you have any leads?"

"Something came in recently, but I haven't read it yet. Let me see." He shuffled through the papers on his desk and picked up what looked like a telex message. His expression changed, and there was something shifty in the man's eyes that worried him.

"I have it right here." He glanced at the text, "Yeah, yeah, I thought as much. It's him, Tran Quang. The guy we want you to eliminate."

"Why didn't you say before?"

"I just got confirmation."

Sure you did.

"There's no mistake?"

He hesitated. "It says here it was Quang. He has enough blood on his hands for a box load of medals. You may as well know the suicide bomber who killed your brother was once his girlfriend. She was carrying his child."

"You're telling me he ordered his girlfriend to kill herself and his unborn kid?"

"That's what it says here. An even better reason to put a bullet in him."

He couldn't argue with that. "It'll be a pleasure. Have you found us a guide, someone who can take us to his base?"

"Nope, not yet, but we're still looking. Ideally, we need a Vietcong deserter, a guy who knows the area, and there're not many deserters around. Not live ones, anyway. Don't worry about it, we'll come up with a name."

* * *

Shortly after he'd left, Clarence Dorsey pushed his way into Curtis' office.

"What did Farrell want?"

A shrug. "Just something about his brother, and I confirmed the telex that came in and said Quang was behind his murder. By the way, how come the telex arrived in my office? I don't recall asking for it."

"You didn't. I made the request."

His eyebrows shot up in surprise. "Why?"

"I didn't want to say this about Farrell, but I'm having doubts about him. He's yellow."

"I understood he'd done okay. Since he joined your squad, you've turned in an impressive body count. I don't see any sign of him being yellow. Work with him. You're going back to Ben Co in a couple of days, and I don't want any arguments to upset things."

"I'll make sure he toes the line. I'm not happy about that second strike. I don't want to end up underneath several tons of USAF bombs."

He nodded. "The timing's gonna be tight, but we have to hit them hard while they're still recovering. Clarence, it'll take guts to go in there and get out before the B-52s return. If Farrell knew, do you think he could duck the mission?"

"That's exactly what I think. Boss, after this one I want him out and Melvin back in the squad. If you want results, Farrell has to go."

He didn't look happy, but Dorsey was in charge, and he had to go along with his judgment. "I don't like it. I don't like changing horses in the middle of the race, but if that's the way want it, that's the way it'll be. Is that all?"

"For now. Whatever you do, don't tell Farrell or Ashe about the bombing."

"You're worried about Ashe as well?

"He's pretty pally with Farrell, and I don't want him passing it on."

"Whatever you say."

* * *

Farrell strolled back through the bustling air base, out through the gates, and turned toward the city. He found the hostel and went inside. The first people he saw were Linh and Luc seated on a sofa in the lounge, and in a short time, Luc was a changed man. They'd acquired him a set of clothes that fitted, the traditional white shirt, black pants, and leather sandals. His hair was cut short, neat, and combed. Most of the lines of stress and fatigue had disappeared. He was still thin, painfully thin, but well on the way to recovery from his ordeal.

Linh looked up and gave him a warm smile. "Paul, why don't you join us?"

He took a seat and they chatted. He noticed she and Luc were becoming close, and they both had only eyes for each other. He felt good about it. They'd both been through hell, victims of the Vietcong, and except for Luc seeing his father die, had emerged alive and with their sanity. Now they'd found each other.

They talked about the future, and she gave him a mischievous smile. "Now I know what you do, I guess the question is who're you planning to kill?"

He wasn't sure he should talk about it, but it was Luc who'd described the whereabouts of Tran Quang, so it was no secret. "Quang."

Her eyes narrowed, but Luc visibly shuddered. "You're going after him? I thought the B-52s plastered the area with high-explosives. You think he's still alive?"

"Alive or dead, who knows? Our mission is to search for the body, and if we don't find it, look for the man. And kill him."

"I wish to come with you."

He smiled and shook his head. "It's not possible, Luc.

You've been through hell. Forget it, stay here with the girls, and recover your health. If you want to do something to avenge your father, sign up for the ARVN."

Linh gently reminded Luc he was in no condition to go waltzing into the Iron Triangle. That he wouldn't be ready to even go for a long walk until he was fully recovered. He disagreed and told her he needed to do something worthwhile. To strike back at the regime that'd used him as a slave and killed his father.

Farrell spent a few minutes more persuading him it was the worst idea in the world and got up to leave. On the way out, a couple of the girls accosted him. Not an unpleasant experience, and they made it clear he was their friend for life. If he'd made either of them an offer of marriage, he had no doubt both would've accepted with alacrity. He didn't make an offer of marriage. Marriage was for life. His destiny was death.

He strolled away, wandered through the bustling streets of Saigon until he'd had enough and found his way back to Ashe's bungalow. The place was empty, and he poured himself a large Scotch from the almost empty bottle from the night before. He felt more alone than ever. Although he was glad for them, seeing Linh and Luc so obviously enthralled with each other reminded him of his isolation. Ashe was out somewhere, maybe meeting a girl. Whatever he was doing, he wouldn't be doing it alone. He was alone.

The coke still burned a hole in his pocket, and several times he patted the faint bulge to reassure himself it was there. It beckoned to him. Calling out for him to snort a couple of lines. Nothing to excess, just take the edge off the urge. He resisted the temptation, but by the evening, Ashe still hadn't returned, and by midnight he felt tired and went into his bedroom. Lay on the bed, but the voice in his head wouldn't leave him.

At 03.30 Ashe opened the front door and he came awake. He swung his legs off the bed and went to greet him.

"You're awake?"

"Kind of. Any news from Curtis about the mission?"

"Oh, yeah. I was eating dinner with an old girlfriend when they came to the restaurant. The mission has been put forward. We go in tomorrow, wheels up at 21.00. They've timed our arrival for after dark, so we shouldn't have any problems with ambushes. But we do have one problem. Curtis still hasn't found a guide. Without the right man, someone who knows the area, we'll have problems." He hesitated, and he couldn't meet Farrell's eyes, "Luc would've been perfect. He knows the area, knows where the tunnels are, there's nobody better."

"The answer is no. The poor bastard's been through hell. He needs time to recover."

"Buddy, we're all going through hell when we go into that place. Without a good guide, the chances are we won't make it back. Doesn't it bother you?"

"Not particularly."

Ashe put the kettle on the stove. "I'm brewing fresh coffee, do you want a cup?"

He shouldn't. He needed sleep, not a caffeine fix. But he accepted, and he felt more wide-awake than ever. While they drank their coffee Ashe was silent, and he got the impression there was something he couldn't bring himself to say.

He fired off the question. "What's eating you, Ashe? There's something you don't want to tell me."

"I know how you feel about Luc, but there was nothing I could do."

"Spit it out."

"It's Clarence. He and Curtis have gone to the hostel to visit Luc. They want him."

"Bastards! They'll offer him everything, and he's in no condition to go back into the Triangle. You know it."

"What can I do? Curtis is running things, and Clarence is the squad leader. If they say jump, we jump."

He wanted to rush out, locate Clarence and Curtis, and put a stop to it, but Ashe pointed out it was too late. By now they'd have collected him and taken him to Tan Son Nhut to prepare for the mission. He awoke after a brief rest and felt like a corpse that'd just risen from the grave. He had jagged flashes of Dao, seeing his bloody body slumped on the floor of the Huey. The son wasn't in any condition to fight a one-legged cripple, let alone go into the Triangle. He couldn't let it happen, except the harrowing experiences of the past few days, combined with stress and lack of sleep had left him unable to prevent anything from happening. He was out of options.

Bar one. He fingered the clear plastic baggy in his pocket, and it possessed him. Offered him the solution. He took it out, trailed two lines on the kitchen counter, and snorted them both. Immediately, a surge of energy surged through his system, his brain cleared.

Maybe I've done the right thing. Even if it's the wrong thing, at least I feel ready to fight. If I can't stop Luc coming along, I can protect him from whatever happens. Including Clarence, and Tran Quang. Ben Co, you can go fuck! Paul Farrell is coming, and he's gonna shit all over you!

Chapter Ten

Ashe chose that moment to enter the kitchen and sized up what he saw. The baggie lying on the counter. Farrell had left traces of white powder on his nose, and his bloodshot eyes were glazed with a manic ferocity.

"I thought you weren't doing that stuff."

He snapped a harsh reply. "It was just this one time. I couldn't sleep."

His lips twitched. "One thing's for sure, coke won't help you sleep."

"I'll sleep when I'm good and ready. Right now, I need the energy."

He didn't say any more. They ate breakfast, checked out their gear, and strolled over to the hangar. They were in for a surprise. Clarence Dorsey and Pablo Batista were waiting for them, along with two others. One was Le Luc, and the other a young woman.

"Linh, what the hell are you doing here?"

"I said I'd come along to take care of him."

"You know where we're going? This is the Triangle, it's a killing ground."

"Mr. Curtis said the B-52 bombers hit it so hard most of the enemy will be dead."

"They'll have taken shelter in the tunnels. Most will still be alive, and madder than a nest of angry hornets."

"I cannot let Luc go without someone to take care of him. I don't think he'd make it back."

"You're both making a big mistake. I'm gonna see Curtis and tell him to put a stop to this."

Dorsey grinned. "He ain't here, Farrell. He went up to Bien Hoa, and afterward, he's due to slot in an overnight visit to Cam Ranh Bay. He'll be there for a couple of days, so if you want to go see him, you're looking at a long walk."

"Clarence, neither of them is up to it."

"I don't agree. Luc will be fine. Besides, I didn't ask the girl to come along."

The cocaine was like a living fire inside him, and he bunched a fist and launched himself at Clarence, who dodged to one side, avoiding the punch. Ashe and Batista pulled him off, pushed him to the floor, and held him down until his rage subsided. When he got back to his feet, Clarence and Batista were busy preparing supplies and equipment for the mission as if nothing had happened. He knew he'd be wasting his time trying to get him to change his mind. All he could do was his best to take care of Luc.

He didn't take long to pack his gear and ensure he had plenty of spare magazines. He left the hangar for a walk around the air base to clear the turmoil in his head. Four two-seat F-100F fighters were on the stand at the edge of the tarmac. No doubt they were preparing for their next Wild Weasel flak suppression mission. Ground engineers were clustered around them.

It started to rain, and before long his shirt and pants were soaked through to his shorts, but he didn't care. He was thinking of Luc and Linh, assumed they were safe, and now they were going back into Vietcong Central. If they thought the B-52s had wiped them out, they were dreaming. They'd be skulking in the tunnels, and when they came out, they'd be spitting nails and fighting mad. Luc was still weak, and Linh a civilian, a schoolteacher. Neither was able to defend themselves, and if he couldn't protect them they were in for a world of pain, more likely a bloody death.

Almost unconsciously his hand reached for the baggie, and he took a pinch of white powder, snorted it up one nostril, and did the same with the other. Once again, the feeling of overwhelming power and strength swept over him. He could do it all, take care of them, and kill Quang. Easy as falling off a log. Nothing could stop him.

He walked the entire perimeter of the air base three times, and when he returned to the hangar, he was so wet the water puddled on the floor. Ashe told him to go get changed. "There's some dry gear of mine in the locker. If you don't change into dry clothes you'll freeze to death."

"Wet or dry, what's the difference? It'll still be raining." The retort came out harder-edged than he'd intended, and he knew it was the coke was talking, "But thanks anyway."

"I mean it. Towel yourself off and change. I know it'll still be raining, but that's why we carry our ponchos."

He glared back at him, and he knew he was handling it badly. Linh looked worried, but Ashe was right. He was starting to shiver after being out in the drenching rain for so long, and he toweled off and pulled on a change of clothes. He felt better, warmer, and when Clarence told them to pay attention, he forced himself to keep his mouth shut and listen.

"You all know why we're going. The mission is to rake over the ashes and the rubble after the visit from the B-52s. Our objective is to locate Tran Quang, dead or alive. If he's dead, I want us to bring back confirmation."

"What kind of confirmation?" Ashe asked.

He looked irritated. "What the fuck do you think? An identity document, or something else that can give us a positive ID. Cut off his finger, maybe they can check the fingerprint, or even better cut off his head. The same goes for Dieu if we find him, and with luck, we'll find them both dead. Farrell, I want you to stay with the Viets and look for Quang, that's the primary mission." He sneered, "I'm giving you this assignment because you seem to hit it off with the natives. Me, Pablo, and Dave will look for Dieu."

He wondered why Dorsey was splitting them up, but it did mean he could stay close and take care of Luc and Linh. They ended the short briefing and trooped over to the cafeteria for a final meal before they left. Afterward, they sat around drinking coffee until it was time to board the helicopter. Night fell over the air base, and they took off into the dark sky that shrouded Saigon. Linh and Luc were seated together, and when they thought nobody was looking, their hands linked together. That was just fine, except they were going into the Triangle. That wasn't fine.

The journey was as uneventful as journeys went in this hellhole. Several times streams of tracer bullets whistled past, like tiny, lethal fireflies. Men got used to them, Vietcong or People's Army shooting at anything that moved across the sky. The pilot didn't bother to veer away. It was routine, SOP. Without the incoming tracer rounds, he'd have suspected the Viets were up to something strange.

The journey was short, and nobody said anything. They were lost in their thoughts, and Luc looked nervous. He'd been keen to help locate Quang, but when the rubber hit the road, maybe it didn't seem such a good idea. He'd been enslaved and brutalized for a long time and hadn't recovered his strength. There was something else, the possibility of meeting up with some of his former pals. They'd welcome a chance to settle the score with a deserter.

All too soon the journey came to an end, and the skids hovered a couple of feet off the ground. They jumped and rushed for the nearby treeline. So far so good, nobody ambushed them, and even Clarence seemed more agreeable than usual.

"All of you make sure you have everything you need. Remember, we don't want to start a war. The plan is to locate Quang and Dieu, put a bullet in them if they're alive, and get out before first light. If anything goes wrong we'll hole up until the next night. Any questions? No? Good. About that gun Luc's carrying. I'm not happy about him carrying a weapon. I don't trust any of them. The only good Viet, you know how it goes. "

They were listening, and they kept their faces expressionless. Farrell grunted. "There's good and bad,

Clarence, same as in America. When and where do we rendezvous?" He hadn't mentioned it, as if it wasn't important.

"We meet right here. One hour before dawn, shall we say 05.00?"

"That's not much time."

"Maybe not, that's why I said we may need to hole up for the day and exfil at dawn the following day. By the way, it's best if Ashe goes with you, in case you need extra firepower make sure you're back here at 05.00. No earlier, I don't want to alert the enemy to our LZ, and the Huey pilot would be upset if he landed in a hot zone. Get moving.

They shouldered their packs and entered the dense jungle. Luc seemed to know the way, and he led from the front, picking his way along narrow paths. When several routes converged, he knew instinctively which one to take. The route they were taking was pulling them deeper and deeper into the Triangle. They made the first three klicks, several times having to duck into the undergrowth and wait while parties of men walked past on adjacent paths. They could've been a hundred meters away or ten meters away, in the darkness. It was impossible to know. All they needed to know was to stay out of their way. And they were alive. The bombing hadn't killed them.

It took them more than three hours to cover those three kilometers, and he silently cursed Clarence. Every step of the way the deeper they went into the jungle, the more it looked like they were going to be inside the Triangle for the next day. He wondered for the umpteenth time if Dorsey had been pulling his chain, deliberately making things difficult for him and the two Vietnamese, but he doubted it. They had a job to do, and Clarence needed results. Charles Curtis appeared to have accepted the body count he'd submitted so far, but sooner or later he'd want something more tangible. Confirmation the more notorious Communist traitors had been eliminated.

He checked his watch, and it was past midnight when Luc suddenly threw up a hand for them to stop.

"What is it?" he murmured.

"There used to be a major Vietcong base up ahead. They abandoned it after a bombing raid and ground attack during the major operation the Americans mounted to wipe out the Iron Triangle. But I don't believe they'll have gone far."

He was talking about Operation Cedar Falls, another notable failure. Employing vast fleets of bombers, batteries of heavy artillery, and thousands of troops, the Communists had retreated into their tunnels, or west toward Laos, and waited it out. When the shit ceased hitting the fan, they returned to their old positions as if nothing had happened.

He scattered around for an hour but found no trace of them, and they kept walking, frequently crawling. The further they went into the Triangle, the more Cong they had to avoid. They stopped again, and he conferred with Ashe. "I reckon we've gone far enough. Any more, and we'll have trouble getting out." He looked at Luc. "Do you have any ideas?"

"I'm sorry, I don't. I knew that base camp had been abandoned after it was destroyed in the bombing, but because of the network of tunnels beneath, I assumed they'd have rebuilt not far away, except we haven't seen them. I'm sorry, I must've been wrong."

"Yeah. Okay, another fifteen minutes, and we're out of here. Who knows, we might make the LZ in time for the helicopter? The last thing I want is to stay in this place through the day."

They started walking again, and fifteen minutes later Luc called another halt. They'd stopped because they'd found it, the new base built by the VCs over the tunnel network, and its size was astonishing. They'd constructed what appeared to be a village, heavily camouflaged beneath scores of mats hoisted into the trees to screen the place from aerial observation. It was nighttime, almost 03.30, and the place was swarming with men. In the dim light cast by a few flickering lanterns, they could see laborers carrying heavy loads on yokes across their shoulders. A wooden bucket on either side and carried them deep into the jungle. Men with picks and shovels were sprawled on the ground, obviously taking a break, until a man wearing the uniform of an officer of the People's Army appeared and shouted a series of orders.

Slowly, wearily they got to their feet, picked up the tools, and started toward a dark hole with a ladder poking out the top. They waited while a host of men emerged, like zombies climbing from the grave. They immediately threw themselves to the ground, too exhausted to take more than a few paces.

"They're tunnelers," Luc told him, "Slaves, like they made me. They'll be expanding the network of tunnels. Probably toward Saigon."

Ashe grunted. "Maybe they're looking for a bar, or even better a brothel. I mean…" He stopped and looked at Linh. "I'm sorry, I forgot."

She winced. "That's okay. What're you going to do about this place? I doubt there's any chance of finding Quang. It's too big, too many people."

She was right, and as dawn approached, they'd have to

melt back into the jungle out of sight. Which would mean they couldn't keep an eye on the place. More and more men were coming in from the jungle as dawn approached, and he looked around for the best route out, except there was none. VCs were thronging in from every pathway, and it was more than just a routine end of the working day; or a working night, in the case of the Vietcong. There was plenty of working time before dawn, and Farrell had an uneasy feeling in his guts.

They're up to something big.

He couldn't skulk in the jungle until he'd worked out what it was. He looked around for a suitable hiding place, somewhere he could maintain observation. He found what he needed and looked at Ashe.

"I'm gonna stay here and keep an eye on them. You get back into the jungle with Luc and Linh, and stay out of sight. Keep them out of trouble."

He gave him a skeptical glance. "Paul, they're everywhere, crawling around like termites. If you stick around, it'll end one way, and it won't be healthy."

"I hear you, pal, but that's what I'm gonna do. Get moving now. Get them out of here."

He didn't like it. Luc and Linh didn't like it, but his chosen hiding place had room for one man, and they reluctantly crawled away into the tangle of stinking foliage.

It was 04.20 when he reached the foot of the tree he'd identified. A gap in the matting suspended from the branches was just big enough to crawl through, and where the branches forked, he'd worked out one man could stay out of sight. He broke off vines and small branches and wrapped them around himself, matted leaves and twigs to make it more effective.

They didn't see him. He was nothing more than twisted foliage, invisible. Several times men walked past without seeing anything untoward. Once, a black-clad, AK-47 toting VC stopped and relieved himself next to him, so close he could reach out and touch him. He gripped his pistol and held his breath, waiting for him to move away. Afterward, he couldn't help but smile at what the guy would think if he knew how close he'd been to death.

He started to climb the tree, and it wasn't too hard. Ropes hung down from the camouflage mat, and he was able to pull himself up, hand over hand. He squirmed through the tiny gap in the matting and squatted in the fork of the branches. Satisfied he was all but invisible from the ground, and he'd have a perfect view of what was going on below at dawn.

When the first glow of the new day began to push away the shadows, what he saw was more than surprising. In the darkness, he'd noticed a few huts and the top of the shaft with the ladder poking out. In daylight, it was much bigger. Not a village, more of a small town. He counted as many as fifty bamboo and palm thatch huts, although most were ramshackle. They'd be accommodation for the laborers working on the tunnel network.

Further from the tunnel the huts were sturdier, roofed with tar paper against the incessant rain. They'd be for the fighting men, or more likely the guards. The fighters would sleep in the tunnels, for they were indispensable. The guards were of little value. The laborers were of no value. Except to work them to death, and they'd round up more suckers to end their lives digging, digging, and more digging.

As he'd suspected, the fighting men disappeared

underground. Leaving the guards and the laborers above ground. Work didn't stop. They entered the shaft periodically, reappearing after a couple of hours to be replaced by the next shift of walking skeletons. More men carried excavated earth out into the jungle to spread around and hide the evidence of the digging.

After a short time, he found it boring, watching the same process over and over, with no sign of the targets. Keeping his perch in the branches was difficult, having to exert the muscle strength in his legs to stop him from falling. Once, he felt his body going numb, and he even started to doze. He dug his fingernails into his palm so the pain would keep him awake. He tried exercising his muscles, tiny movements that wouldn't alert anybody below who chanced to look up. By midday, he was all in, and despairing of finding anything valuable.

He hung on through the early afternoon and continually checked his watch, waiting for the time when nightfall would allow him to slip away.

I've seen everything I need to see, except Quang and Dieu. Too bad, if the B-52s carpet-bomb this place, it'll slow them down, but little more. This is a major project they've been working on for many months, and they'll be prepared for the worst.

His mouth was parched, and he took a sip of water from his canteen, enjoying the cool liquid sliding down his throat. He looked for a change of position so he could take some of the pressure off his leg muscles. When he looked down again, he was staring at Quang. There was no question. The grainy photos he'd seen at Tan Son Nhut were poor but good enough to recognize him.

He'd found him, he was alive, and there wasn't a damn

thing he could do about it. He was so startled, he almost fell, but what happened was almost as bad. He'd been holding his canteen, and it slipped out of his fingers and fell to the ground. Several men standing a few meters away heard rather than saw the small object fall, and at first, they didn't take much notice. Fruit fell from these trees all the time, so why should one more mango or coconut, or whatever the hell grew in these parts, make them suspicious?

Four men nearby chatted to each other, and one walked to inspect the fruit that'd fallen. Farrell saw him rummaging below him, and at first, he thought he might not spot the canteen. His hopes were dashed. The guy stooped, picked it up, held it up, and shouted for his pals to see what he'd found.

In another few seconds, he'd look up. He had to look up, and Farrell looked around desperately for a way out. There were just the camouflage mats, and with no choice, he crawled along a branch, took hold of the rope supporting the camouflage, and pulled himself over to the mat. He fell when the intertwined vines and leaves, rotted after so much time out in the open, collapsed, and he dropped six meters to the ground, landing in front of an astonished Vietcong.

For what seemed like an eternity, but was closer to ten seconds, all movement ceased. Men stared down at him, frozen like statues. He looked up at them and realized he'd dropped his rifle, for all the good it would've done. He had the Colt in the shoulder holster, and wisely, he kept his hand away from the butt. When they moved, it started slowly and became a swelling surge of men rushing toward him.

There was death in their eyes. Most unslung their AKs, and held them by the barrel, smashing the butts down on his body in a rain of blows. He curled up in a ball to protect himself from the worst of the beating. Although he wondered if it would've been better to let them beat his brains out. A quick death would be merciful, compared to the brutal end they tended to inflict on many of their American prisoners. A man barked a command, and the beating stopped. Cautiously, he uncurled his body and looked up.

He was staring at the implacable face of Commissar Tran Quang, perhaps not so implacable, for the man's lips softened into a ghastly semblance of a smile. He said something to the man closest to him, and they chuckled. He had a feeling it wasn't anything good.

"Who are you?"

"I, uh, I was out for a stroll, and I was interested in what was going on."

The ghastly smile vanished, and what appeared in its place was an expression as cold as the Arctic depths. "You are an American spy."

He shrugged. "That's not entirely true."

"You are an American, and you were spying on my camp. American spy!" he uttered triumphantly, looking around at his men.

If you want the truth, I was planning to kill you. Which makes me an assassin, not a spy.

"What do we do with spies?"

Not being conversant in Vietnamese, Farrell didn't understand the words. He understood the meaning, and he didn't bother to reply. What could he tell them, the truth? Tell them he was employed by the CIA to kill traitors and men like Quang? If they learned the truth, God help him. Besides, he didn't want to give them the satisfaction of knowing he'd failed in his mission. They were Commie gooks. And Quang was the worst of the Commie gooks. He was also the man who'd issued the order that resulted in Mark's death.

Leaving his brother unavenged troubled him more than dying, and if there was any way he could've pulled his pistol and shot the man dead, he'd have done it. His death would have been quick, riddled with scores of bullets. But they were already searching him, and they extracted his gun and combat knife.

Quang shouted another order, and they dragged him to a nearby tree. He hoped they'd put together a firing squad and finish him, but it wasn't to be. They roped him to the tree, with his arms and ankles tied back around the trunk, so he was unable to move. They fetched a pot of some treacly sweet-smelling substance and smeared it around his boots and his pants legs. Then they left him.

He knew what they'd done, and he wished he was dead. This place would be alive with red ants. In minutes, they'd catch the scent of the substance they'd smeared over him, and a long procession of crawling insects would arrive and climb over him. Red ants were not poisonous, not as far as he knew, but their bite was painful. Multiply that by a hundred, or a thousand, and it didn't take a huge imagination to work out by nightfall his body would be in an agonized torment of fiery hell.

They left him, returning to their labors. He knew they'd be back once the ants had arrived and started work on his body. They wouldn't want to miss the fun, the spectacle, to see a man suffering beyond any human endurance. It was an hour before the first tiny visitors arrived. He saw them coming, a long procession of insects getting closer until they reached his boots.

They hesitated, enjoying the anticipation of a hearty meal. It wouldn't be long before they started up his pants. Before they crawled inside his pants, up his legs, biting their way higher, until they reached the openings in his body. His penis, his anus, and they'd continue up until they reached his mouth, his ears, his nostrils, and his eyes.

Quang reappeared and nodded in approval when he saw they'd arrived. He looked at Farrell. "You killed my wife."

He shook his head. "Mister, I never met your wife."

Besides, you killed my brother, as well as your girlfriend and her unborn child.

His eyes slitted; "American bombers buried her in the rubble of our home. You are an American, and you must pay. You must all pay."

"Mister, I don't fly a plane. Never learned how."

"This is my country, and I will not rest until every one of you is either dead or has left."

He could've explained to Quang he didn't want to stay in Vietnam, any more than he wanted him to. Just until he'd put a bullet in him, and that didn't seem likely, not now. He doubted telling him he wanted out as much as the next man would've made a difference. He had him trussed up like a Thanksgiving turkey ready for a celebration. The Viet stalked away, leaving him the butt of amusement for passers-by, although not all of them. The VCs found his parlous state hilarious, but the laborers walked past with closed expressions. He suspected in the past this punishment had been meted out for slacking off, and they didn't find it amusing.

Red ants crawled past his knees, and he looked down at his pants legs. They were covered in crawling insects, as if his clothes were coming alive. He forced his gaze away, not wanting to look at the thousands of tiny instruments of his torture. They headed toward his crotch, and he did everything to stop himself from thinking about what was about to happen. They'd invade his body, and it would be very bad. Excruciating. Probably not unlike being branded with a red-hot iron.

He was condemned to die in agony while the Vietcong looked on, enjoying the show.

Fuck you all, and fuck this stinking, disease-ridden shithole of a country. You're welcome to it.

Chapter Eleven

They'd almost reached the top of his legs when the rain came. Water poured through the camouflage netting in torrents, dousing him in blessed, cool liquid relief. He was parched, and he tilted his head up to catch some of the water in his mouth. It was a relief, but wonder of wonders, the rain stopped the red ants from crawling any further. But they didn't go away. He prayed the deluge would go on, preferably forever.

Drown, you nasty little six-legged bastards. Dear Lord, keep them away from me. Let the rain never stop.

It rained all through the night, and the ants waited. They weren't about to give up their tasty meal. The dawn arrived, and it was still raining. He knew it couldn't last, and it didn't. Slowly, the torrential downpour eased until it was no more than a light shower. Not enough to dissuade the red ants from enjoying their meal, and they crawled higher, exploring his crotch, and he wanted to scream. He banged his head against the trunk of the tree, trying to beat out his brains and kill himself, without success. All he managed was to give himself a headache. The fire of hundreds of bites swamped him, and his imagination ran wild.

More grinning soldiers walked past. He couldn't stop himself and raved at them, cursing and swearing. Told them they were a heap of stinking shit, that Ho Chi Minh had been a worthless piece of scum, that the best thing that could happen to Vietnam was for somebody to nuke the place. Probably they didn't understand English, and they walked past, leaving behind the echoes of their laughter. He was desperate for anything, and he felt a surge of relief when a soldier approached, wearing the uniform of the People's Army. Water trickling down from the matting above blinded him so he couldn't his face, but he saw the AK-47 held hip-high pointed toward him.

He was coming to kill him. A quick death, and he thanked his lucky stars. Felt like he'd won the jackpot at Las Vegas, and soon he'd be reunited with his brother Mark. He'd apologize to him for not getting Quang, and all he could offer was he'd tried. Done his best, and maybe somebody else would deal with him.

The soldier came closer and stopped with the muzzle of his rifle touching his belly.

Farrell snarled, "Do it, you stinking, worthless piece of shit. Don't you have the guts? You puke-faced motherfucker, I spit on you, and I spit on every piece of filth that crawled down from the North. Pull the trigger, you yellow-bellied piece of vomit."

Although he wasn't a religious man, he silently recited the only prayer he could remember from when he was a kid. The Lord's Prayer, and it wouldn't be long. A few seconds and it would all be over.

Pull the fucking trigger!

'Give us this day our daily bread. Forgive us our trespasses, as we…'

"Mr. Farrell."

The voice was a low murmur, barely audible. He blinked a dozen times to clear his eyes, and something about the soldier looked familiar. His tortured, agonized mind couldn't believe it. After everything he'd been through, he was having hallucinations.

"Whoever you are, shithead, shoot me! Are you man enough to do it or not?"

"It's me. Luc."

He still couldn't work it out. "Luc who?"

"Le Luc. Dao's son."

At first, he was lost for words. He was here, dressed in the uniform of the People's Army.

What the fuck!

"You've turned traitor again and rejoined the Communists. Fuck you. Pull the trigger."

Luc leaned in closer and spoke again, his voice barely audible. "I've come to get you out."

He shook his head to clear it, still convinced he was hallucinating. Yet it was no hallucination, the face staring at him was Le Luc.

"Luc, you're crazy. There's no way you can get me away from here. They'll see you, and they'll kill you same as me."

"I won't leave you like this. Don't worry. We have a plan. Ashe is waiting nearby with Linh. They'll create a diversion, and while the enemy is busy, I'll cut through the ropes and get you away." He paused and glanced around, but nobody was taking any interest. He was a North Vietnamese soldier, a tree hiding in a wood, "Can you walk?"

"I can run the marathon if you can get me out of here. What kind of diversion are you planning?"

"I don't know. But it's due to start in…" He glanced at his watch, "Three minutes."

Farrell felt his hopes soar. There was a chance he'd get out of this place, and he could hardly believe it was happening. Provided Quang didn't happen along any time soon. He wouldn't want to miss the long, slow death of his American prisoner.

Luc moved away from his line of sight and disappeared behind the tree. Farrell waited and waited. Satisfied it would soon be over, no matter which way it went, one way or the other. He could feel the red ants nibbling at his crotch, and some were crawling behind him, between the cheeks of his ass. It wouldn't be long, and he hoped to Christ Ashe's plan succeeded.

He counted the seconds, and he reckoned more than three minutes had passed. Nothing had happened, no explosions, no bursts of machine gun fire, and he wondered if it'd failed.

Nothing's gonna happen. Maybe Luc was a hallucination after all.

A murmured voice behind him said softly, "It's started. It won't be long."

He didn't know what was happening, and it sure as hell wasn't somebody shooting up the camp. He smelled it first, the odor of grass burning, damp wood smoke, and out of the corner of his eye he saw a tendril of smoke wisp in front of him. It billowed through the trees, building up like a thick, Atlantic fog. Worried voices were raised, and the smoke became a huge cloud, engulfing the camp as if the entire jungle was on fire. Not flames, but burning enough to produce the great clouds of choking smoke blotting out much of the camp. He felt movement behind him. Luc had cut through his bonds.

"You're free. We have to leave."

No shit.

Luc escorted him away, pushing him out of sight into a clump of trees, and he pulled him deeper into the thick foliage. Behind him, everything was chaos. The Viets didn't have a clue about what was going on. Men coughed and choked, shouting and screaming, barking orders, panicked men running every which way, and they had no trouble slipping away. They'd made several hundred meters when they ran into Ashe and Linh, who'd stepped out from behind a huge, gnarled old tree.

Ashe gave him a worried look. "You look like hell."

"I look like dinner for a few thousand red ants. Get me to a stream, fast. They're all over me."

The girl suddenly noticed the insects still crawling over him, and she gasped in horror. "Are they inside?"

He didn't know if she meant inside his clothes or inside his body, but he said, "Damn right they are. I need a stream, fast!"

Ten minutes later, they came across a dank, muddy stream wide enough for him to rip off his clothes and plunge in, completely naked. He wasn't worried about a female being present. All he wanted was to get those damned ants off his body. He clawed at the insects, rubbing them off his body, using his shirt to scrub them away. It took him a quarter-hour before he was satisfied they were gone. He washed his shirt in the stream, checked it again for signs of insect life, and checked it once more to be sure before he pulled it back on.

Only then was he able to still his racing mind and thank them for getting him away. "That smoke was a stroke of genius," he told Ashe, "Better than a machine gun."

He pointed to the girl. "It was her idea. Worked like a charm."

"Linh, it was brilliant. I thought it was all over for me. Luc, that took some guts, masquerading as a North Vietnamese soldier and coming into the camp to get me out. Where did you get the uniform?"

He pointed at Ashe. "He took it off the body of a dead soldier."

"I take it he wasn't dead when you ran into him."

"He wasn't. Thankfully, he was the same size as Luc, which made him the ideal candidate."

He nodded. "We've missed the rendezvous with the Huey. I guess that means another night in the jungle, but in the morning we can head back to the LZ, and we'll be ready when it comes back."

Ashe's eyes narrowed. "I doubt the helicopter will be coming back."

"What're you saying?"

"After you climbed that tree, I decided to head back to the LZ to let Clarence know what was going on. We were still several hundred meters away when we saw the helicopter arrive. They climbed aboard, and it took off."

"Dorsey and Batista? You're telling me they've gone? Left us?"

"That's what I'm telling you, buddy. We're on our own. If we're gonna get out of here, it'll be a long hike."

"But why has he abandoned us? We're part of his squad.

How will he explain it to Curtis when he gets back?"

A shrug. "He'll find a way. And I doubt Curtis will give a shit. Men come and men go. There're plenty of vets looking for big paydays. We're expendable."

"I still don't get it. What does he have to gain?"

"Gain? The guy's a psycho, a sociopath. He doesn't need to gain anything. He enjoys the killing." A shadow crossed Ashe's brow, "Wait a minute, I'm thinking there's Melvin."

"His brother? I thought he was injured."

"He was, and they brought you in to replace him. But Clarence wants him back. If he bumps you off, he'll come back like nothing had changed."

Farrell was still puzzled. "I still don't get it. How does leaving us out here make sure any of us die? There's a good chance we'll make it back. It's not that far to Tan Son Nhut or Bien Hoa. Unless he's playing stupid games."

He shook his head. "Clarence doesn't play games."

"Maybe the Huey will return. There could be a simple explanation for them pulling out. We should make the LZ at dawn and see what happens."

He agreed, and they retreated inside the treeline to find a place where they could wait out the night. The rain returned, but he didn't give a damn. His clothing was soaking wet after he'd scoured the ants in the stream, and it was still soaking wet. In some strange way, he enjoyed the pure, cool feeling of the water soaking through to his skin, anything but red ants.

Luc and Linh made no secret of their growing attachment, and he made her a simple bower from palm leaves, insisting she shelter beneath it to protect her from the worst of the deluge. She refused until he joined her, and they spent the long, wet night huddled together.

Ashe had a waterproof poncho in his pack, and he sheltered beneath it. At times, Farrell heard him checking his rifle, extracting the bullets from the magazine, and replacing them one by one. Then he'd do it again. Like a ritual, the kind soldiers do before going into action. By the early hours, it was getting on his nerves, the constant rattle of cartridge cases.

At last he gave up and looked at Farrell. "I don't think he's coming back. We may have to hike out, and it's gonna be a hard slog. Our chances of making it aren't good. The VCs are everywhere."

"At least I'm not tied to a tree with red ants queuing up to eat me alive."

"There is that," he agreed, "Damn, it wouldn't be so bad if we had so much as a recognition flare we could send-up. There're plenty of helicopters passing overhead. If we could send up a flare, we'd be out in no time. As it is, they don't know we're here, and if we're unlucky, we could find ourselves on the wrong end of an M-60 if a trigger-happy door gunner decides to spray the area with bullets, or a fighter jock decides to unload his napalm. What is it some of these guys say? 'If they move, they're hostile. If they don't move, they're targets.' That's us, targets."

An idea was trying to surface in Farrell's brain, some thought at the back of his head, something to do with an aircraft dropping ordnance like napalm over their heads, but try as he might, he couldn't work it through. An hour before dawn they were silent, watching the sky, listening, waiting the unmistakable 'whump whump' of helicopter rotors, the roar of a turbine engine that would announce their imminent rescue. It didn't come. An hour after dawn, flights of a half-dozen Hueys had passed several clicks to the south, but nothing to suggest their ride was on the way.

Two hours after dawn, they had no choice but to face facts. Ashe grimaced. "They're not coming. Clarence fucked us over."

"But why? Why would he…" Suddenly, everything clicked, and he'd worked it out. Napalm was ordnance. Bombs were ordnance, like the eight-engined monsters that dropped hundreds of tons of bombs daily over Vietnam. Automatically he looked up at the sky, searching for the groups of contrails that would indicate a cluster of incoming heavy bombers. He saw none, but that didn't mean they weren't up there somewhere. Heading in to plaster the area with high-explosives, "They're gonna flatten the place."

"The Viet compound? Fucking hallelujah."

"Not the compound. Here, the LZ. That's what Clarence is up to. The bastards are coming, and soon."

Ashe looked up, and the two Viets looked up. The girl's face wore a puzzled expression. "American aircraft would bomb us?"

"Not knowingly, no. But that's what I think they're about to do, and real soon. We need to get out of here, and fast. Start heading east. The nearest base is Bien Hoa, around thirty klicks. Get on your feet. We're moving." They were packing up their meager gear ready to leave, when he sensed something rather than saw or heard it. He couldn't explain it, like a feeling in the air, a sense of menace. He looked up, and they were there, contrails. There were eight of the monster Stratofortresses, each aircraft carrying enough bombs to wipe out an entire city block.

Jesus Christ!

"Run!"

"Which way?"

"East, toward Bien Hoa."

"Too late. Look!"

Farrell looked up again. Black objects were falling like a meteor shower, and they were out of time. He estimated the bombs were targeted on the LZ, thanks to Clarence. He looked to the north for a way out, and men were coming toward them, black-clad men, carrying AKs. He spun around to look south. A wide river lay in front of them, almost certainly impossible to get across in such a short time. Which left one alternative.

"West."

"That's the way we just came. We'll walk straight into them."

"Any other direction and we're toast. Move out, fast, before those bombers get here!"

They ran back into the jungle, and the bombs seemed to take an age before they hit the ground. They made four hundred meters from the LZ before the first bombs hit, and it was worse than they could've imagined. The ground seemed to shake and swell up like a gigantic earthquake. A hurricane wind swept across the jungle, punched into them, trees shook, and some fell. Followed by a roaring noise, and then the after-shock hit, slamming them to the ground.

He shouted at them to keep going. "There's no other way. We'll have to crawl. Keep heading west, and forget the Vietcong. They've got enough problems without worrying about us."

He led the way, crawling along the ground. Despite the appalling bombardment threatening to obliterate them, it wasn't as bad as the thought of coming into close contact with more of those little red six-legged critters. They crawled on, and every time a stick of bombs detonated from behind, they had to curl up and cover their ears to protect them from the enormous blasts.

He kept moving, his brain foggy mash, battered and beaten by the immense blast waves that pursued them, and it couldn't get any worse. Yet it did. One B-52 unloaded further west, close to where they were crawling. He saw Linh tossed into the air, as if by a giant hand, and Luc rushing to protect her, covering her with his body as if that would be enough to stop the bombs from reaching her.

The nearby explosions ceased, as the entire quantity of bombs dropped from the aircraft detonated, and they crawled on. He glanced back, and they were still too close to the bomb's target zone.

"Keep going. Don't stop!"

All they could do was stare back at him with shell-shocked eyes and crazed expressions, like a bunch of lunatics who'd escaped from an asylum. He didn't recognize the familiar ground, didn't recognize the compound until it was in front of him. To his astonishment, they'd crawled so far they were back at the Vietcong base.

It was still intact, incredibly. Clarence had given them coordinates for the LZ, ignoring the real prize, and the huts were still standing, the matting still suspended overhead. Although the place was empty of VCs, they'd gone underground, all of them. He revised the estimate. They hadn't all gone underground. Thin, emaciated, and ragged men were peering out fearfully from beneath the huts. They were the slaves.

Ashe caught up with him. "They'll be back when the bombing ends. We still have to get out of here."

"Give it a minute. Luc, Linh, are you guys okay?" Unable to speak, they both nodded, "I think it's over. Give it a few minutes more, and we'll start back."

He was wrong. It wasn't almost over. The eighth B-52 had yet to unload, and for some reason they'd never understand, the bomb aimer decided to hit a patch of jungle to the west of the designated target. Maybe some of the camouflage matting had been blasted off by the blast and the hurricane winds created by the previous seven bombers, and he'd seen something below that looked interesting. Once again a stick of bombs fell toward them and exploded over the area. The huts disappeared in a storm of high-explosive, and all that remained were broken, lifeless bodies and debris scattered over the ground. As if a giant hand had swept the pieces from a chessboard.

Luc and Linh had crawled some distance away, so they were on the edge of the blast radius. When the explosions died away, he crawled to where they lay huddled in each other's arms.

"It's all over. We need to get out of here before they pop up out of their holes." There was no reply. Maybe the blast had damaged their eardrums. He crawled closer and tapped Luc on the shoulder, "Get up. We don't have much time."

They still didn't move, and he turned Luc face up. He was dead; mouth open wide, and eyes open wide. There was no sign of injury on his body. He knew what'd happened. The enormous blast had burst his lungs, probably his heart as well, and killed him immediately. The girl had suffered the same fate, and he felt a terrible darkness clamp down over him. She'd gone through so much. They'd both gone through so much, and they were here because sheer guts and bravery had driven them to volunteer to guide the mission in. Now they were dead, more bodies to stack up toward the grisly total.

He was aware of Ashe standing over him. "Dead?"

"The poor bastards. They'd just found each other."

"It's the fucking war," he spat, "Paul, we need to leave. Like you just said, they'll come crawling out of their holes, and we need to be someplace else, preferably a long way away."

"Give me a moment." He couldn't look away.

She'd been a schoolteacher, for Christ's sake. This shouldn't have happened. After everything she's done, it's ended here. Killed by an American bomb.

"Paul, the jungle's on fire. We have to get out of here. Look!"

Ashe was pointing toward the camp. Despite the rain, the bombs had started a fire, and it wasn't just smoke. The flames had caught, sheets of yellow fire. They were feeding on themselves. The fire was becoming bigger and hotter, the flames already above the trees, which had become flaming torches. The fire was sweeping toward them, engulfing the entire region. Scores of corpses lay on the ground, turned into blackened charcoal, but he guessed most of the bad guys had survived underground.

He returned his gaze to the bodies of two Viets, his friends. They shouldn't have died. He wanted to assuage his grief by swallowing enough cocaine to put him into orbit, but he resisted the urge. Still looking at Luc and Linh. They were noncombatants, yet the Vietnam War had soaked them up like a giant, evil sponge. Ashe was tugging on his arm.

"We gotta go."

241

He'd like to have spent more time, to mumble some long-forgotten prayer over them, but Ashe was right, it was time to leave. He took a last look around. The multimillion-dollar bombing mission had resulted in the deaths of maybe a hundred VCs, and the destruction of a few score of bamboo huts.

Okay, it'll set them back awhile, but they'll recover and rebuild, SOP for Vietnam.

He was about to turn away when he saw a movement on the edge of the burning camp. A gap opened between the flames, just a few meters wide, and the shape of a man appeared. The man was staring at him, not aiming a rifle, just standing and staring like a statue. Rigid, unmoving, until he raised an arm, and his finger pointed at Farrell. He stayed in place with that finger pointed at him. Not moving, and he wondered if the guy was in shock after the bombing. He wasn't in shock. He was sending a message.

The message was unmistakable. He'd been staring at Tran Quang, and the guy had spelled out what he had in store. He'd focused his war on one man. Paul Farrell, and from here on in, he'd better keep looking over his shoulder. Sooner or later, Quang would put a bullet into his guts and condemn him to the tortured death he should have suffered.

Tran Quang. He recalled him standing over him when he was tied to the tree. Stocky, built like a wrestler, yet he moved with a fluid grace. Despite being older than most of the men around him, he looked superbly fit. What distinguished him more than the raw, physical power he exuded was his expression. Lips fixed in a snarl as if he'd examined the world and found it wanting. At least, he'd found the world of his enemies wanting, and this was a guy with plenty of enemies.

Including most South Vietnamese, and every American. Like he wanted to tear them apart, limb from limb. His cause was right, and he'd kill any man who said different. He was cruelty personified.

Farrell started walking toward him, knowing this wouldn't end until the bastard was dead. Until he completed the mission Phoenix had sent him here to accomplish, and Ashe grabbed him.

"You're crazy. You won't even get close."

"I'll tear his guts out."

"Later, maybe, but if you go after him now, you'll burn. We're leaving."

A thick cloud of smoke roiled across the scene of destruction. When it cleared, he'd gone, as if he'd never been there.

Did I imagine it? No, it was him, no question. From this moment on, my fate is inextricably linked with Tran Quang. There isn't room inside Vietnam for both of us. Either Quang will die, or me.

Chapter Twelve

There wasn't time to bury the bodies of the two Vietnamese. The fire was spreading fast, and they had no choice but to run. They headed east, and the jungle was clear of hostiles. Which suited them just fine. They walked for ten klicks, toward the nearest American base of Bien Hoa. A Bradley M113 picked them up and gave them a ride the rest of the way.

They made it back to Tan Son Nhut by the end of the following day. They went straight to Ashe's bungalow, cleaned up, and wolfed down as much food as they could find. For Farrell, the war in Vietnam had become even more personal.

Sure, I signed on with CIA as one of their paid assassins, and I've crossed a few names off their target list, but not all. Xuan Dieu may still be alive. I know Tran Quang's alive. In Quang's case, he's made it as personal as me, locking us in a deadly duel that will never end until one of us is dead. There's also the problem of Clarence Dorsey. The bastard left us for dead, stranded in enemy territory. But how can I deal with him?

He looked at Ashe. "Does Clarence know you saw him leaving in the Huey?"

He shook his head. "Not possible. We were inside the treeline, so there was no way he could've seen us. Why?"

"Because when I deal with him, I want to make sure he doesn't see it coming."

"Paul, you're not gonna do something stupid, like kill him?"

"Negative. That would be murder. That's not the way I operate. But I'm gonna cause him some grief, something that'll pay him back for what he did to us."

"Like what?"

"I'll let you know later. Right now, it's time to check-in with Curtis."

They strolled through the gates and found him in his office. Farrell watched him carefully to see if he had any idea about what'd happened, but he just nodded a greeting.

"You're back, that's good news. Clarence told me you failed to make the LZ, and they had no choice but to leave without you. He thought you were both dead."

"The Vietcong tried hard, but we're still here, and we're still alive. Which is more than I can say for Luc and Linh. They're dead."

"The Vietcong got them?"

"Not the Vietcong. USAF."

He grimaced. "You got caught up in that bombing raid? That's a real shame. How come you guys survived?"

"Luck, is all. Where are Clarence and Pablo?"

A shrug. "They're in the city, doing some sightseeing." He smiled, "Eyeing up the girls is my best guess. I guess there're worse ways to spend your free time."

"What do you have fixed up for our next mission?"

He picked up a manila file from his desk and leaned back, perusing the contents.

"You'll like this one. It's local, Saigon, a guy who's been moonlighting for the Communists, name of Trung Binh. He works for the National Police as a civilian employee in the archives, and we found out recently he's been passing information to Charlie. Details of police operations, forthcoming security sweeps, you know the kind of thing. He warns them, the military goes in, and they've vanished into thin air." He passed over a sheet of paper with a photo clipped to it. A thin, severe-looking man with round, wire-rim spectacles and crew-cut hair unusual for civilians inside Vietnam, "You have the address, so all you need do is pay him a late-night visit, and make sure he never wakes up."

Farrell took the paper and glanced at the address. "This is in the center of the city. Hai Ba Trung."

"I believe it is. What of it?"

"It's around the corner from the hostel where the girls are staying."

"Girls?"

"The girls we rescued from the VC, remember? They were using them as whores."

Understanding came to him. "Right, yeah. I remember." He chuckled, "Clarence said they were onto a good thing, plenty of willing customers. A captive market."

"They were the captives, slaves, held prisoner in a Vietcong tunnel. I wouldn't call it a good thing."

"No, no, of course not. When you do Binh, it's essential

you do it during the night. The cops will likely blame it on the Communists, and if they don't, we'll point them in that direction. Good luck."

He looked down at his desk in dismissal, but they stayed where they were. "We need weapons and ammunition. A lot of our stuff got left behind."

"Sure, sure." He delved in the drawer of his desk and pulled out a set of keys, "These're the spare keys for the hangar. You know where everything is, so help yourselves. Let me have the keys back when you're done."

They left the office and walked outside. The rain had returned, a reminder for Farrell of what he'd gone through when he was tied to that tree. He stopped, enjoying the feel of the cool, fresh air. The downpour also hid many of the odors of the air base, grease, and burned gasoline. As well as the background taint of backed-up sewer pipes.

He thought of Quang. He had unfinished business, and no idea how he'd go about getting it. He pushed it to the back of his mind.

Quang will likely find me first. That's fine. I'll be waiting.

The hangar was empty. They unlocked the gun rack and helped themselves to fresh, newly oiled AR-15s, together with spare magazines. In the locker, he found jeans, jungle boots, a shirt, an OD combat jacket, minus unit markings. When he'd changed his clothes, he felt better. More like a mercenary assassin in the pay of the CIA.

He strapped on a shoulder harness, tucked a Colt M1911 into the holster, and glanced at Ashe. After some misgivings, he'd also helped himself to the gear.

"Clarence regards this stuff as his personal property, and

he decides who takes what."

"The stuff is the property of CIA, so he can go hang. You ready?"

"Almost."

Ashe went to a drawer and opened it. Inside was a selection of knives. Combat knives, including Fairbairn Sykes, tactical Bowie knives, and small machetes. They helped themselves to the Bowies, long, single-bladed, and heavy. Designed for killing, the tools of their trade.

* * *

The Vietnamese entered the building by the fire escape at the rear and climbed to the fourth floor. His face was cold, etched with cruelty, a man who went through life with death in his heart, carrying the stench of death everywhere. He entered the corridor, found the room number they'd given him, and knocked. Two men were waiting for him, seated on a sofa. They were both Americans, and he had to fight down his distaste for the people he'd made it his life's work to destroy.

The older, bigger man pointed to an armchair. "Take a seat, pal. How about a beer?"

"No beer." The voice was as hard as stainless steel, filled with menace, and both Americans instinctively dropped their hands to their sides, close to the holstered automatics. It was a reflex action, and the hands remained empty. They stayed seated, waiting, and the Vietnamese stared at them in stony silence. His expression spoke volumes as if he was fighting down the urge to pull a gun and kill these two enemies of his regime.

After several minutes, he chose to speak. "You failed."

"Excuse me? What do you mean, we failed?"

"He lives. You called in your bombers, and they failed to kill one man."

"It's not possible. Nobody could've survived that bombing raid."

"I survived, and I'm here. He survived."

Clarence looked at Pablo. "I'll be damned. I can't believe it."

"I want him."

He grimaced. "Mister, we all want him dead. He's a royal pain in the ass."

"Not dead. I want him alive. I want you to bring him to me. I don't care what it takes."

A sly expression came over Clarence's face. "What's in it for me." He glanced at Pablo, "I mean what's in it for us?"

"I can make you rich."

"I'm listening."

"Drugs. As you know, North Vietnam distributes large quantities of illegal narcotics to the South." The harsh faced softened in a cruel smile, "We find it is an effective weapon against the imperialists and their puppet government in Saigon. Assist me in this matter, and I will ensure you have control over supplies for Saigon."

"And Tan Son Nhut."

He inclined his head. "Saigon and Tan Son Nhut, agreed."

"In return, you want Farrell? That's it?"

"I want him alive."

A broad smile crossed Clarence's face.

I could have told him I'd have done it for free, just to get the bastard out of the way. This man's offering to make me rich for doing something I planned to do anyway. It couldn't be better. Farrell out of the way, and Melvin back in the squad.

Pablo shot him a nervous glance. "What about Ashe? He hangs around with Farrell. They've become buddies. He may get in the way."

He glanced at the Viet. "We may have to kill him, is that a problem?"

"As long as I have Farrell alive. Do we have a deal?"

"Not so fast. How do I know you can supply these drugs? This could all be talk."

The Vietnamese reached his hand down, and the two Americans once again moved their hands toward their guns. And once again they relaxed. The man was picking up a plastic briefcase. Instead of pulling out a gun, he extracted a stained oilskin pouch and handed it to Clarence. He opened it, and his eyes went wide. White powder, and inside that pouch there had to be at least a kilo.

"Cocaine?"

"Of course. Pure cocaine. We also have large quantities of marijuana, which comes in from Afghanistan and Pakistan, but cocaine is more valuable. Try it."

"I don't mind if I do."

He took a pinch between his fingers and snorted it into his nostrils. The familiar feeling swept through his body, and he passed it across to Pablo. "Your turn."

Batista helped himself, and he snorted deeply. "Damn, that's good. Where do you get the stuff?"

The Vietnamese didn't answer, but he didn't need to. They already knew. Their Communist pals in Russia and China would be more than happy to supply as much cocaine as they could take. Despite the Chinese dislike for most things Vietnamese, they disliked the capitalist West more, and if the drugs weakened the American military capacity, they'd regard it as a worthwhile return.

Neither Clarence nor Batista paused to consider they were conspiring to undermine their own nation. What mattered was the bottom line. The balance both men were building in their secret bank accounts, and if they had sole rights to the distribution of drugs in Saigon and Tan Son Nhut, their days of petty larceny, stealing from the villages they raided, were over. One year, and they could retire, wealthy beyond their dreams.

"It's a deal."

Clarence offered him his hand, but the Vietnamese declined with a cold stare. As if the very prospect of touching the skin of an enemy offended him deeply. He shrugged, and the Vietnamese walked to the door.

"You know how to contact me. As soon as you have him, call, and we will make arrangements for the handover."

"You'll bring us the first shipment?"

"You have my word."

He exited the room and walked back to the fire escape. As he descended, Tran Quang was supremely satisfied. His escort had been waiting in the shadows behind the building, and they fanned out around him to make sure he returned to his hideout, a house belonging to a Communist sympathizer. He planned to stay in Saigon until they gave him Farrell.

If those Americans think I'll hand over the cocaine in return for Farrell, they're more stupid than they look. Once I have my hands on him, I'll give my men the order to kill them.

He arrived safely and before he went inside, he dismissed

his men to go back to the hotel where they were staying and get some sleep. He ordered them to return the following morning.

"We have an important day ahead of us. I will get my hands on Farrell, and you men will deal with those Americans who will give him to me.

* * *

They locked the hangar and strolled away. They called in the PX and bought fresh supplies of food and booze. With everything they needed, they returned to the bungalow, enjoyed a meal washed down with a couple of beers, and climbed into Ashe's bright red Pontiac GTO for a drive into the city. The streets were crowded, and he threaded his way through the heavy traffic, avoiding cyclos, suicidal pedestrians, military jeeps driving like there was no tomorrow, and cop cars trying and failing to control the chaos.

The first place they visited was the hostel. They walked inside, and several of the girls were seated in the lounge. And English lesson was taking place, and they were listening to a tape cassette, repeating the words in English.

'Where is the nearest hotel?'

'I would like a double room with bath.'

'Can you direct me to the railway station?'

They were so absorbed in listening and repeating the words they didn't notice them at first, but when they did they jumped up, screaming with pleasure.

"Paul, Dave, how do you do?"

Ashe grinned. "We do good. Are you okay?"

"Yes, we okay. Where're Luc and Linh?"

His grin faded. "I'm sorry, they're dead."

Their English didn't stretch that far. "What mean dead?"

He mimed shooting with a rifle, and they understood. One girl sobbed, and the girls looked shattered at the news. Linh had been their savior, had got them to this place of safety, only for it to end in some stinking stretch of jungle; even worse, victims of an American bombing raid. They spent time with them, correcting their English, but a dark cloud had descended.

The girls insisted they joined them for drinks.

"In memory of Luc and Linh," one girl said. She'd introduced herself as Mai, and although her bright expression had darkened when she heard about the deaths, after a couple of drinks she recovered. Life had to go on, and if they wanted to honor Tan Linh, the best way would be to work for what she'd fought for. Do everything possible to destroy the Communists.

He finished his third beer and declined any more alcohol. He got to his feet. "I have to get back. Ashe, if you want to stay it's no problem, I'll call a cab."

"Why not wait for your friends to come down?" Mai asked him, "I'm sure they won't be long."

"Friends?"

"Of course," she smiled brightly, "They're in a room upstairs, some kind of a meeting."

"Who're we talking about?"

"Clarence and Pablo, of course. Didn't you know? They rented the room for four hours and met with an older man, a Vietnamese. That was three hours ago, so I expect they'll be finished soon."

Something was going on with Dorsey and Batista, and

whatever it was, it was nothing good. He looked at Ashe and kept his voice to a low murmur. "I'll pay them a visit. Maybe we can have a friendly chat about that bombing raid."

"I wouldn't. If they think you suspect, they'll kill you to make sure you don't take revenge."

"It looks like they plan to kill me anyway, so what difference does it make. Mai, which room are they in?"

She gave them a number on the fourth floor, and he started to walk away. Ashe made to join him, but he told him to stay with the girls. "Like I said, it's just a friendly chat."

He went up to the fourth floor, strolled along the passage, and reached the door. He knocked. "Room service."

A moment later the door opened, and Clarence stood there with a grin on his face. The grin faded, his eyes widened, and his mouth dropped open. "When did you get back?"

"Not so long ago. I thought we could have a chat about things."

"Things?"

"That's right." He shouldn't have said it, and he'd told Ashe he wouldn't bring it up, but he was raging inside, "Things like calling in a B-52 strike over the LZ, after you and Batista left us out on a limb. By the way, where is Batista?"

"He went out."

"Will he be back soon?"

"I guess. Look, Farrell, tell me what you want. I don't appreciate you calling in like this."

"I…" He paused. He'd noticed the white powder around Clarence's nostrils, and there was enough of it to know what it meant. And feel the familiar urge, "Having a party?"

Dorsey involuntarily glanced at the oilskin package on the

table. It looked like a lot of cocaine. "No."

"Why all the coke? You must be expecting company."

"Nope, it's just me and Pablo."

Farrell was wary, but he needed to take a look. Needed to know what was inside that pouch and satisfy himself he didn't need it. Keeping his eye on Clarence, and one hand close enough to snatch out the pistol from the shoulder holster, he picked up the pouch and flipped it open. Cocaine. Enough to keep a battalion of Marines awake for a week. "You going into business?"

He looked around the room as if searching for a way out. "Of course not."

Farrell looked closely at the handwritten symbols on the outside of the pouch. Chinese, had to be. He fought down his need while at the same time trying to work out what Dorsey was up to. It was too much for personal use, which meant he had to be dealing.

He kills people on a regular basis, the guilty and the innocent, so what difference does trafficking a few drugs make? A lot of difference! The look of guilt on his face is so strong, whatever he's doing has to be something bad, but what? The Chinese characters are a giveaway.

"You're dealing with the Chinese? I doubt Curtis would be impressed if he knew."

The denial shot back so fast, he was surprised. "It's not the Chinese."

"Then who?" He didn't answer, but he looked so sneaky, so evasive, he didn't need an answer. He already had the answer, "Hanoi."

Clarence began to stutter about how he wouldn't deal with the enemy. It would be immoral, he gabbled, and more stuff like that. For a man who'd pillaged, raped his way across South Vietnam, the denial didn't count for peanuts. The guy was dealing with the enemy.

"You bastard, you worthless piece of dog shit. What does Hanoi get out of the deal? Money to support the Vietcong?"

"No money changes hands!" he blurted out. Once again, the answer was too fast, and Farrell was watching the effects of cocaine on the man's thought processes.

He's talking too fast, spitting it out without thinking. Another push and maybe I can get him to admit the truth.

"Then what?"

"I just trade a few baggies with the troops, keep them happy. Keep them awake when they need it."

He'd read about the effect of powerful stimulants on soldiers during wartime. The Nazis invented methamphetamine and branded it Pervitin. The plan was to keep them fighting during the appalling privations on the Eastern Front. It worked, until increasing doses caused widespread addiction. Men suffered terribly when the drug ceased to work on their ruined metabolisms. Intense cold and snow cut them down in swathes, and for those who survived, they still had the Russians to contend with. The rest was history, but scientists and governments had learned the lessons. Stimulant drugs taken regularly by troops in battle were a short-term solution and a long-term catastrophe.

The Communists may be lowdown scum, but they're no fools. Every American soldier they turn into a drug addict is an American soldier they don't have to fight. Why waste bullets when you can poison the enemy with hard drugs? That's the deal Clarence Dorsey's made, a deal with the devil.

"You bastard! I'm calling a halt to this."

He sneered, and Farrell could see the coke working on him, so he'd feel all-powerful. "You're not calling a halt to anything. If you think I'm letting you interfere with my operation, you can forget it."

"We're going back to Tan Son Nhut and have a cozy chat with Curtis. See how he feels about your little sideline with the North Vietnamese." Farrell's hand went to the shoulder holster and froze. He'd felt something hard jab into his back, like the muzzle of a gun. He turned slowly, and he was looking at Pablo Batista, holding the muzzle of his automatic against his body.

"I don't think so, hombre. Take the gun out, and put it on the floor. Slowly."

He obeyed, eased out the gun, and it was inches from the floor when Clarence's next words made him pause. "Did you follow Tran Quang and see where he went?"

"Sure. The house belongs to a guy by the name of Trung Binh, and it's in a street named Hai Ba Trung."

"Good work. When we've taken care of Farrell, we'll get back to the hangar. We have a kilo of product, and as soon as we've cut and bagged it, we can have it on sale by tomorrow. We're gonna be rich, Pablo."

"Fucking hallelujah!" Both men whooped with glee, and the room echoed to their laughter.

Farrell didn't need to hear anymore. Quang was here, in Saigon, and staying with the man Curtis had assigned them to eliminate. Trung Binh.

These bastards are responsible for the deaths of Luc and Linh, and conspiring with Quang against the American military.

He acted instinctively, and he should've died. He kept hold of the gun, jerked around, squeezed off a round that took Pablo in the right shoulder. He screamed and dropped his gun. Farrell swung back around to deal with Clarence. A pistol had appeared in his hand, and he brought it up to get off a shot. He dived to the side, the bullet whined past him, and he pumped three bullets into Dorsey's chest. The force of the bullets threw him back, but Pablo was scrabbling on the floor to retrieve his gun. He jerked his gaze around, and he'd grabbed it with his left hand.

Farrell fired first and finished him with a double-tap to the chest. He fell to the floor, and both bodies lay still, with blood pooling beneath them. Footsteps pounded on the staircase, the door was wrenched open, and Ashe pushed through, gun out.

"What the hell happened?"

"We had a disagreement."

His eyebrows shot up. "Some disagreement. Paul, why kill them? They're supposed to be on our side?"

"Not any longer. They'd just made some kind of a deal with Quang."

"Tran Quang?"

"He's here in Saigon. Staying with the target, Trung Binh, fixing up to flood South Vietnam with drugs."

He shrugged. "Plenty of our guys smoke Mary Jane, so what?"

"Not grass, cocaine. Probably they'd follow it with large quantities of methamphetamine. The plan is to undermine our troops."

"Jesus! You said he's staying with the target?"

"That's correct. If we take them now, we can nail two for the price of one."

"What're we waiting for?"

They ran down the fire escape and circled the building to

where Ashe's GTO was parked. They'd left their AR-15s in the trunk, and they retrieved them, and started hiking toward Hai Ba Trung. Farrell had stuffed the pouch of cocaine into a pocket before they left, and he rationalized he didn't want to leave it in the hostel to get the girls into trouble. It wasn't the only reason. A kilo of cocaine was forbidden treasure. The temptation to take just one snort was powerful. As powerful as the drug itself, and as they walked through the darkened streets, his mind was preoccupied. Fighting off the urge, the terrible temptation tormenting his brain, and he was surprised when Ashe pulled him off the street into the shadows of a darkened doorway.

"It's across the street, you see it?"

He snapped his mind back into gear. They were looking at a single-story villa, built in French colonial style. It was sandwiched between a gas station on one side and a small hotel on the other. "I see it. Ashe, cover the rear. I'll go in through the front."

"You think that's the best way to do it? If they see you approach, they'll start shooting."

"They'd better make it fast. I'm gonna start blasting before the door opens."

He gave him an uncertain look. "You seem all fired up. Did you snort some of that coke?"

"Negative. You ready?"

"Give me half a minute."

He jogged across the street, threaded his way past the gas station, and went around the back of the bungalow. It was time to move, and he'd worked out he had one chance, and one chance only. He held his assault rifle at the hip, gently knocked on the door, and stood back. Someone called out from inside in

Vietnamese, and he guessed they were asking who was there. It was time to introduce himself, and he squeezed the trigger, sending a long burst through the woodwork. He heard a scream from inside, and he simultaneously shoulder charged the door, threw it open, and leaped inside the villa.

A body lay in the hallway, and it wasn't Quang. Which meant it had to be Trung Binh. He'd taken most of the bullets, and his body was torn apart.

Score one for the good guys, and now for Quang.

He raced through the villa, kicking open the doors and searching the rooms. He didn't find him, but he heard a cry from the back, and he charged out the kitchen door into the rear yard.

Ashe lay on the ground, and he shouted, "I'm okay. It's nothing serious, but the bastard got away."

"Where'd he go?"

"The gas station."

"I'm on it."

He raced across the yard and vaulted a fence. He was running toward the gas pumps when several pistol shots echoed through the night. Bullets whistled past him, and he rolled on the ground and came up shooting. Quang was standing beside a pump, holding the nozzle, and pumping gas onto the forecourt. He holstered his pistol, but he didn't need it. In his hand, he held something far more dangerous. A Zippo lighter.

"Farrell, if you come any closer, I'll set fire to the gas. You'll roast."

"If you start a gasoline fire, the entire area could catch fire. You'll die, and scores of people will die as well."

"They are nothing!" he spat, "I will take my chances, but you're finished."

Farrell was working out how he could take him, without burning down half of Saigon. It wasn't going to be easy, but it had to be done. The range to Quang was around thirty meters. Not a difficult shot, and so far he hadn't ignited the lighter. If he could take him quickly, he'd be dead before he had a chance to set the gasoline alight. He had to risk a shot. The alternative was to let him get away, and he'd probably fire the gasoline anyway. He'd have one chance to put him on the ground, but first, he needed to make the Viet believe he had the upper hand.

All he needed was an opening, a tiny window. He'd chance getting caught by the flames to kill Quang if it didn't mean the potential loss of many lives. He had to keep him talking, and he kept his voice calm and reassuring.

"We can make a deal, Quang. Just you and me, we can strike a bargain."

"First, put down your gun. Then we will talk."

Sure, I put down the rifle, and you'll snatch out your pistol and pump me full of bullets. Then you'll set fire to the gas as you leave.

"I'll put down the gun, if you put down the hose. Stop pumping gas."

The Viet couldn't help it. His gaze involuntarily strayed to the pistol on his belt. With the Zippo in one hand and the muzzle in the other, he'd need a hand free to pull the gun and kill Farrell. Dropping the hose would suit him just fine. Drop the rifle."

Farrell bent down to lower the rifle, and it was an inch off the ground when Quang let the hose fall and his hand dived to his holster. He was fast, and he almost had him. Farrell hit the deck still holding his rifle, threw it to his shoulder, and took aim. Three bullets whined past the Viet, but he was running, clicking the lighter to torch the gas when he was clear of the spreading pool.

He stopped when his feet were clear of the gasoline, continuing to click the lighter. It still didn't ignite, and Farrell aimed at Quang's chest. Slowly, carefully, he squeezed the trigger. He shouldn't have missed. The range was too short, the shot well aimed, but at the last moment, Quang moved. He clicked the lighter again, and it flamed into life. He went to toss it into the pool of gasoline, but Farrell's bullet took him in the wrist. He screamed, dropped the Zippo, and it slid across the concrete, closer and closer to the flammable liquid flooding the ground.

Farrell froze; Quang froze, both men waiting for the flames to engulf the entire area, including them. It didn't happen. The air was thick with fumes, with insufficient oxygen for combustion to take place. The lighter went out. Quang recovered and started to run, but the gasoline was everywhere, and he slipped and fell. Farrell was on him in a flash.

I have ideas for this worthless piece of shit. Not as painful as the death he planned for me, but it'll be a certain poetic justice.

He beat him over the head with the butt of the AR-15. It wasn't heavy enough to split his skull, but enough to leave him semi-conscious, and he dragged him back to the villa. Ashe was sitting in the rear yard, his back to the wall. His lips twitched in a smile when he identified Quang.

"He's dead?"

"Not yet. Can you hold out for a few minutes more?"

"If it means you finish that bastard, I can manage for a few hours."

"It won't be that long."

One hour later, he picked up the telephone inside the villa and persuaded the operator to patch him through to Tan Son Nhut. A military ambulance arrived, and two paramedics helped Ashe into the back. They asked Farrell if he was accompanying his friend, but he told them no. When the vehicle drove away, he went back into the villa, to the kitchen where he'd roped Quang to an iron cooking range, with his head tilted back. He'd stuffed a wooden ladle into his mouth to keep it open, and his lips were coated in white powder.

Quang's eyes bulged, and he was shaking his head, moaning and gurgling, but Farrell ignored him and spooned more white powder into his mouth. With no choice, he had to swallow. When he estimated he'd swallowed a half kilo, he sat back to watch.

"This is for Mark."

His eyes were bulging, his body thrashing and writhing, his system fired up like an F-4 Phantom on afterburners. Except he wasn't taking off anywhere, for the ropes and the weight of the kitchen range kept him secure.

"I want you to know, Quang, this is for Linh and Luc."

He watched for another hour, and his struggles became so fierce he managed to lift the heavy iron range several inches off the floor. He possessed the drug-fuelled strength of a madman. It was also the strength of a dying man.

"This is for the girls you enslaved, and for everybody else you murdered and brutalized. You deserve worse, but it's all I have."

He watched him until the end. When daylight came, he untied Quang and laid him out in the yard. The rain fell again, and he watched him from the shelter of the kitchen doorway.

He wasn't surprised when Curtis entered through the front door, stepped over the body of Trung Binh, and found him. He nodded a curt greeting. "Ashe told me you were here."

"I guessed he would. Is he okay?"

"He'll be fine. They've patched him up, and he'll be ready to go back to work in a few days. Which is more than I can say for Dorsey and Batista. No amount of patching up is gonna fix them. A pity, they were two of my best people."

"They were traitors."

He nodded slowly. "Yeah, there is that. Ashe told me. I had my suspicions about Clarence for some time, so maybe it's best this way." He looked at him keenly, "Which means I have a few vacancies to fill. I'll bring in a couple more men to make up the numbers, but I need somebody to head up the squad. Even though you're new, I'm offering you the job. What do you say?"

"I don't think so."

"We're doing important work. It could change the course of the war."

"You can change it without me."

"Is it a question of the money? Clarence earned a big bonus as topkick."

"I'm not interested in the money."

"Then what?"

He swung around to face Curtis and met his eyes. "I got what I came for."

"Justice?"

"Fuck the justice. Vengeance."

The CIA man nodded. "I hear you, and like you said, you got what you came for. Now I want you to think again. Take a couple of days, and we'll talk. Don't forget, I got you out of Leavenworth to join Phoenix. You're the kind of material we need to make a difference. Give it some thought. I wouldn't want to rock the boat if I were you."

He left, and Farrell went back out into the rain to look down on the body of Tran Quang. He was reminded of the time he'd been tied to the tree, with red ants crawling over him, and he shuddered. But he was free, and he looked up at the sky, enjoying the feeling of the fresh, clean rain.

Were Curtis's last words about rocking the boat a threat? Probably. The reason they put me there in the first place, my drug habit. Cocaine. I have another task to complete.

He went back into the kitchen and retrieved the pouch. Took it outside and paused, giving it a long, hard look. The urge was still there, but not so bad. The death of Quang had exorcised at least some of the demons; along with the terrible need that'd tortured his body didn't seem so terrible.

He tipped the pouch and emptied the powder onto the wet ground, where it soaked in.

Let the insects have it. Maybe they'll enjoy it.

He left the villa and started walking back to Tan Son Nhut. Until he recalled Ashe's GTO was still parked nearby. He climbed into the driver's seat, started the engine, and pointed the hood toward Tan Son Nhut.

First, I'll check up on Ashe, tell him I've brought his car back safe. Afterward, what then? I don't know. I'm without family, and all I have left is… Nothing. What is there to go back for? Nothing. What is there to stay here for? I need to think hard about Curtis' offer. It's not the kind of work I prefer, but I've made a good friend in Ashe. I'll decide my future in the next few days, and make the decision with a clear head and a clear conscience.

I'm cleansed of the need for vengeance and the need for cocaine. Aren't I? Time will tell.

THE END

Made in the USA
Las Vegas, NV
04 October 2022